PRAISE FOR *BREAKING SKY*

"An action-packed thrill ride that smashes through all kinds of barriers at a Mach 5 pace."

—Carrie Jones, *New York Times* bestselling author of the Need series

"A nonstop thrill ride...will keep you reading at the speed of sound. *Breaking Sky* is one of the most exciting reads of the year."

—Thomas E. Sniegoski, *New York Times* bestselling author of The Fallen series

"Had me in its grip from takeoff to landing. Chase is a kick-butt female and the swoon-worthy flyboys kept me up way past my bedtime."

—Joy N. Hensley, author of *Rites of Passage*

"*Breaking Sky* ticks all the boxes: love, war, friendship, action, and danger—I was left wanting more, more, more!"

—Jessica Shirvington, author of *One Past Midnight*

"Replete with fighter pilot jargon, plausible science fiction elements, and nerd-friendly literary allusions, this taut, well-crafted novel should have broad appeal, for fans of everything from Roth's *Divergent* to Wein's *Code Name Verity*."

—*The Bulletin for the Center for Children's Books*, Starred Review

"Strong characterizations, action, adventure, and emotion combine to produce a sci-fi novel that is more than just the sum of its parts."

—*School Library Journal*, Starred Review

"Smart, exciting, confident—and quite possibly the next Big Thing."

—*Kirkus Reviews*

"McCarthy puts her characters in increasingly tense situations, testing them to the breaking point and giving what could have been merely a popcorn thriller sudden gravity. This crazy-cool story should soar."

—*Booklist*

"McCarthy deploys breath-stopping depictions of high-stakes piloting with enviable ease, and the in-your-face personal confrontations are nearly as taut."

—*Publishers Weekly*

ALSO BY CORI McCARTHY

Breaking Sky

YOU WERE HERE

CORI McCARTHY

sourcebooks
fire

Copyright © 2016 by Cori McCarthy
Cover and internal design © 2016 by Sourcebooks, Inc.
Cover illustrations by Sonia Liao
Cover image © Elisabeth Ansley/Trevillion Images
Internal illustrations by Sonia Liao
Internal images © Szantai Istvan/Shutterstock; JJ Studio/Shutterstock; Jason
Yoder/Shutterstock; Eky Studio/Shutterstock

Published by Sourcebooks Fire, an imprint of Sourcebooks, Inc.
P.O. Box 4410, Naperville, Illinois 60567-4410
(630) 961-3900
Fax: (630) 961-2168
www.sourcebooks.com

Library of Congress Cataloging-in-Publication Data

Names: McCarthy, Cori, author.
Title: You were here / by Cori McCarthy.
Description: Naperville, Illinois : Sourcebooks Fire, [2016] | Summary: On
   the anniversary of her daredevil brother's death, Jaycee attempts to break
   into Jake's favorite hideout, the petrifying ruins of an insane asylum,
   where her eccentric band of friends challenge her to do the unthinkable:
   reveal the parts of herself that she buried with her brother.
Identifiers: LCCN 2015022867 | (alk. paper)
Subjects: | CYAC: Brothers and sisters--Fiction. | Grief--Fiction. |
   Psychiatric hospitals--Fiction. | Friendship--Fiction.
Classification: LCC PZ7.M47841233 Yo 2016 | DDC [Fic]--dc23 LC record avail-
able at http://lccn.loc.gov/2015022867

Printed and bound in the United States of America.

VP 10 9 8 7 6 5 4 3 2 1

This is for
Matthew Wakefield.

August 15, 1982 — June 7, 1997

You were here, Matt.
I remember.

ruin

[roo–in]

noun

1. the remains of a man–made
   structure that has succumbed
   to decay and abandonment

2. the god–awful downfall of a person

THE RIDGES

CHAPTER 1

JAYCEE

I HAD BEEN DRIVING ALL AFTERNOON, TRYING TO GET LOST.

The road blurred. My foot was a stone on the gas pedal, and I took the turn too fast. Tires growled and spit gravel, almost sending my car sideways through the Saturday evening traffic.

I came to a slamming stop in the playground parking lot and pressed my head to the steering wheel, cursing. The pause was short-lived. I tightened my ponytail and got out.

Trudging toward the swing set, my face burned and my breath stung in my chest. That's what regret does well and grief does better: rips out your energy and leaves you feeling each and every heartbeat. Plus, well, I'd failed once again. Getting lost in my hometown was turning out to be as easy as disapparating—something I'd once wasted an entire lightning bolt–foreheaded summer attempting.

I sat hard on the swing. My endeavors to get lost were getting extreme. Just last week, I'd night-trekked into the woods where the cross-country team practices and chugged three inches of rum. I'd left the path behind, only to run into my equidrunk classmates, taking their idiotic dares to make out with a tree and underwear-roll through a patch of poison ivy. I emerged hours later on the road behind the middle school, the same spot where years earlier I used to pump my bike into dirt-sneezing speed, trying to spin out. In short, my earliest attempts at getting lost.

I itched the length of my arm. The poison ivy welts *were* starting to fade, even though a few hours earlier, my mom complained about how blotchy I would look in all my grad-uation pictures. "Photoshop," I had assured her following the ceremony. "I promise you won't have to remember me as rashy every time you marvel at my monumentous achievement in surviving standard education."

Surviving was the wrong word. My mom started to weep, and I ended up taking a three-hour drive on Easy Death Road. Which is exit 13 off Guilt Highway if you're curious. And then after all that, I surrendered to a seizure of loneliness and came here to the oddly placed Richland Avenue Park.

I scuffed my Chucks on the stubbly turf, drawn to the spot beneath the swing set where Jake died. Of course, it wasn't rubber back then. It had been good, old-fashioned, unforgiv-ing blacktop. My mind hummed, and something inside me screamed *Run!* as if my worst memories were zombies, and if I were quick enough, I could outstrip them. But I stayed where I was, kicking into gear on the swing instead.

The sunset was taking forever to get over itself, and I pumped my legs like a ten-year-old. I could have been at any number of graduation parties, sneaking beer into Sprite cans and cheersing the end of high school. But no, I was here. Killing time. Waiting for dark, when I'd break into The Ridges and meet up with Mikivikious for our bizarro anniversary. It had been five years. That's something special, right? What's the traditional present for five years? Silverware? A couch? Flat screen?

The sun's blaring rays made me squeeze my eyes until the whole universe went orange-red. *Killing time.* What an expression. *How* does *one kill time? Anesthesia? Time travel? Lobotomy?*

The last one made me snicker as I stared up at The Ridges, the decrepit Victorian mansion on top of the hill. Until recently, it had been known as the Athens Insane Asylum, but the state had demanded a rebrand when they shut it down, as if a new name could erase a hundred years of inhumane abuse, death, and yes, copious amounts of lobotomies. I should know; I'd tried it once or twice. Not a lobotomy—changing my own name. Anything to escape being the infamous girl who'd had a front-row seat in watching her big brother snap his neck.

I would rather be known for frenching a tree.

My feelings flared as I imagined my mom on her way back to her own asylum, Stanwood Behavioral Hospital. She was most likely weeping for Xanax, a wreck because I wrecked her with my sarcasm. And my father was probably holding her hand and saying nice things, because that's how he dealt with Jake. My dad was a grade A deflector. Everything he said was ripe with the exact same sentiment: *So we don't have a son anymore, but hey, look at our daughter!* To be honest, I preferred my mother's tears.

I turned to the half-shadowed redbrick towers of The Ridges peeking over the tree line and wondered where I'd left off on my easier thoughts. Oh yeah: lobotomies. The guy who performed them, nicknamed Dr. Lobotomy, traveled from asylum to asylum in the sixties, living out of his *lobotomobile*—he seriously called it that—while banging out twenty procedures a day. Apparently it only takes a few minutes to destroy someone's frontal lobe. True story. Google it.

I kicked harder, faster, higher on the swing, and then turned into a board, locking my elbows and knees. I tracked the blue sky with each swinging pass, waiting for gravity to get predictable. To bring me back to earth.

When it finally did, I was no longer alone. A kid glared from a few feet away with that dog snarl only middle schoolers possess. Behind him, his buddies hung from the monkey bars, faux whispering. Clearly he'd been sent over. Chosen to poke fun at Jaycee Strangelove.

Yes, that's my name. No, you may not make fun of it.

I stared him down. "You're too old to be on the playground. Take off before you freak out the little kids," I said even though I was the only other person there.

The boy's hair was unevenly shaved on the sides, and he'd Sharpied rap lyrics up his ropey arms. "I dare you."

I exhaled for roughly ten years. "Dare me to do what, Eminem?"

He pointed to the top of the swing set, smirking.

"No."

"I can do the backflip," he bragged. "So can two of my friends."

I took the bait even though I knew better than to talk about the accident. "Jake could do it too, you snotwad. The flip that killed him was probably his thirtieth."

My thoughts went graphic. I couldn't stop imagining my big brother standing atop the swing set. He wore his cap and gown from graduation and was also half-drunk—a detail the coroner threw in later. Jake's classmates were cheering him on in a way that made me think he was the coolest human on the planet. I mean, I had only finished seventh grade, so that seemed entirely possible.

I remembered in slo-mo how he crouched and sprang backward. The flip was so fast that it had turned into one and a half flips, and then…

"Is it true that his head snapped off?" the Sharpie kid asked.

I glared.

"Well? Do the backflip," he said. "I dare you."

I got up and walked away.

"But you're supposed to do any dare," he yelled. "That's what everyone says."

"You've got the wrong Strangelove," I called back. "Jake was the one who did every dare." *I only do the ones that aren't suicidal,* I added in my thoughts. *Mostly.* I turned to walk backward and spoke my next words loud enough for him and his little thug friends. "Jake's head didn't snap off. His neck bent ninety degrees." I held my arm up, crooked. "Like an elbow."

Maybe that would keep them from mimicking the flip that broke Jake. But probably not. More likely, it'd make them even more interested. Middle schoolers make no freakin' sense.

I pretended like I was leaving, but I didn't go anywhere. Instead, I hooked around the small wooded area and back to the playground. To the swing set. Lil Eminem and his posse had bugged off, and I felt myself edging too close to the supermassive black hole inside that Jake had left behind.

Five years ago. Five. *Five.*

I eyed the playground like I might catch a glimpse of his ghost. He would probably be pissed to know that I imagined his spirit in that ridiculous cap and gown. Also barefoot, but then again, he never wore shoes.

I flipped off my bashed-up Converses and climbed the support beam of the swing set without another thought. The cool metal gripped my palms, and I looped my legs around the top bar and hauled myself into a sitting position. *Easier than it looks.* I wriggled my butt down the pole.

The sunset was lapsing into a cherry-stained twilight. A breeze came in from somewhere and set itself against my radical heartbeat. A few dozen people had watched Jake flip; none of them had tried to stop him, least of all me. And now I was alone. No one was going to stop me either. *I'm lost without you, Jake*, I thought, followed by, *What sentimental crap.*

"I'm always right here," I muttered. "How lost is that?"

Crazy and cursing, I stood up.

CHAPTER

2

BISHOP

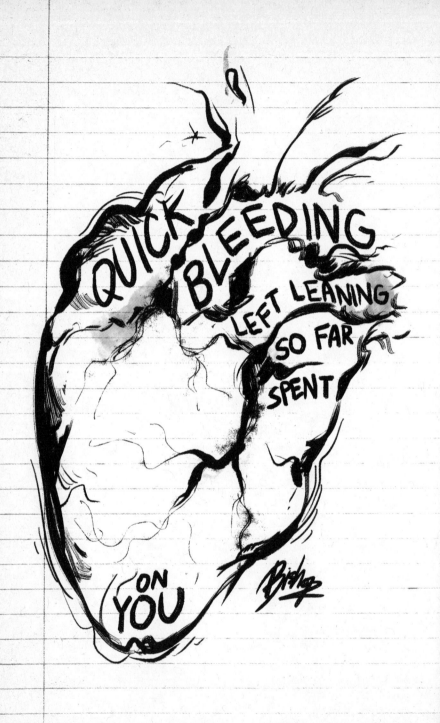

CHAPTER 3

Natalie

NATALIE COULD SEE THE LIGHT AT THE END OF THE TUNNEL. Really it was the far streetlamp over the Richland Avenue Bridge, but it shone like a beacon. This was the route by which she'd escape town in two short months, heading to Cornell University. In *New York*. Which blissfully felt like an entirely different country from Athens, Ohio.

I am Natalie. I can do this.

It had become a mantra to get her through all this meantime. *I can do this. Yes.*

"No," she told Zach, flicking his hand off her thigh. "I'm driving." Natalie didn't glance at his fish pout even though she knew it'd be there. Fishy and cute. Zach was reaching for her a lot these days. It was the beer he'd guzzled at the last party. It was the fact that she was leaving. And it was that All Things Ending feeling leftover from graduation that afternoon. Good thing she didn't think of it that way—that'd be a mess. She missed the stoplight turning red and had to brake hard before the bridge. Her glasses slipped down her nose.

"Maybe I should drive," Bishop said from the backseat. He

hadn't spoken since they got in the car, probably because Zach had spent most of the night making fun of Bishop's heartbreak. Zach was probably too drunk to feel bad now, but when he woke up tomorrow, she'd remind him, and he'd cry. Zach was a weeper.

Bishop was not.

"I'm fine to drive. Are you all right back there?" Natalie eyed him through the rearview mirror, taking in the distance in his brown eyes as he sketched.

"Many people with holes in their hearts don't even know it," Bishop said, his black pen paused over a notebook. "As adults, they have a stroke and die, and then the coroner says, 'This guy had a big hole in his valves and no one knew. Least of all him.'"

Zach groaned and threw his head back. "No Marrakesh talk. Not tonight. You promised."

"Did I mention Marrakesh?"

Natalie put a hand on Zach's arm. "Maybe lay off the Discovery Channel, Bishop."

"Small minds," she heard him mutter. Bishop went back to his drawing. She thought she saw a heart—a literal heart with ventricles and twisted muscle. Bishop had fractured over Marrakesh, a study-abroad student whose name, in Natalie's opinion, was as overly staged as her behavior. Bishop and Marrakesh had only dated for three months, but the pieces he'd fallen into since she left actually made Natalie doubt the validity of her four-year relationship with Zach. Which didn't make sense because four years *mattered*. Didn't they? They had to.

The light turned green, and she drove across the bridge.

"Kolenski has three kegs and his parents are so cool," Zach slurred. Too much flip cup at the last party. He was close to useless.

"Sober up or we're not going to Kolenski's." She pushed a Red Bull into his hand. "I'll get you a calzone at D.P. Dough."

"Thanks, Mom."

"Oh, you really don't want to start that shit with me." Natalie eyed him until he relented. Zach snapped the tab and drank most of the narrow can in one go. Then he belched. And laughed. And Natalie had to literally bite her lip from screaming, *You're a boy. I get it.*

She retreated into her Cornell dreams and took the roundabout too fast. Zach pitched against the passenger window. Natalie ignored his dramatics, driving up Richland Avenue and around the park—until something made her freeze. She screamed, "Stop the car!" before she remembered that she was the one driving.

Natalie spun into the playground parking lot, Zach slamming into her for real this time.

"What the—" Zach said, but Bishop spoke over him.

"Jesus Christ, that girl's going to kill herself!"

Jaycee balanced precariously on top of the swing set.

Standing.

Natalie was out of the car and running. Jaycee's eyes were closed, her chin tucked. She crouched and sprang backward just as Natalie screamed, "DON'T!"

Jaycee flew through the air in a lame arc and landed on her back so hard that Natalie heard the air *whoosh* out of Jaycee's lungs.

Then she was still. Dead still.

Natalie's memories stabbed, making her imagine the exact grotesque angle of Jake's neck as he lay in this same spot. She flung herself to her knees, grabbing Jaycee's shoulders, shaking her and suddenly crying.

Jaycee's eyes flew open, and she sucked in a breath. She blinked a few times. "Natalie? Oh God, if you're here, I must be in hell."

Natalie dropped Jaycee on the playground turf, shocked.

Jaycee laughed. "You know, I don't think you're supposed to be so violent with someone who might have a back injury."

"But you just…you could've…" Natalie's voice dwindled out and came back in a growl. "I'm going to *give* you a back injury if you try anything like that again."

"Oh, you care?"

Natalie could tell that Jaycee had meant for the words to come out drenched in her usual sarcasm. Instead they sprang out like a startled truth, wedging a silence between the girls that was stained with history.

Jaycee looked away first. "I'm having a bad day. You might want to shove off before I unleash on you."

Natalie gave a short laugh. "Must be really bad. You don't usually give warnings."

Bishop and Zach jogged to the swing set. Natalie scooted away from Jaycee, scrubbing away the tears that had appeared way too fast.

"Is she all right?" Bishop asked.

"She's rather insensitive, considering what she just reenacted, but she's fine," Natalie said.

Jaycee sat up, wiping her jean shorts. "Sheesh. You'd think it was *her* brother who cracked his neck." She flashed that stupid, infectious Strangelove smile. "Am I right?"

Zach grinned, and Natalie smacked him in the kneecap before she stood up.

"Why do you have to be so dark all the time?" Natalie

motioned to the top of the swing set. "And what the hell was that? A sick joke?"

"A dare."

Natalie rolled her eyes. "You see what I'm doing, Jaycee? I'm rolling my eyes at you. Because *come on*. We're high school graduates. We're not idiot kids anymore."

"Speak for yourself," Zach said. "I want to be an idiot kid for at least four more years."

"That's why you're going to OU," she snapped. "To drink away your life at frat parties."

Zach's glare had more fire than usual; Natalie could thank the Natty Light. "OU is a good enough school for your mom to teach at."

"Yes, and definitely a good enough school for someone who ends sentences with a preposition."

Bishop offered Jaycee a hand, hauling her up.

"They always this loveydovey?" Jaycee asked Bishop. He nodded, and Natalie bit back a retort. At Cornell, no one will have heard of Jake and Jaycee Strangelove. Just like no one will have heard of Natalie Cheng. She could be anyone. *I am Natalie. I can do this.*

Jaycee jammed her feet into her limp canvas shoes, and then the four of them stood there, trading looks and bowing to awkwardness. Natalie could tell that Jaycee was about to overshare like she always did, but Natalie couldn't think of something else to say fast enough.

"Natalie was my best friend from preschool through seventh grade," Jaycee said to Bishop. "You wouldn't've guessed it, would you?"

Natalie poked Jaycee in the shoulder. "I was the only one

who put up with how you let whatever's in your head fall out of your mouth."

"And I put up with you turning forty on your eighth birthday."

They narrowed their eyes on each other.

"Let's get along now," Zach said. "Or hey, better idea, let's go to Kolenski's. Three kegs. *Three.*" He held up three fingers like the gesture might prove essential to his suggestion.

Natalie pushed his hand down, but she polished a smile. "Good idea, Zach." Maybe Jaycee would come and be social. They'd hang out like old times and get beyond this…*whatever*…that was between them. "You should come with us."

"I'm busy." Jaycee walked away. "I have an anniversary to celebrate," she called back.

"Jayce!" Natalie was surprised to hear Jaycee's nickname jump out like that and even more surprised that Jaycee stopped and turned around. The girl's hair was in a mess of a ponytail, and her worn button-down shirt with the rolled-up sleeves had most definitely been Jake's. Natalie wondered if the baggy jean shorts were Jake's too. "This is all super morbid."

Jaycee shrugged.

"You going to his old hideout?" Natalie asked. "You'll get caught."

"Oh yeah, the campus police. I'm shaking in my Chucks." Jaycee started walking again, up the hill toward The Ridges. It was getting dark, and Natalie watched her get smaller and duck through the trees. Jaycee's shoulders had a bad hunch to them.

"That girl is an atomic bomb," Zach said. "Full of explosives. Scary."

"An atomic bomb isn't full of explosives. It's all about

fission, a process of nuclei division." Bishop paused. "Unless you're talking about an implosion device, which often uses high explosives in order to trigger the fission."

"That girl is just like an implosion device." Zach popped Bishop in the shoulder.

Bishop frowned and turned to Natalie. "Why is she sneaking into The Ridges?"

"Her brother loved breaking into abandoned places. The stain room was his favorite."

"The *what* room?" Bishop asked with more than a little wonder in his voice.

Natalie shook her head. "Don't ask. Jake was…intense on the good days, insane on the bad. He died the summer before you moved into town. An accident. Sort of." The memories were there, waiting to spring. She shoved them down and screwed the lid tight.

"The kid who died on the playground?" Bishop asked, glancing back at the swing set. "Wait, was she really doing what killed—"

"Yes," Natalie said to hopefully put a stop to all of this. Jaycee's misery sometimes felt like her own, a leftover bond from their tangled childhoods.

"Always wanted to look around in The Ridges," Bishop said.

Zach bounced on the balls of his feet. "I broke in once."

"No, you didn't." Natalie crossed her arms. "You went on a haunted hayride around the grounds with Cub Scouts."

"It was still creepy," Zach muttered.

She sighed. "We should follow her. I have a bad feeling."

"Like she's going to kill herself?" Zach asked. When Natalie glared up at him, he added, "Well, she did just try."

"She wasn't trying to kill herself," Natalie said quickly.

"She's not like that. She just doesn't have a whole lot of respect for staying alive."

Bishop laughed, and it was a sound that Natalie hadn't heard in months—since before Marrakesh went back to England with Bishop's heart in her pocket like a souvenir. "Well, I'm in." Bishop started after Jaycee, leaving Natalie and Zach behind.

Natalie closed her eyes tight. Breaking into The Ridges on the night of graduation was not what she wanted, and yet, following Jaycee appealed to her in some aching way. Maybe they could talk tonight. Get all the history out in the open so that when she left in three short months, she wouldn't have to drag any guilt baggage with her. All the college prep books agreed: travel light.

She took a measured breath and looked to Zach. His sweep of blond hair was touched with gold from the very last of the sun, and his features were sweet. "If I go in there buzzed, the ghosts will freak me out, babe. I'll piss my pants."

"I'll protect you," Natalie said, taking his hand and heading up the hill. They were good at being alone. When it was just them, she could see under all the manboy to the Zach she'd fallen for at the eighth grade science fair. The Zach she'd gone with to every football game and to whom she'd given her virginity on her eighteenth birthday. And who, just as logically, she'd be breaking up with on the night before she left for Cornell. Long-distance relationships never worked.

Natalie pictured her mantra in Cornell red: *I can do this!*

The words helped, but not as much as holding on to Zach more tightly. He held her back, which suddenly made her feel awful. The plain truth was that she was cheating on Zach; that's exactly what it felt like. She was cheating on him with the sexy allure of out-of-state college.

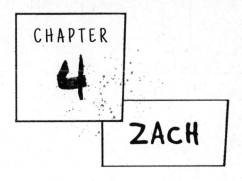

CHAPTER

4

ZACH

Zach Ferris had never regretted a beer so much in his life. The last beer he'd drank, the one he'd shotgunned before they got in Natalie's Oldsmobile, was now churning in his stomach and making him notice all the things about The Ridges that he usually avoided.

Like the sound—or lack thereof—up on the hill.

The wind roughed up the trees, but it did nothing to the huge building. Not a thing. It was almost like The Ridges ate it. And then there were the shadows that reached down from the red brick like arms… His imagination got his brain in a headlock, and the tower shifted to life over him, suddenly hailing punches. He shook his head until his Natalie-styled hair covered his eyes. *Too much* Transformers, he thought bitterly. *Balls to you, Michael Bay.*

Natalie, Bishop, and Zach followed Jaycee toward the nicest side of The Ridges, where Ohio University had bought and rebuilt part of the main mansion. The daylight took off like a coward, and Zach glanced past the renovated section to the endless stretch of broken, barred windows. Twilight showed off the wingspan of vulture hawks leaving the front tower, and he imagined them swooping down and pecking him in the head.

Why did everything in his imagination always seem like it was about to attack him?

Stupid last beer.

"I'll freak out, Natalie," he whispered. "I swear I will. I don't like the dark. I don't like decaying things. I couldn't even go into the nursing home when my pappy was dying. All that paper skin and old bones…"

"I'm scared too, but I need you with me," she whispered back, her hand as tight on his as it'd ever been. He huffed. Natalie didn't give him much credit for being smart, and he had half a mind to point out that she wasn't scared of the old insane asylum. She was terrified of Jaycee.

Zach didn't blame her. The suicidal girl was freaky. Jaycee had a centerfold body skewed by tomboy clothes, and her speeding-slick sarcasm could nail you to the spot just for glancing. Her constant cloud of *I eat men alive* kept every guy at school from taking a swing, but it never stopped Natalie from attempting to make peace with her old best friend. Plus, when Natalie was more than two beers deep, she'd talk about Jaycee and cry about needing to get out of this town. Natalie never mentioned that this would also take her out of *his* life. And if Zach pointed it out? Forget it.

"Too tight. You're hurting me," Natalie said, shaking her fingers free from his.

"Sorry."

Zach watched Bishop reach the spot where Jaycee leaned on the redbrick building, arms folded. They began to talk, but Zach couldn't make out their words. He stumbled over a large stone in the gravel.

Natalie grabbed his elbow. "Act sober," she whispered. "Hey," she said to Jaycee, her voice smooth.

"You two aren't coming," Jaycee replied just as smoothly.

Zach took Natalie in his arms, pressing her against his chest and turning her into part shield, part security blanket, a maneuver he'd perfected over their four years together. It really did make him feel better. Natalie Bear, he'd sometimes call her. She hated it, which was a secret perk.

"I'm not letting you in there alone, Jaycee," Natalie said. "You'll never come out."

"Who said I'd be alone?" Jaycee asked. "I'm cool with Bishop coming. He has genuine interest, unlike you." Natalie glared as Jaycee added, "Besides, Margaret Schilling is always with me up there."

"Don't be crazy!" Natalie aimed her pointer finger at Jaycee. Zach knew this mom-warning really well. Apparently so did Jaycee.

"Are you going to ground me, Natalie Cheng?"

Now they stared. Everyone stared. And Zach started to daydream that they might make it to Kolenski and his three kegs after all.

"They'll be cool," Bishop said to break the stalemate, and Zach scowled. He didn't need his buddy to speak up for him. Natalie thought the crap between Bishop and Zach was all about Marrakesh. Nope. Which was proof that Natalie *didn't* have a spy hole into his brain like she thought. Ha. So there.

Jaycee let her hair down, and just like that she was gorgeous under the three-quarters moon. Natalie elbowed Zach in the stomach, and he wondered if he'd made a sound.

"I'll let you tag along on one condition," Jaycee said, her

eyes on Natalie as she locked her messy light-brown hair back into its ponytail. "Truth or dare, Nat?"

Natalie broke out of Zach's arms and got in Jaycee's face. "Truth."

"Wrong answer," Jaycee said with all sorts of venom in her voice.

"It's *my* answer," she snapped. "That doesn't make it wrong."

Zach's attention swung from girl to girl, sensing that they'd time-warped into a private childhood war. And he knew his girlfriend well; Natalie was close to exploding. How'd Jaycee manage it so swiftly? Should he be taking notes?

"Let me show you how it works, Jaycee," Natalie continued. "Truth or dare?"

Jaycee laughed hollowly.

"See!" Natalie said. "You're just as predictable as me. And you know what? I can follow you in there, so if you really want to celebrate this *anniversary*, you're going to have to accept that Zach and I are coming."

When Jaycee spoke again, her voice was Indiana Jones–styled. Resigned with a whip of anger. Zach couldn't help but like it. "All right. I'll let you come. But only because you need to live a little."

"As long as you *keep* living," Natalie said, still in Jaycee's breathing space. Zach had the craziest flash of the two girls sinking into a mad, hot kiss. He shook his head free of the image—stupid, stupid last beer.

Jaycee stepped around Natalie, grabbed hold of the decorative bars on the first-floor window, and hauled them free.

"Whoa," Zach said. "How'd you do that?"

"The administrative assistant in this office is a smoker. A lazy smoker." Jaycee's words seemed to wink at him. "This whole side of the building was renovated a decade ago. They turned it into offices, and whoever works here"—she handed the bars to Bishop—"likes to pop out for a smoke without having to walk around to the door. Jake found it years back." She slid the window open, her dead brother's name hanging in the air like she'd conjured his ghost.

Jaycee stooped through the narrow opening and onto some OU employee's desk. Bishop squeezed through behind her. Then Natalie disappeared.

Zach wasn't as smooth as the rest of them, damn it. He dragged himself in on his stomach, spectacularly clearing the desktop of all papers before he dropped over the edge.

"Balls!" he yelled as his shoulder connected with the floor.

"Shhh!" everyone said, peering down at him with all their church-worthy judgment.

"We need to be quiet. It's possible someone's here," Jaycee said. "No more screeching."

"I didn't screech." Zach stood up. Natalie put a hand on his chest. Could she tell that his heart was about to rev out of control? This was the last thing in the world he'd like to be doing on the night he'd graduated from motherfucking high school. He bit back his words as usual and forced a maniac's smile. People liked it when he smiled.

They followed Jaycee down the dim hall, up the renovated stairs to a set of nursery-green double doors with a mighty lock. Jaycee pulled a key from her pocket.

"Why do you have a key?" Natalie asked.

"Stole it a few years back," Jaycee said. "From the office we just came through."

She unlocked the door and hauled it open.

A different world awaited.

At first, it was the smell. Old fabric. Peeling wallpaper. Dust. So, so, so much dust that the moonlight streaming through the windows was peppered by it. Zach coughed while his eyes adjusted to the unrenovated side of The Ridges. Yellow, frayed curtains hung raggedly, and the tile at their feet was chipped, piled up like gravel. The light fixture was easily from the fifties. And in the middle of the floor. Zach couldn't tell if it had fallen last year or twenty years ago.

"Jesus!" he said.

"They've cleaned it up a lot," Jaycee replied pleasantly. Natalie didn't say anything, which was such a first that it muddied Zach's nerves.

"I had no idea that it was like this," Bishop said.

"OU tries to clear these halls out, but it's slow going. Lots of asbestos," Jaycee added.

"What?" Zach covered his mouth. "Am I going to get cancer from being in here?"

"Your chances have already gone up," Jaycee said, making her way down the hall.

Zach stared at Natalie. He suddenly realized that he didn't love her enough for this.

"An hour or two of exposure to asbestos won't hurt you," Natalie said. "It's probably not airborne."

"Probably?"

Natalie took his hand from where it gripped the door, keeping it from closing and locking him in. "It's like when you go geocaching and find things. Think about all the things you could find here."

"That's low. I know how stupid you think I am for going geocaching."

She narrowed her eyes. "Not true. I don't think you're stupid. I think geocaching is a little stupid. There's a difference."

If there was, Zach couldn't see it. He didn't budge from the doorway.

"Okay, what do you want?" Natalie whispered. "We can go to Kolenski's after this, and you can get sloppy drunk and I'll take care of you. Or we can have sex. Not both."

Zach looked away, more embarrassed than angry. Natalie knew him well enough to know the dumb things he wanted, but she couldn't figure out any of the reasons he wanted them. And you know what? That made her dumb.

"Okay? Come on," Natalie said like they'd agreed on something. She walked after Jaycee, who was already at the far end of the hall. "I don't want to lose her," she called back to him.

"Right." Zach complimented himself for catching the more than literal meaning.

Bishop was hanging back, which surprised Zach after the boozed-up lipping he'd given him at the last party. "You'd think Marrakesh stole his balls!" Zach had yelled. That should have been a good, old-fashioned fistfight right there. Air out some grievances, you know? But nope. Bishop had ducked into his sketchbook, and Zach chalked it under the things he kept messing up.

Connecting with a post-Marrakesh Bishop was turning out to be an art form, and Zach Ferris had totally failed art class. Mr. Caponi said that his self-portrait looked like the Kool-Aid man and wouldn't buy that that was how Zach saw himself. What? Maybe he did. He certainly felt like a wrecking ball whenever he tried to join one of Natalie and Bishop's "deep conversations."

"They call it *ruin porn*," Bishop said. "The fascination people have with urban decay."

Zach snorted. "*What* porn?"

Bishop turned away, looking buff in the shadowy light. A good-looking guy—that's what Natalie called him. He'd moved to Athens freshman year, and being the son of OU's new president as well as built and black, he'd immediately become a hot commodity. Bishop and Zach really had nothing in common except for a love of old-school Nintendo and a general hatred of sports. Natalie called them anti-teammates, which always kinda sounded like a bad thing.

Maybe that's why Bishop was leaving Zach. At the end of the summer, he'd be off to school in Michigan—five hours away—instead of staying in Athens and going to OU *for free*. Natalie's mom worked for the university too. She could go to OU tuition free as well.

But no, they had to leave Athens. *Had to*, they both said.

Zach walked by a moldy stuffed chair and kicked it. The springs exploded through the polyester.

"One too many beers?" Bishop asked.

Zach growled a response. That stupid last beer had burned away, leaving him feeling distinctly unbuzzed, and he already missed the way alcohol blunted things. Natalie had thrown out that *What do you want?* like he should have his order ready to go. *Yeah, I want two all-beef patties, special sauce…a girlfriend who acts like my girlfriend instead of my mom, and oh, how about a best friend who answers my texts?*

Zach did that thing he'd taught himself during the hellish

years of his parents' divorce. He pushed his bad thoughts outward. Animated them. Gave them pixels and sound effects until he was no longer in a dying building but down a pipe into Mario Bros.' black-and-blue underworld. He threw on his maniac grin like a plumber's cap and even started singing the theme song. "Do-do, do-do, do-do. Do-do, do-do, do-do…"

Jaycee and Natalie whipped around in unison to *shush* him. Bishop didn't even notice.

Zach kept on singing quietly, to himself.

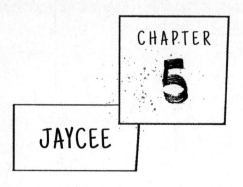

CHAPTER 5

JAYCEE

I COULD FEEL NATALIE AT MY HEELS. SOMEWHERE FARTHER back, her boyfriend and his boyfriend were grumping at each other.

I'd let them in, and I didn't know why. It was nice, I supposed, not to be alone in the freaky creaky Ridges, but then Mikivikious always popped up at some point. I was never truly alone on this night; my brother's bizarro childhood best friend made sure of that. Of course, allowing my own ex–best friend to tag along was a whole different level of weird.

I hated Natalie.

Well, not really, but I certainly didn't want to be in the same room with her. Jake had died, and she'd stopped being my friend. Tandem tragedies. It still made no sense. It still burned, and boy, was that getting old. What was the statute of limitations on being angry anyway?

I focused on the broken building around me. The years had drawn cruel illustrations on the walls, ceiling, and floor, depicting how things *really* return to dust. I crunched through glass shards and trespasser's garbage: beer cans and McDonald's wrappers. Drunken frat boys got in here sometimes, swigging their

Natty Light and telling ghost stories. Mik and I had sent a host of them squealing out the window last year simply by banging around in one of the padded-walled rooms. I chuckled at the memory, and Natalie looked at me like I was a Chihuahua humping her ankle.

On the way to the old stairwell, I was disappointed to find that OU had stripped many of the small patient rooms. I missed the rusted metal bed frames and broken ceiling fans. The cracked sinks and spiderweb-smashed mirrors. But item by item, things were being thrown out. The row of Dumpsters behind The Ridges was always overflowing with the past.

Which made me think about Jake's favorite sandwich. I swore that it was peanut butter and jelly and potato chips. Mom said it was peanut butter and banana, and I said that she was thinking of Elvis. Dad asked how I knew a thing about Elvis, since he died about the same time as the tyrannosaurs. And I told him he was stretching to sound cool. What I didn't say was that they were both wrong, and now they had me wondering if I was wrong as well.

If I was losing Jake, memory by memory.

"This feels so spookily lived in, you know? You can really sense the history." Natalie's shoulders hunched toward her ears, and she kept combing through her straight dark hair as if she needed to check for creepy crawlies. "What does this place make you think about, Jayce?"

She had to stop using my old nickname. I was liable to kick her.

"Peanut butter," I said.

She gave me a motherly look. "I wish you'd just be honest with me. You don't have to protect my feelings."

"I wish you'd figure out that I'm always honest," I muttered. Brazen truth was my biggest problem. When Natalie had asked, "How do you feel?" after Jake died, I said, "I feel like someone used a pumpkin scoop to take out my insides, filled me with gasoline, and set me on fire." Then she cried and ran home. Later, Dad gave me a lecture on answering *Fine* to that question because it hinted at optimism and made other people feel better about "our loss."

Natalie looked away first. Maybe she was losing *me* memory by memory. And maybe that was a good thing. I tossed the rest of my thoughts on Natalie Anna Cheng out the window and in the general direction of the crowded Dumpsters.

After all, today wasn't about Natalie. It was Jake's death anniversary, and this was Jake's favorite place on the planet. The barred windows threw shadow patterns across the stairwell as we climbed. The ironwork of hearts and diamonds cast black lines on each step, and I wondered about the people who built this place. Did they seriously think that pleasing shapes would make the bars seem less like a jail?

We passed a room stacked high with old computer monitors.

"Looks like OU is using these rooms for storage. That's smart," Natalie said.

I cursed and hurried up. If OU was messing with the rooms, they might have touched Margaret's room. They might have touched the windowsill. When I reached the tower room of ward twenty, I didn't pause in the doorway and greet Margaret like usual. I rushed to the window.

Natalie waited for the boys to enter, and then I heard Bishop swearing about the body stain, but I was too busy using the moonlight. Searching.

"Whatcha looking for?" Zach asked, leaning over my shoulder.

"The Holy Grail. Now move out of my way."

He moved back. A little. But I couldn't find it. I couldn't find it! I started to breathe hard, and the only thing that kept me from knocking Zach's balls into his abdomen was that he spoke in a whisper. "What are you looking for, Strangelove?"

"A footprint," I said.

"Was that so hard?" He turned to the half circle of the tower room's windows and checked each sill. "Here," he said, pointing.

I rushed over. The mark was under new layers of dust and more faded than ever, but it was there: Jake's dirty footprint. I knew it was his because my brother was the only person crazy enough to be barefoot in The Ridges. Plus Jake's second toe popped up in a way that didn't leave an impression. My hand hovered over the spot where Jake had been. *He was here climbing on the windowsill. He was* here. Remembering that was getting kind of fuzzy.

I breathed in the foul air of this dying place and closed my eyes, not even caring that Zach was staring. I drew my brother in my thoughts, bare feet first. Then hairy legs in shorts and a baggy, ripped T-shirt. But when I got to his face, I couldn't remember the exact angles.

I gasped and reached out. I wound a fist up in the front of Zach's shirt. "What are my eyes like?"

"Greenish?"

"The shape!" I whispered.

"I dunno! Eye shaped? Oval?"

"My brother had the same eyes," I said, but I didn't know that for sure all of a sudden. I let go of Zach slowly. Were Jake's eyes a little different? Did he have my dad's? My mom's?

"What are you looking at?" Natalie asked from the far side of the room, and I shifted my body in front of the footprint, blocking her gaze.

"We're checking the lawn for cops," Zach invented. I squinted at him. Why would he lie for me?

"You see cops?" Natalie asked in a rush. "Do you think they know we broke in? My parents will murder me if I get arrested."

"Oh, untwist your panties. No one is out there," I said, right before something big and hard and heavy *boomed* several rooms away.

Natalie screamed.

Nope. It was Zach.

"What was that?" Bishop said.

"Ghosts!" Zach spun around, searching.

"A raccoon, most likely," I said. "There are animals all over this place." I wasn't going to tell them about Mikivikious. Odds were that he wouldn't show himself anyway; Mik wasn't crazy about people. Which also meant that I needed to get these guys on the way to their next keg stand if I wanted to see him, which I did. Especially after last year.

I crossed the room and sat in front of the stain. Bishop was staring down at it like he couldn't believe what he was seeing.

"That's a person," he said. "A real person. At least it *was* a person."

"Bishop, this is Margaret Schilling. Margaret, this is… What's your real name?"

"Eric," he said.

"Margaret, this is Eric Bishop and Zach Ferris and—"

"Don't tell it my name!" Natalie said.

I eyed Natalie. "*Margaret* will be less cool if you don't

introduce yourself. Remember, years ago, her spirit followed that freshman home. Made the girl write devil runes all over the walls in her own blood and then kill herself. Or so she said in her suicide letter."

Everyone was staring at me now. "Sit."

They did.

"Hello, Margaret," I said sincerely. A stain in the shape of a small woman lay before me. Her story flooded my thoughts, and I let it spill out. "In 1978, a patient named Margaret Schilling was playing hide-and-seek from the nurses. She hid too far away, in the closed-down ward formerly used for infectious patients, and they forgot to go find her. A month later, a maintenance worker discovered her body, her clothes folded neatly beside her."

"Bodies put out some serious chemicals when they decompose. Look at how she burned herself into the concrete." Bishop's eyes were wide. "This is *real*. Not a ghost story or a television show. A real life that left an imprint on its way out of the world. Amazing."

"So she died from the cold or dehydration?" Natalie seemed genuinely saddened. "That's awful. She was probably terrified up here."

"Wait, so this ward was used for infectious patients?" Zach asked.

"Germs don't stay alive that long. You're *fine*," Natalie said.

I winced at the word. When Natalie used it, it did not hint at optimism.

Natalie inched toward me. "What do you see when you look at her, Jaycee?"

I glanced at each of them. Bishop's dark-brown eyes reflected the moonlight, and Natalie's face seemed tanner and slightly more Asian in the dark. Zach was playing with his boy band bangs, unable to look at Margaret.

"What do I see?" I asked, turning back to the halo effect created by Margaret's splayed hair. "It was a game. She died because she was playing a game."

"Just like Jake," Natalie said.

"Right," I quipped, trying to mask not only my annoyance at Natalie's psychoanalyst tone but also a flare of grief. My chest grew tight. Why wouldn't it go away? Why did all this still buckle me to the ground? Tears burned my eyes, and I took my hair out of my ponytail. This never happened when I came here with Mik. Mik didn't talk or prod. Mik let me be while we walked around Jake's old haunt, wondering if he was actually haunting it.

"My dad said that OU will raze the TB ward." Bishop pointed out the window toward the building on the very top of the hill, by far the spookiest and most unkempt in The Ridges compound. "It's the only fully abandoned building."

"Raze?" I asked, suddenly angry. "When?"

"End of the summer, I think. My dad said it was going to cost a ton but that leaving the old building there while it was falling in is just asking for lawsuits."

"Jake loved the TB ward," I said. "They haven't stripped it down like this building."

"TB?" Zach asked.

"Tuberculosis," Natalie said.

Bishop squinted at his friend. "TB has been one of the leading terminal diseases in society since the dawn of civilization, Zach."

"But it doesn't exist anymore," Zach said. "Like leprosy."

"It totally exists," Natalie said. "And so does leprosy. Where do you learn these things?"

"TB is still the leading cause of death for all people with HIV," Bishop said. "But don't worry, Zach. You won't get it."

I was surprised to find Zach looking at me. "What kind of things are in there?"

I shrugged. "I've never been, but I know it's more dangerous. All the windows and doors are boarded up to keep drunk undergrads out."

"So there's no way in?" Bishop asked.

I shook my head. "Didn't say that. Every building in The Ridges compound is connected by basement tunnels. If we get into the basement, we can get into any building."

We all shuffled to our feet and stood around the last portrait of Margaret Schilling.

"I'm in," Bishop said, and I nodded. Bishop was cool; we'd been partners for two semesters straight in woodshop. He said odd, grandiose things sometimes, but I liked him for it. Plus there was a pretty good chance that Mik would show himself with only Bishop around.

"I'll take you two to the exit," I told Natalie and Zach.

"Well, hey," Zach said. "What if I want to come?"

Natalie looked at him, stunned. "You want to go? What about Kolenski's three kegs?"

"Kolenski gets kegs every couple of weeks." Zach shoved his hands in his pockets. He had sobered up since they'd entered The Ridges, and now he just looked worn down. Even his hair had flattened. I'd written him off years ago, but the way he'd helped me find Jake's footprint and waylaid Natalie…maybe he wasn't such a garden-variety "dude."

"Who else can say that they did this the night of graduation?" he added with a shrug.

"So Natalie's the loose end?" I said. "Big surprise."

"Wait a second. It was my idea to follow you in the first
place. And I...I want to see it."

"Really?" Zach asked her. "Even if it's dangerous?"

"I'm going to minor in history. It'll be like walking around
inside of history."

I knew Natalie well enough to know that she was deluding
herself, but when I opened my mouth to point it out, I saw
something instead. Bishop did too.

"Apple." He pointed to the ground. "Guys. There's an apple."

A shiny, green Granny Smith apple sat in the doorway. I
picked it up.

"Where the hell did that come from?" Zach asked, fear trill-
ing his voice. "Is someone else here? That wasn't there a few
minutes ago, right? Right?"

They all looked up and down the hall. Nothing.

"Maybe Jake's ghost put it there. Or Margaret's," I said. A
thump of what could only be described as happiness resounded
through my chest. It was foreign and weird, and yet welcome.

"You're smiling," Natalie said. "Why are you smiling? You
never smile."

I rubbed the apple on my shirt and took a huge crunching
bite. Natalie looked like she was going to pass out. I winked.
"This way to the basement."

CHAPTER
6

MIKIVIKIOUS

AT LEAST THERE ARE LIGHTS.

CHAPTER 7

Natalie

THE MOMENT THE LIGHTS WENT OUT, NATALIE WAS BODY-slammed by two guys twice her size.

Bishop and Zach clung to her, and she was shocked enough to—briefly—believe in ghosts. But then she remembered that ghosts were stupid. Impractical. What she believed in was people. Cruel people. Dumb people. And whoever turned off the lights was a cruel, dumb, *idiotic* person. She was definitely going to call his or her parents.

Then a rolling *snip* sounded through the dark, and a large flame danced into existence. It illuminated a tall, older boy in a trench coat. He lit a cigarette.

"*You!*" Natalie crowed. She pried Bishop off her right side so that she could put her most threatening finger in the intruder's face. "You!"

"Is he dead?" Zach asked, trembling. "A dead guy who smokes?"

"Oh, he's alive," Natalie said, her tone scorching. "Aren't you, Mikivikious?"

Mik waved his cigarette like a greeting. Jaycee stood there

crunching. God, she was still eating that apple she'd found *on the floor.*

"Mik-a-whatikous?" Zach asked.

"He goes by Mik," Jaycee said. "Told you I didn't break in here alone, Natalie."

Natalie peeled Zach's arms from her waist. "Mik was Jake's best buddy when we were kids. He once poured glue in my hair," she couldn't stop herself from adding.

"Elmer's," Jaycee threw in. "It washed out, didn't it? Besides, don't blame Mik. That was all Jake's idea. You shouldn't have tattled on him for the flaming arrow thing."

"The flaming arrow thing?" Bishop asked Jaycee.

"It was great," Jaycee said. "We were shooting arrows into old Halloween pumpkins—"

"Oh, *we* were not. Jake and him"—Natalie pointed to Mik—"were doing that. Jaycee and I were in the middle of a controlled reenactment of the discovery of King Tut's tomb— which had taken us weeks to prepare, I might add—when Jake got the brilliant idea to fill a pumpkin with gasoline and try to shoot a flaming arrow at it. So I tattled. That's right, I tattled, and we're all still alive, so you're welcome." She realized what she'd said way too late. "Well, not all of us, but…" She glanced at Jaycee and was stunned to find her beaming.

"I'd completely forgotten about the gasoline. Think about the explosion!"

"King Tut? Flaming arrows? I wish I grew up with you guys," Bishop said.

Natalie took a deep breath, and her lungs filled with cold rot. Even worse, her emotions were snagging on all this reminiscence. The past was the past. Period. "We need to keep going."

Bishop ignored her and slap-shook Mik's hand in that way boys have for ascertaining coolness. Mik seemed to pass. "Were you following us this whole time?" Bishop laughed, shaking his head. "That's the most scared I've ever been in my life. Fantastic."

Mik sent a smirk Jaycee's way. Jaycee flashed her equivalent of a smile—lips twisted tight—and then they looked at each other. And *looked* at each other. Natalie was nothing short of astonished. Bishop glanced at Natalie and shrugged, and then Zach interrupted because he always missed social cues.

"Did you go to school with us?" Zach asked Mik. "You look like…like I know you."

"You're probably thinking of Judd Nelson in *The Breakfast Club*," Natalie said.

"He graduated two years ago," Jaycee said. Mik held up three fingers. "Three years ago. Oh yeah, forgot. He was a senior when we were freshmen."

"Let's get into the TB ward already," Natalie said.

Mik went deeper into the tunnels, his Zippo held out like a torch. Jaycee followed him.

"Use your cell as a flashlight," Natalie told Zach and Bishop.

"Can't," Zach said. "Battery's almost dead. Had to turn it off." She handed her illuminated phone to Zach.

"Does this Mik guy talk for himself?" Bishop asked, flicking on his screen.

"He's a selective mute," Natalie said quietly to the boys.

"A what?" Zach sputtered, the tunnels echoing his voice.

"A guy who doesn't suffer fools," Jaycee called back, making it clear that both Mik and she had heard the whole exchange.

The five of them rounded corners as the tunnels grew colder

and reeked of mold. At one turn, Natalie tripped into a rusted metal gurney. The hair stood on the back of her neck, and she surrendered her forced calm to grip Zach's hand.

The group came back into contact with the moonlight at the bottom of the creepiest set of split-level stairs in existence. Two seriously disconcerting signs awaited. The first:

WARNING
Lead Work Area
POISON
No Smoking or Eating

Followed by the even more encouraging:

DANGER
Asbestos
Cancer and Lung Disease Hazard
Authorized Personnel Only

"Found your lung cancer, Zach," Jaycee said. She plucked the cigarette from Mik's mouth and ground it out. "I keep telling you, Mik. You're too smart to be a smoker."

He took the apple core from her hand and threw it into the black of the tunnels. Wherever it landed, it didn't make a sound, which was almost as weird as watching the two of them interact. So relaxed. Natural. No one relaxed around Jaycee; Jaycee usually made sure of that.

Mik snapped his Zippo closed and ascended, followed by Jaycee, Bishop, and Zach. Natalie went last, and the piled dirt and debris made her nearly lose her footing. Mik grabbed her arm and helped her the rest of the way. His expression was nice without smiling, almost like he knew she was flashing back to all the torments of their youth. Natalie could admit that he'd grown up quite a bit since the last time she'd seen him, and she might even be tempted to call Mik sexy if he wasn't so damn mysterious-looking. She loathed mystique; it felt too much like a disguise.

"Thanks," she said, pushing away from him.

Natalie held her elbows as she stepped into the moonlight-soaked TB ward. The lead paint peeled from ceiling to floor, and an upright piano rotted in the corner. Her anxiety started to crescendo just as she turned toward Jaycee.

The girl stared at her, green eyes bright. "Don't step anywhere that seems damp. The wood is probably rotted through in some places."

"Hey, Jayce," Natalie started, watching the three boys venture into a larger room. "Are you with Mik?"

Jaycee cocked her head, confused. "As much as you are."

"No, I mean…*with* him."

Jaycee made a distinctly reptilian noise and walked after the boys. Zach came out at the same moment, passing Jaycee too closely and getting a hard knock to the shoulder. "Oww," he said. "Is she always this intense?"

"Yes." Natalie sighed. "Always."

Zach stepped over to the rotting piano. He ran his fingers over the bones of the existing keys, and when he pressed one, a low sound moaned through the air. "Freakin' amazing."

Natalie entered a large room punctuated by a huge brick fireplace. Beside it, a graffiti artist had spray-painted a black angel with a golden halo. The shadows from the windows reached for it like devilish hands, and Bishop stood before it as though he were having a spiritual awakening. Mik and Jaycee were on the far side of the room, turning in circles as they took in the ruination. Everyone was bewitched. Everyone but Natalie.

Her nerves were rising, getting the better of her. She needed facts. Questions and answers. Her hands fumbled to do a search on her phone as she crouched on the cobbled floor in front of the skeletal remains of an iron bench.

"Typical," Jaycee said from the far corner. "We're in the coolest place in Athens, and Natalie is on her phone."

Natalie looked up, feeling struck. "I was Wiki-ing the history of this place."

Jaycee turned her back, but Bishop looked her way. "What does it say?"

Natalie's voice was too loud when she found it, trying to cover up how much Jaycee's dismissive remark had hurt. "I wanted to see if this was a hospital for tuberculosis patients or for mental patients who also had tuberculosis."

"And?" Bishop asked.

"The latter."

"That's a tough break. Mentally unstable *and* dying of lung disease." He rolled his shoulders and cracked his neck from side to side.

"How many people died in this building, you think?" Zach asked.

"Hundreds," Jaycee said from where she stood by stairs that led to the second floor. "TB is a pretty terrible death. Not quick. Months or even years of pain." Jaycee spoke of death like it was both banal and a treat. Like potato chips.

Something creaked on the floor above, and they all froze.

"Hundreds," Zach murmured.

Bishop moved to the stairs, looking up longingly. Then he climbed, and Mik followed. When Zach started to go, Natalie grabbed his arm.

"Don't go upstairs," she said. "It's too dangerous. The floor could fall in."

"I want to see what's up there." Zach looked at her anew. "Wait, are *you* scared now?"

"Hey, you were terrified when we first got here, and I helped you."

"You helped me do what you wanted to do. Now I'm going to do what I want." All those beers had finally burned out of Zach's system. He was no longer childlike and silly.

"Don't leave me alone," she tried.

Zach motioned to the girl at the foot of the stairs. "Jaycee will stay with you."

"She won't," Natalie said to herself as Zach took the steps too hard.

Jaycee was watching Natalie. Half of her face was in shadow, but it only emphasized the reflection of her eyes. "You should have left. You could be doing things you like by now."

Truth, Natalie told herself. Only truth worked on Jaycee Strangelove. Natalie took a leveling breath. "I'm leaving soon for New York. I thought we could bury the hatchet."

"You bury yours. I'm still using mine." Jaycee started up the stairs, and Natalie surged forward and grabbed the back of Jaycee's shirt. Two of the buttons popped off when it pulled tight, and Jaycee swore. "Damn it, Natalie. This was Jake's!"

"It's falling apart," Natalie said. "That's not my fault!" Jaycee straightened her shirt, and words started to fly from Natalie's lips. "It's time, Jayce. It's been a million years, and I don't want you to hate me for the rest of your life."

"Five. It's been five years since my brother died and you dropped me. Put the real number on it, Natalie. And stop calling me 'Jayce,'" she said. "That was Jake's name for me."

Natalie felt that push of wild anger all over again. "No, that was *everyone's* name for you. Don't you remember? Or has our whole childhood been hijacked by Jake?"

Jaycee scowled, and Natalie felt the urge to get the truth off her chest. She made a fist instead, because none of this was in her plan. They were supposed to find some sort of peace and then go their separate ways, and yet there was nothing peaceful in the way Natalie wanted to shake Jaycee. Wanted to scream that what had happened was beyond everyone's control. But that would mean talking about Jake's accident. And Natalie did *not* do that.

Jaycee took the stairs, leaving Natalie to grope for composure. She breathed in through her nose and out through her mouth. Three times. *Calm.* It didn't matter if Jaycee didn't forgive her. In two months, Natalie would be in New York, so none of this mattered, right? *Right?*

"I am Natalie," she said to herself, ignoring the way her voice trembled on her own name. "I can do this." Her mantra scored a fat zero, and she fled for the stairs to find Zach. She found him in the hall and wrapped her arms around his waist. Nothing made her feel better faster than leaning on him; it's what their whole relationship was founded on. And that had to be okay too.

Zach and Natalie wandered down hallways dotted by rooms. Metal bed skeletons leaned into themselves, and tilted bureaus vomited old drawers. At one point, she heard a series of squeaks that made her grip Zach's belt. "You hear that squeaking?" she whispered.

Zach pointed into the farthest room, where they found Bishop scribbling poetry on the square panes of an old window. Natalie read a line about Marrakesh and tugged Zach away before he went off. "Let him do his thing," she said.

"Don't I always?"

They found the largest room, a gathering place of sorts that had wide windows and a door that led to a second-story wrap-around porch. Mik and Jaycee were on the porch, excitedly hunched over something.

"What did you find?" Natalie asked.

Jaycee turned her back, climbing up on the brick railing and onto the roof. Mik followed.

Natalie ran for the porch and yelled at the sky. "Get the hell down! That's dangerous!"

"Let them be," Zach said. "You can't control her." His words hinted an accusation.

Natalie felt red and breathless. Everyone else had started to enjoy themselves since they stepped into the old TB ward. But not Natalie. Why couldn't she just chill?

Zach moved past her and climbed onto the railing.

"Get. Down," she said between her teeth.

"I want to see what they found." Zach's legs disappeared, and Natalie spun in a circle.

She was alone again. No one wanted to stay with her. And did she blame them? No. She was too type A. Always bossing people around. This was why she had to go to New York. No one would know her, and she could just hit the restart button.

Natalie had beautiful plans. She'd let people call her *Nat*. They always seemed to want to. And she'd bought a whole new wardrobe. T-shirts and jeans to replace her camisoles and cardigans. She'd be relaxed in New York. She wouldn't study all the time. Maybe she'd find a boyfriend who didn't make her cringe so much. Or maybe she'd enjoy being single.

"Sky's the limit," her dad used to say when she was little. She cradled those words as though they were her only hope. In two months, the sky would truly be her limit—unlike now, with limits everywhere. What would they all say if she just climbed up on the roof?

Insane. She could literally die. Like Jake. She remembered the sound of his neck snapping and put her hands over her ears, shaking.

Bishop found her a few minutes later.

"They're on the roof," she said, pointing to the way they'd climbed out and up.

"You all right?" he asked.

She ignored the question and wiped her face even though there were no tears. "I saw what you were writing…was that about Marrakesh?"

He leaned against the wall, and plaster fell to reveal the brick underneath. "Maybe it was about Margaret Schilling."

"Don't mock Jaycee," she said. "She's been through a lot."

"I *wasn't* mocking her." He stood up and reached for the balcony. "Can I give you some advice? Go easy on Zach. Let the leash out. He hates transitions, and he *hates* that we're leaving Athens for college."

Natalie nearly spun out. "*You're* telling me this? You're the reason he's so feisty. You never want to hang out with him anymore. We basically had to drag you out tonight, remember?"

Bishop's scowl deepened. "I'm trying to cut ties before I leave, Natalie." His hand reached higher on the roof. "Question is, why aren't you doing the same?"

"What?"

"You are going to break up with him when you leave, aren't you? So why are you dicking him around now?"

Natalie opened her mouth, but nothing came out.

Bishop climbed onto the roof like everyone else, his words floating down on her. "Zach knows what you're doing. He's not as stupid as you treat him."

She sat on the floor and pulled her knees into her chest. She knocked her palm against her forehead, trying to rearrange Bishop's words into an order that didn't hurt. Was she being awful by staying with Zach this summer? Should she just break up with him? She'd have to do it carefully. He was so tender-hearted. And no matter how she did it, he'd undoubtedly spend the rest of the summer in his basement bedroom, drinking away the world. She couldn't do that to him.

And she didn't really want to part with Zach before she had to. He steadied her—even when he was invoking her mom tones. Was it so selfish not to want to be alone all summer?

The anxiety attack came on with a red head rush. She stood and turned in a circle, finding the scribble of a chimney on the wall that Jaycee and Mik had gotten excited about. Beneath it was a signature:

JAKE

Natalie touched it. All of this started with him...all the nightmares and emergency trips to her counselor. All the loneliness and ruptures in her personality that made her desperately realphabetize her books or iron every piece of clothing she owned. She combed her hair with her fingers over and over again, but it wasn't enough.

Reaching for the balcony, her hands shook, and she felt like something was ripping inside, but maybe this had to happen. Maybe she had to break free now, embrace everything that scared the crap out of her. It was a long list, starting with Jaycee and ending with the world.

But before she could, the ceiling beams started to scream.

And the roof split open, dropping Zach hard and revealing the black sky beyond.

CHAPTER

8

BISHOP

WE ARE
ONLY WE UNTIL
WE RUIN INTO
YOU AND ME

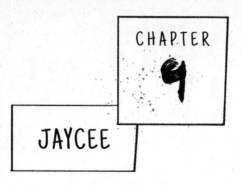

CHAPTER 9

JAYCEE

FINDING JAKE'S HANDWRITING LIT ME UP INSIDE.

All of a sudden, I could picture his left hand curled around a pen, his tongue pointing out to the side, and his hair growing scraggly over his ears. I could even hear his laugh. It was high when he was a kid, but by the time graduation rolled around, his laugh had dropped to a growl, and my dad bragged that puberty had turned Jake into part grizzly bear. The deep laugh also made Jake's sense of humor seem like it had matured, which, of course, it hadn't. He was still pretty damn amused by his own farts.

The memories came back strong as I climbed the TB ward roof, and I couldn't believe the bright rush of details. Mik was right beside me the whole time, and I felt emboldened and a little wild. I scrambled around soggy spots, taking Mik's offered hand as we shimmied toward the apex. He seemed stronger or maybe broader than he had been last year. Definitely taller.

Definitely still Mik, which was what I loved about him. People in town talked about Mik's selective muteness as if it was a psychological injury from seeing his best friend die, but I knew the truth. Mik had never liked to talk. That's why he hung out with Jake. My big brother did all the talking for both of them. And sometimes they let me tag along on their adventures, although it always caused a fight between Natalie and me. She didn't approve of climbing trees, walls…or heinously steep, decrepit roofs…

Mik's foot went through, and I grabbed his trench coat before realizing that that wasn't going to keep him from falling. We ascended more slowly, moving to one of the many chimney stacks.

"Jake was up here, wasn't he?" I couldn't keep the thrill out of my voice. "That picture of the chimney seemed like he was leaving a note behind or something."

Mik's silence said yes.

"Good. I'm not imagining it." We reached the chimney, and I clung to it. Mik held out his Zippo, and I used the flame to look over every inch of the brick until I found a tiny black arrow.

"I think he means for us to climb up," I said, acting before I was thinking. I grabbed the top of the chimney and hauled myself half onto it, only pausing when I realized that Mik's hands were pretty firmly on my waist. "It's okay. I'm not going to fall."

I tried to wiggle free, but he held more tightly. I ran with it, ignoring an extra double thump in my pulse while I used his arms for balance. Crouching on the top of the chimney stack, I couldn't help thinking, *Jake was right here.* And he probably stood up like it was nothing.

I closed my eyes briefly before standing tall. My breath vanished as I glanced around, because I swear I could see the night. Not just the darkness but the wind on every shadowy tree. I could see each light on in Athens below and the serpentine gleam of the Hocking River.

"Amazing," I said to my brother, and I swore that he replied, "*I know, right?*"

It was nuts, and yet, I could sense Jake. He was here. Right on the edge of suicidal crazy, waiting for me. "Jake?" I murmured, closing my eyes and leaning forward.

"*Why not?*" he seemed to say back—his favorite phrase. The very words he had tattooed on his right arm the day of his eighteenth birthday. Four months before he died.

The old brick beneath my feet began to lose its mortar.

To tumble.

Why not?

Whirling black and a slam to my shoulder later, I opened my eyes and found Mik on top of me, pinning me to the roof. He gasped, and his hands were so twisted in my shirt that I could feel his knuckles against my collarbone.

Natalie's words came back like a finger snap. *Are you* with *Mik?*

His mouth was open like he was going to say something. Or because he'd just said something.

"What?" I asked. My cheeks were hot, and I suddenly felt little beneath him—a schoolgirl with a lame crush on her big brother's best friend. But that wasn't even quite it: I pushed him off of me. "Thanks for the superhero save," I mumbled.

Zach was picking his steps through the dark on the roof's edge. "It's unbelievable up here!" he yelled. "You can see all the lights of the city!"

"Shhh," I said, laughing at the way he Gollumed and crept. "There're security patrols we need to worry about."

"What happened there?" Zach asked, pointing at the now-halved chimney. Bricks were still tottering and rolling off the roof.

"Just a dare," I said, relishing the words. *A dare from my brother.* I glanced over my shoulder and found Mik coolly smoking a cigarette. He arched an eyebrow at me that was supposed to mean something, but I didn't follow, and I wasn't going to beat myself up to figure it out. To be quite honest, I was annoyed by the way he'd pulled me down. Maybe I was supposed to fall off that chimney. Fate has a dark sense of humor.

A few minutes later, Bishop climbed up to join us. "Natalie is in a *mood*," he grumbled.

"What else is new?" Zach and I said at the same time.

He held out his fist to do one of those bumps that I always see guys doing, but when I leaned in to connect, he disappeared.

Right through the roof.

Natalie was screaming long before the dust settled and long afterward. Bishop and I looked through the hole to where Zach had landed on his back, laughing and moaning.

Natalie kicked him.

"Stop laughing," she yelled, hysterical. "Zachary Frederick Ferris! This is it. IT. We're done!"

Bishop started laughing at that, and I couldn't stop myself from joining in. Honestly, it was the best breakup I'd ever seen...up until the point when the campus security patrol car pulled around out front.

"Oh shit. Get down!" Bishop whisper-yelled. "Natalie, turn your cell off. They'll see it through the window."

"I see you already!" the cop called up. A seriously strong flashlight beam reached all the way to our faces. "Come down slowly and carefully! The Athens PD is on their way to pick you up for breaking and entering."

"Jaycee!" Natalie hissed through the hole in the roof. "You said that the campus cops handle this!"

"They do until they call the real cops," I snapped. "Natalie, take Zach out back. We'll come down through one of the windows on the far side and make a run for it through the woods."

"You better be right about this, Jaycee. My parents will—"

"Just go!"

Mik was gone, and it took a few precious seconds to find his all-black clothes on the far roof. I slipped through a small window where two buildings were joined in an L. Natalie yelled all over again when Bishop and I came running through the hallway to meet them.

"This way," I said.

"Mik?" Natalie asked.

"He went his own way." *As always*, I refrained from adding.

I led them out through the backyard to a narrow break in the chain link. "We should split up," I said. "Bishop, head for the woods. For the hiking trails."

I had to peel the fence back with all my strength to get enough space for Bishop's shoulders to squeeze through. He ran off toward the woods, and I turned to Zach. "Go to the cemetery. I'll meet you there." Zach wedged himself through, getting stuck. I pushed him with my foot and faced Natalie. "Follow Bishop. Stay out of sight until they leave."

"Maybe I should turn myself in," Natalie said in a trembling voice.

"What?" Zach and I cried out together. I shooed him away from the fence. "To the cemetery!" I snapped. "I'll take care of her."

I spun around, surprised to find Natalie crying. Hard.

"They'll go easy on me if I cooperate," she said.

"Natalie. They'll make you tell them who you were with and get us all busted."

"You think I'll rat you guys out," she said, her voice strangled. "Don't you?"

My face was so close to hers that I knew my words would slap, but I didn't care. Not now. Not after five years of radio silence. "I don't think. I know."

I tried to leave through the fence, but she took hold of my arm.

"Jayce, let me come with you." Her hand gripped so hard that I felt the bite of her nails, and I had a flash of little kid Natalie. She was always smooth and in control until something snapped—and then she could barely breathe. "Please don't leave me alone right now."

"Don't be a baby," I said. "Lay low until they're gone. You'll be fine." Something banged behind us, and I whipped around, but no one was there. "To the woods. Find Bishop." I flung her hand off my arm and ducked through the fence.

The security cop's flashlight was coming around the building, and I heard another patrol car pulling around front. I made myself visible to give the others a chance, running across the road before I leaped down the hill and into the endless rows of identical limestone graves. I found Zach's blond head and flattened him to the grass just as a flashlight beam swept over us.

For a solid few minutes, we listened and waited. From some far-off place, I swear I could hear Natalie crying, but that couldn't be true. She'd made it into the woods; I'd watched for that much. And why was she even crying? No, *sobbing*?

I looked at Zach. He was pressed into my personal space

while my back was against a cold headstone. "Does she usually cry when she dumps you?"

"Huh?" Zach blinked. "Are you high? When did you get high without me?"

I shook him by the shirt. "Answer."

"No, she's usually pretty pleased with herself."

"You have really bad breath."

"You have really nice boobs," he countered.

I pinched his shoulder so hard that I had to cover his *ow* with my hand. "What do you know about my boobs?"

"A whole lot when they're pressed up against me."

I pushed him away, bristling all over as the two patrol cars drove toward the other side of The Ridges. "The cops'll keep circling. We should get out of here." Something rustled close by, and this time, Zach knocked into me, pulling me down.

"What was that?" he whispered.

I peered over the eerie white bricks, all numbered, all without names. No wonder the poor souls who died in The Ridges were never at rest. A bit of black turned around from the edge of the woods and looked at me with eyes shining like deep wells. Mik. He held his hand up in a half wave, and I knew that was the best I was going to get for a goodbye.

"See you next June, Mik," I muttered, frustrated by the way he ghosted in and out of my life—and by the sudden daydream I was having about following him. About what might happen if I saw Mik more than once a year.

Instead, I hauled Zach to his feet by his shirt. "Let's go. I'll give you a ride home."

CHAPTER 10

ZACH

"WHAT ARE YOU DOING?" JAYCEE ASKED.

"You got to hear this. It'll rock your face off." Zach plugged his phone into the auxiliary line of her car stereo. He was about two seconds from crying, and like hell was he going to let Jaycee see him cry. "I've only got twelve percent battery. Enough time to get 'Vindicated.'" He cranked the volume way up.

An electric guitar slammed through the car, and Zach liked Jaycee more in that instant because she didn't turn it down. The lyrics filled the space between them with bleeding angst, and Jaycee drove with a strange, paused expression, like she was taking in every single word.

Zach drummed on his legs and gave in to the chorus at the top of the lungs, his voice barely heard over the screeching volume. When it finished, he flipped on some Modest Mouse, that song about missing the boat, and turned the volume back to human levels.

"I had to vent a little," he said. "Natalie gets right under my skin."

"We have that in common," she said. "Where do you live?"

"The Plains. Behind the elementary school."

She turned toward the neighboring town, speeding into the turn so fast that the tires squealed. "Was that Dashboard Confessional?"

"My answer to that depends on if you're going to tease me for listening to them."

"I've never teased anyone in my life."

"Well, then it is Dashboard. From the *Spider-Man 2* soundtrack."

"Ew."

He looked at her full on. "You're being for real, aren't you? About not teasing people? You're missing out on the fun."

Jaycee didn't bite. She took her hands off the wheel to tie up her hair, and the car almost went off the road. When Zach reached over to straighten them out, she hit him in the arm. "Don't think about it. You're drunk."

"I *was* drunk. Like three hours ago." Zach frowned. "Now I'm painfully sober." He rubbed his face. "My back is killing me, although I have to admit, this was a pretty epic night. Up until that last part."

"The cops?"

"The Natalie."

Jaycee scowled as she drove. "She'll take you back. She's done it before. You two are rather infamous for breaking up and getting back together."

"Oh, you know my work?"

She didn't laugh, and holy hell, could the girl drive fast.

Zach held on to the handle above the window and pretended he was in one of the Fast and the Furious movies so that he didn't barf. "Natalie and I have a harder time staying apart than we do being together. She's dumped me thirty-something times in our four-year relationship. That's like…every two months. Or something. I'm not good at math. Basically, every few weeks, I just wait for the boom."

"Sounds like love," Jaycee deadpanned.

"She can't get enough of me. What can I say?"

Jaycee looked at him from the side. Twice. Then she went back to scowl-driving. "What do you know about her? What do you *really* know about her?"

"Enough. I know she's scared of her own shadow and that she works hard to make sure that no one sees that side of her. I pay attention, and she does confide in me. Sometimes."

Jaycee nodded. Whatever he'd said had pleased her in a weird, indefinable, Jaycee kind of way.

They entered The Plains, and Zach's phone died completely, the music cutting off. He glanced at it. He really needed a new phone; the funky battery on this one would take hours to pick up a charge again. "Guess she won't be able to text me later when she changes her mind," he wondered aloud. "Maybe it'd be good if we had some time apart. These days, we're either having sex or trying to tear each other down. I could use some middle ground, you know?"

Jaycee's cheeks were cherry red, and Zach swore that he'd embarrassed her with the sex talk. He didn't think anything could make Jaycee look like that. She turned down the street near the elementary school, and Zach directed her toward his driveway.

"Why are you confiding in me?" she asked abruptly.

"It's just some girl talk."

"That isn't my forte."

"Oh, but it's mine," Zach said with his most confident smile.

"I see that. It's probably what's encouraged Natalie to keep you as a pocket pet all these years." Jaycee pulled to a stop, and he looped his hands behind his head instead of getting out.

"Natalie and I...we are what we are. She knows me."

"What happens when she goes to New York?"

He glared forward. "She goes to New York."

"You're working hard to convince me that you and Natalie are pretty laid-back," she pointed out. "It's backfiring. You're going to be messed up when she takes off."

"You would know. You're kind of the expert on life post–Natalie Cheng. Got any tips?"

Now Jaycee was glaring. "What happened between Natalie and me was different. Plus, I was her best friend for eight years. I've got double the time on you." Jaycee began to act strange. Nervous. She ran a finger around and around the steering wheel. "Natalie didn't look right at the end of the night. Did you notice anything?"

"Oh, she'll be fine. She was probably just pissed because we all went up on the roof, and she didn't have the guts. She really doesn't like being left behind. Whatever the problem, she'll probably just deal with it in an orderly fashion like usual."

"I'm not so sure," Jaycee said.

"Hey, want to come in? Hang out?" he asked, surprising even himself. She glanced at him like he'd asked her to get naked. "No funny business, I swear. I usually hang out with my little sister when Natalie goes postal, but she's at a sleepover. I...I don't know what to do when I'm by myself."

"That's the saddest of the very sad things you've said tonight."

He unbuckled his seat belt and got out of the car, his back tight from the fall through the roof and his chest now aching for reasons he'd rather not deal with.

"Hey." Jaycee rolled down her window and called out to him. "When we were up in the stain room, thanks for not saying anything to Natalie about the footprint. If she knew why I go up there, she'd just call me morbid."

"Aren't you morbid though? That's like your thing, right?"

"Good night, Zach."

He couldn't help himself. He leaned on the driver's window, making Jaycee lean back. "So you and Mik, huh?" Zach made his pointer fingers kiss and completed the effect with smooching sounds.

"How old *are* you?" she said, but there was the tiniest hint of a smile. "Natalie grilled me on that too," she admitted after a pause. "Why?"

"Because he likes you. It's obvious."

"How?"

Zach shrugged. "Dunno. Just is."

"You guys are insane. He's practically my brother," she said. Zach lifted an eyebrow at her, calling her bluff. "All right," she relented. "*Not* a brother. More like a stranger. We spent a lot of time together as kids, but since Jake died, I've only hung out with him four times. Every year on Jake's death anniversary, we meet up in The Ridges. It's not romantic, believe me."

"Do explain." Zach sat down on the driveway. Jaycee opened the car door and swung her legs out. It was almost friendly. "Only four times?" he led. "You exaggerating?"

"Five if you count that first night, which I probably shouldn't." Jaycee's face was misleading. It was normal. Casual even, and Zach walked right into the trap.

"Why shouldn't you count that night?"

"We went to the hospital together. He put his trench coat

over my head to help drown out my parents' screams when they ID'd Jake's body."

"*Jesus.*" Zach rubbed his hands over his eyes. "You really do just talk about all that stuff like it's no big deal, huh? That's what weirds everyone out, you know."

"You think I should change my grieving process so that I don't weird everyone else out?" she asked.

"Well…of course not."

"Good. That makes you smarter than Natalie."

Zach tugged his shoes off and splayed his toes on the cement, accidentally thinking about Aquaman before he remembered what had led to this rather depressing turn in the conversation. Mik and Jaycee. Misfit love.

Zach stood up and dug his hands in his pockets. "There's more to this story, Jaycee. I saw you guys stare at each other like star-crossed lovers in those basement tunnels. If I hadn't said something, it would have gotten real awkward real fast."

Jaycee's face went cherry again, and she looked even more intriguing than usual. "Last year when I saw Mik, it was different." She paused and shuffled her Converses on the pavement.

"Don't get shy now."

"After we met up in the asylum, we had fun scaring off some drunk frat boys who had broken in. They had Burger King bags with them, and it made the whole place smell like fries, and I got hungry. For some reason, Mik had all these apples in his backpack, so we ate them and walked around laughing about what had happened."

"Ah, the origin story of the apple. I thought Natalie was going to have an aneurism when you ate that off the floor."

Jaycee kept talking like he hadn't said anything—like she

was both anxious and relieved to tell someone what had happened. "We walked the whole bike path around campus and saw how quiet Court Street gets after the bars close and everyone stumbles home." She squinted like she was trying to remember even smaller details. "Mik came in and out of focus under the streetlamps, and I talked forever. I told him about my senior year nerves. About my parents and missing Jake. He listened until past dawn."

Jaycee looked up at Zach, a strange yearning on her face that made her seem a heck of a lot younger than eighteen.

"Yep. Mik likes you. No guy spends a whole night listening to a girl talk unless he likes her. It's one of the Ten Man Commandments. Number four, I think."

"But Mik never said a word to me that whole time. And afterward, he disappeared to wherever he goes and didn't reappear until tonight." Her voice dropped. "And now I won't see him again until next year."

"Nope. He'll show up when you least expect it. *And* it'll be soon."

"You have absolutely no basis for that assumption."

"Ah yes, but when I'm right, you owe me one pint of Ben and Jerry's. AmeriCone Dream is my favorite." He smiled and waited. It took a lot longer than with a normal person, but Jaycee smiled back.

"Fine," she said.

"Told you I was good at girl talk."

She pulled her legs back into her car and closed the door. "I take it back, Zach Ferris. You're not entirely worthless."

"And you're not entirely batshit crazy, Jaycee Strangelove." He held out his fist through the window, and she bumped it.

And then she drove away, and Zach was alone. Even his father was out—at his girlfriend's house no doubt.

Zach turned on every single light and popped open the lock on his father's liquor cabinet. Then he retreated to the basement and flicked on his old-school Nintendo with his big toe, wishing that Natalie would crawl through the window and get right under his skin where she belonged.

CHAPTER
11

MIKIVIKIOUS

WHAT THE HELL DO *YOU* WANT?

MOONVILLE TUNNEL

CHAPTER 12

Natalie

NATALIE AWOKE FEELING TORN IN HALF. SHE WAS SPRAWLED out on a foreign bed, a wretched taste in her mouth. She dragged herself into a sitting position before the events of the night crashed over her. Where was she? What had she done? *Where was she? What had she done?*

Her head pounded until she had to hold on to it with both hands, peering between fingers that reeked of vomit.

Answer one question, she told herself. *Take it slow.* Where was she? Natalie looked around at a boy's room, having a whipping flash of the frat boy she'd been with hours earlier. She'd been in his bed too. But no, this was a different boy's room. This was a room she'd been in before…a lifetime ago. Jake's room?

Jake?

She scooted up in the twin bed and looked down to where Jaycee slept all curled up with her hands wrapped around her cell phone. Natalie's throat ached, and she tried to remember how she'd gotten here, but the only clear memories were even harder to swallow than drunken flashes. She remembered wandering through the woods behind The Ridges, never finding

Bishop. Torn up, she'd gone to Kolenski's to find Zach and collapse into him, but he wasn't there, and she went uptown. She went to find someone to make her feel something else.

Anything else.

Natalie wrapped her arms around her chest. Her shirt was missing, and she was only in a bra. What was worse, she could totally hear Mr. Strangelove walking around the hall. She stood up, and her legs shook. She opened a dresser drawer and pulled at the clothes inside, but suddenly Jaycee was on her, knocking her hands away.

"I fall asleep for an hour and wake to find you in Jake's underwear drawer?"

"I need a shirt," Natalie said, one arm over her bra. "Your dad is out there. Imagine his face if he came in and saw me like this."

Jaycee's fury settled. "True. I'll get you something. Stay here. Don't touch anything."

Jaycee ducked out of the room, and Natalie slunk back to Jake's bed and pulled the covers over her head. She wanted to cry, but her body couldn't muster it. Her mind was stuck on that moment she'd been standing on the couch at the frat house, screaming and dancing—right before she threw her arms around that bastard and kissed...

Jaycee returned and tossed a black T-shirt to Natalie. She pointed to the trash can. To what was left of Natalie's baby-pink camisole. "Don't think you're going to want to save that one. I had to pull it over your crying, miserable head at four in the morning. Remember?"

Natalie felt like she was melting. The shirt was so soft and the bed was warm. She curled up in a ball, knees to chest. "Jayce," she said softly, "please go easy on me."

Jaycee sat on the edge of the bed and handed Natalie a glass of water.

Natalie sipped at it, but for all her apparent dehydration, her body didn't want anything. "You took care of me last night." She reached up and touched the rubber band in her hair, recalling how Jaycee had fastened it into a ponytail while she was throwing up. "What about your precious hatchet?"

"I don't hate you, Natalie. I'm mad. There's a huge difference." Jaycee's voice was as gentle as it could be, which only made Natalie want to cry. "You have to tell me if someone hurt you. If something happened."

"No, no," Natalie started. "Nothing like that. But Mik. He…"

"What about him?"

"Mik brought me here, right? What happened before that?"

"You're supposed to know that," Jaycee said. "Did he find you at Kolenski's?"

Natalie forced the words. "I was at Kolenski's, but then some people were heading uptown to a frat party. I went with them."

"You went to a frat party with strangers," Jaycee said flatly. "Jesus Christ, you're lucky you didn't get raped, Natalie."

Natalie turned her face into the pillow. *Breathe, breathe.* "I was with Zach's brother's friends. They were looking out for me. I wasn't even drinking at first."

"Then why were you crying when Mik brought you here? You didn't…" Jaycee shook Natalie's shoulder sort of hard until Natalie looked at her. "You hooked up with Mik. Is that it?"

"No!"

"Then how did you end up half-dressed and hanging over his shoulder?"

"I don't…remember," she said, which was a lie. A necessary lie, because she was not going to think about *who* she had been with. No. Not ever. Never. She could shove that down and ignore it. Leave it all behind when she went to New York. The only problem was that the further she pushed her secrets down, the more she felt things ripping inside. Just like last night.

She ran her fingers over the frayed edge of Jaycee's old T-shirt. "What did Mik say?"

"Nothing, per usual."

"But you're his friend, right? You can ask him."

"Selective mute, Nat."

Natalie sat up and squared her shoulders, finger-combing her hair. She could do this. She could just push through it. "Yes, he's *selective*, which means that he does talk to some people."

"Well, Mik doesn't talk to me." The words made Jaycee's face do a weird thing. A sour thing. "I'm not one of his people." She checked her text messages and tossed the phone onto the end of the bed with a little too much force.

"Who are you waiting on?" Natalie's heart thumped hard. "Did you text Zach?"

"I don't have your boyfriend's number. Besides, the state in which you arrived did not suggest that you wanted him around."

"State," Natalie repeated.

"Crying your face off. Saying you were sorry. Puking your guts out."

"I'm sor—"

"I *don't* want to hear it again. You scared the hell out of me. I've never seen you so…destroyed. And you kept saying that thing."

"What thing?" Natalie felt cold all of a sudden. She held on to herself.

"*I'm not Natalie. I can't do this.*" Jaycee paused. "Over and over. *I'm not Natalie! I can't do this!* What the hell was that about?"

Natalie stared out the window. Her whole life felt like it was waving, teetering in on her. She had reverse vertigo…whatever it's called when it feels like the sky is falling on you.

"Natalie." Jaycee's voice was strong and surprisingly caring. "What does that mean?"

"Nothing," Natalie whispered. "Sounds like gibberish."

There was a long pause, and Natalie could feel Jaycee's eyes on her, but she couldn't look at them.

"I'm sorry," Jaycee finally said. "About last night. About taking all your friends away from you and up on the roof. I understand that that probably bothered you."

"You all could have died. That's what bothered me."

"But it was an amazing view." Jaycee looked at Natalie with that superiority thing she always did so well. "Next time, just climb the roof. Then maybe you won't feel like the world is passing you by."

"That's not how I feel. The world is breaking." She hadn't meant to say that.

"Explain," Jaycee ordered.

Natalie busied herself with her hair. "I'm just hungover. It's nothing. What's that?" She pointed at a small triangle of folded paper on the rug, desperate to distract Jaycee.

"Must have fallen out of the drawer," Jaycee said, picking it up and turning it over in her hand. "It's Jake's."

"Open it."

"I don't like to go through Jake's things. I found his porn

stash in his closet a few years ago, and I think it's best not to know everything." Despite her words, Jaycee kept looking at it, so Natalie scooped it out of her hand and opened it.

"It's just that stupid map he used to carry around. Look."

"What?"

"Jake's urbex map." Natalie smoothed it down on the bed. "Don't you remember? He used to scribble on this and talk to himself. He had that journal too."

Jaycee blinked at her.

"There's no way you don't remember this! Remember that one time he came home from being out all night, and he'd mangled his knee. He was icing it at the kitchen table and said he'd been in an abandoned mall up in Cleveland. Your mom was so mad."

Jaycee was still staring, practically enraptured.

"That was the time he explained his urban exploring fascination—how he'd been hiking through man-made ruins every weekend. You said you wanted to go with him, and I said that's insanely stupid, and he said you had to wait until you were eighteen to tag along. And then he told me that I couldn't come no matter what."

Bright tears spotted Jaycee's eyes. "Why don't I remember that? I mean, I can see it now when you say it, but before it was like....gone."

Natalie folded up the map into its tight little triangle. "Don't know, Jayce. Sounds like you've got some emotional road-blocks." Nice one; her therapist would be proud.

"You remember lots of things, don't you?" Jaycee scooted closer on the bed. "Like you were saying in the tunnels. You remember that stuff with the pumpkins and the gasoline."

"What I *remember* is how hard you and I worked to dig out the sand pit and plant all those old garden tools and vases. Remember? We were going to recreate the discovery of King Tut's tomb and film it and become a YouTube sensation. I was going to be Howard Carter, and you were going to be the Fifth Earl of Carnarvon. Remember the costumes?" Natalie crossed her arms and looked down. "I did a lot of research for that. We never did get to finish it after Jake got pissed and Mik put glue in my hair."

"I forget stuff," Jaycee said, her eyes glazed. "No, it's not even forgotten. It's more like things just disappear. *Poof.*"

Natalie watched her carefully. Jaycee didn't look quite right. Distant and sort of *starving*. "Maybe you're just moving on. I mean, you're a day past graduation now. You've already made it further than Jake ever did."

Jaycee's mouth fell open. "What a fucking thing to say, Natalie."

"Hey, it's true. Isn't truth the only thing you respond well to?"

Jaycee strode across the room to Jake's desk. She dug into a drawer and came back with a Mead journal. "This is the journal you were talking about?"

Natalie nodded, unsure of where this was going.

Jaycee opened it and flipped around to a few pages, then she sprang back onto the bed and unfolded the map. "You see that marker over Athens? It says *TB ward*, and there's the little chimney he drew."

"Like the doodle you found on the porch," Natalie said, thankful for this distraction.

"All of these…look at them!" Jaycee flipped open the journal next to the map. "These are all places that Jake went and left messages. Dares."

"Dares," Natalie deadpanned.

"I can go there and do them. And I can read what he thought in his journal."

"Jayce…"

Jaycee wasn't listening. "I bet Mik would know about it." She grabbed at her phone and checked the screen, growling, "I gave him my number and nothing. Nothing!"

"Who? Mik?"

"Yeah. Last night after he dumped you here, I chased him into the street to ask what was going on. He just stared at me. So I grabbed his cell phone out of his pocket and put my number in it. I told him to text me."

Natalie paused with her mouth on the water glass. "Pants pocket or trench-coat pocket?"

"How does that matter?"

"In boyland, reaching into a pants pocket is the flirty equivalent of flashing your boobs," Natalie said.

Jaycee's cheeks turned lava red, and her face looked like it might melt off.

"So, pants pocket," Natalie interpreted. "And now he hasn't texted. And you're upset."

"Wouldn't you be?"

"So you do like him."

Jaycee scowled. "*Like* him? I barely know him. And that's beside the point. I chased him down because I wanted to know what happened to you. I mean, do I need to call the cops or take you to the hospital or anything?"

Natalie looked down, her own cheeks going scarlet. "I'm okay. I'm…"

The door opened after a swift knock, and Jaycee's dad

popped his head in. "Is that Natalie? Natalie Cheng?" He swept into the room and gave Natalie a crushing hug. "I thought I heard someone in here. How are you, Miss Graduate?"

"I'm all right, Mr. Strangelove. Just hanging out with Jaycee. We went to a party last night," she invented.

"It was, like, the best time ever," Jaycee valley-girled.

Jaycee's dad put his other arm around Jaycee, squeezing them together. "I'll tell you what. It's a dream to see you two together. I knew nothing could keep you apart forever."

"Dad," Jaycee said. "We're busy."

He moved to the door, still smiling hugely. "All right, ladies. I'm going to make pancakes. What do you all think of that?"

Natalie forced a grin, nauseated by the mere mention of food. Jaycee tried to shut the door behind him, but he pushed his head back in.

"Hey, Natalie, maybe you can get Jaycee to move out of this room."

"Jake's room," Jaycee snapped back. "It's Jake's room, Dad. Not 'this room.' Don't act like he was never here."

"Yes, fine. Jake's room. But still not *your* room."

"Bye, Dad," Jaycee said. He closed the door, and Natalie felt sorry for the man. Jaycee went back to the map, tracing her finger from the chimney to the next nearest marker. "Jake did something in Moonville—that old haunted railway tunnel out in Vinton County. That's not even a half hour away. Bet Mik knows how to get there." She glanced at her phone and frowned. "I've never been so desperate for someone to text me before. Feels like hell."

"Jaycee, your dad—"

"Tries too hard. Makes me twitch."

"Don't be so dismissive. Grief is atypical, and you can't expect everyone to have the same process as you."

"Thank you, Dr. Cheng."

"Well, I *am* majoring in psychology at Cornell."

Jaycee squinted at her. "Which makes so much sense, considering the fact that you've wanted to be a history professor since birth."

"Well, I'm minoring in history. Academia is unstable. Getting tenure is all but impossible these days. The market is flooded with graduate students who can't get jobs elsewhere."

Jaycee sat back on her heels. "How does your mom do it?"

"Do what?"

"Turn you into a ventriloquist dummy and throw her voice from your house. Isn't it a little cruel for her to tell you not to go into the same profession that she has?"

"It was *my* decision, if you must know. And fine. You want to smack each other every time we talk? Then I get to point out that you act like Jake's *still here*, Jaycee. He's not. He's dead. This room is like a weird shrine. And let's not forget the way you wear his clothes."

Jaycee's face went dark, and she pulled on her shirt. "Leave, Natalie."

Natalie put her shoes on and kept all her words down. All her sadness pressed in. She was at the door when Jaycee snapped a look up from the journal. "Do me a favor. Take Zach back, will you? He's irksome, but he needs you. Don't dick him over when you go to New York. Don't turn your back on him like you did to me."

Natalie shut the door hard. One arm instinctively wrapped around her chest, and the other went around her waist. She was going to hold herself together. She was. But first she needed a plan to get through this damn summer, and before that, she had to figure out how to walk downstairs and past Mr. Strangelove without throwing up or bursting into tears.

CHAPTER 13

ZACH

DESPITE BECOMING BFFS WITH A DUSTY BOTTLE OF SHERRY, Zach hadn't slept all night.

And now he was at church, hungover and stiff with exhaustion.

Silent prayer filled the chapel with shuffles and sniffles. Zach glanced around at his fellow worshippers while they dropped their faces toward their laps, shoulders hunched. Across the aisle, Mrs. Elderly, who matched her name spectacularly, mouthed every word of her prayer, and Zach tried to figure out what she was saying. Something like, *Jesus, save my cat.*

Pastor Allen cleared his throat into the mic, and Zach's older brother, Tyler, started playing a guitar riff that whined through the old wood church. This whole "rock worship" thing was losing popularity fast, although not fast enough for Zach. Zach's dad had been so damn proud when Tyler was named lead musician, but then, his dad didn't know that the only spirituality Tyler got from his role was an infamous on-the-altar hookup with Eleanor, the tambourine and triangle girl, after practice one night.

Zach looked over the altar with its fake candles and flower

basket. How had Tyler done that exactly? The altar was pretty high. Were they both on top of it or was Tyler standing? As if his brother knew what was happening in Zach's mind, Tyler made eye contact with him and puckered his lips in a mock kiss.

Note to self: never, ever attempt to figure out the logistics of Tyler's conquests.

Zach tried to think about something else, but his thoughts dropped on Natalie so fast and hard that his back ached. The fall through the roof had been nothing compared to Natalie's latest and greatest attempt to flatten him.

That's always what happened. She'd dump him and piss him off, and then the next morning, after being alone with his blinking Nintendo screen all night, he'd feel her loss like she'd been ripped out of his chest. It didn't make sense. How could he want to be with her and not want to be with her at the exact same time?

It didn't help that without Natalie, he had to sort through the trail mix of crap in his life all by himself. What to major in at college. How to handle his mom's new boyfriend. When to tell Tyler to piss off. How to keep from strangling his always-judging father. You know, the usual.

Zach loved Natalie—but not remotely like Bishop had loved Marrakesh. Zach felt red just imagining how Marrakesh and Bishop had had that crazed look for each other. He'd once overheard them screwing and been completely blown away by their R-rated pleasure screams. Zach's blush made his face feel like a furnace. Was he supposed to make Natalie sound like that? If so, he was doing a horrible job. Then again, could anyone make Natalie that wild?

Zach put his hood over his head and pulled the strings tight. He wasn't supposed to think about sex in church, so of course, all he could think about was sex.

Alianna elbowed him in the ribs. "You're making weird noises," his little sister whispered.

"No, I'm not," he said back.

"Shhh," their father said from the other side of the pew where he held his girlfriend's hand. Zach's father was wooing the freshly divorced Mrs. Dowen, and Zach was pretty sure they'd be married by next summer.

Pastor Allen ended silent prayer, and yet Tyler's guitar just kept on weeping. The pastor cleared his throat in the mic again, and Zach snorted a laugh.

Zach's father growled a warning.

"I'd now like to invite the children to head to their Sunday school classes with the grace and love of Jesus," Pastor Allen said.

Alianna took Zach's hand. "I have a plan," she whispered. "Trust me." She got up without letting go. She stepped around Zach and into the aisle, the whole while tugging him behind her like a leashed puppy.

"Hey, let go," Zach said. "I'm not a child."

"Let go, Alianna," Zach's father said. "You're holding up the service."

Alianna pouted in the general direction of Mrs. Dowen. "I want Zatch to walk with me," she said, purposefully using the name she'd given Zach when she was learning to talk. "Please, Dad?" she added just loud enough to get a thousand *awws* from the surrounding parishioners.

"Oh, that's sweet," Mrs. Dowen said. The woman had two

boys in college who wouldn't attend church with her, and she found Alianna to be the most precious thing on the planet. Big mistake. "Let them go, Joseph," she said to Zach's father.

Zach stood up, and Alianna led him down the aisle and around to the side door—but not before Tyler instigated a whole new round of *awws* at the sight of the inseparable Ferris siblings.

Once they were in the hall and the door clapped closed, Alianna let go. "It's good for your image to be nice to me. Now that you're back on the market, you've got to look like a sweet guy. You've got to seem like the opposite of Tyler."

"That's not hard." Zach started to walk her toward the Sunday school classrooms, but Alianna grabbed his elbow and swung him into the girls' restroom. She locked the door and sat on the counter. The place reeked of potpourri and gas. *Flower farts*, he thought, mildly amusing himself.

"Get comfortable," she said. "We're not leaving here until you're out of the hoodie."

Zach glanced in the mirror. His hood was drawn so tightly over his head that only a small circle of his face was visible. Great. Was that what everyone was *awwing* over? "I'm just tired, Ali. I didn't sleep last night."

"You never sleep." She motioned to his wardrobe situation. "And believe me that *that* is not helping you find someone to get over Empress Natalie."

Zach tried not to snicker. "She hates it when you call her that." Alianna ignored him and took a bottle of neon-blue nail polish out of her small *Frozen* purse. "You know, at some point, Dad's going to catch on to the fact that you're about twenty-five years old beneath all that fake kid behavior. Mom is already onto your tricks. Natalie never bought them to begin with."

"Hence my dislike of her." Alianna shook the small bottle. "I'll cross the Dad bridge when I come to it. Now tell me everything that happened last night, and don't leave out why Tyler's being a bigger butthole than usual this morning."

Zach collapsed on an overstuffed chair in the corner of the bathroom. "Hey, why do you girls have lounge seats in here?"

"For nursing moms."

"*Ew.*"

"Talk."

He told her about Jaycee and the swing set, about Natalie's insistence that they follow the girl into The Ridges, and then Mik's crazed appearance. He finished off by describing his fall through the TB ward roof, Natalie's reaction, and his run from the cops.

"I don't know what's up Tyler's butt," he added. His brother had woken him up by sitting on Zach, reeking of booze, and saying something about how freshly graduated girls were the hottest drunks. Zach took that to mean that Tyler had hooked up with one of the girls in Zach's class, which made him want to puke. "I hate our brother."

"Tyler hates himself," Alianna said, kicking off her shoes to paint her tiny toenails. "That's enough for me."

Zach checked his phone. No texts from Natalie. Nothing. Would she actually stick with the breakup this time?

"You need to stay broken up," Alianna said eerily. "Trust me. You're both better off with someone else. By the way, I'm supposed to talk to you about your major. Mom wants to get to the bottom of this before you sign up for classes."

Zach responded by pulling the strings tighter on his hoodie until his face completely disappeared, nothing but the tip of his nose sticking out. "I don't know what I want to major in. Isn't that why they have an 'undecided' major in the first place?"

"Mom doesn't buy that."

"Are you really going to be her snitch?" he asked. "That's not your style."

"I don't think it could hurt you to make some decisions. Come out from the hood, or I'm going to paint your nails."

Zach held out his hand, and his little sister scooted along the counter until she was sitting with her feet on his knees. She painted his fingernails carefully, and Zach loosened his hood until he could see what he called her "constipation scowl." Alianna was blond and fine boned like Zach. Both replicas of their mother. Tyler was the one who was all shoulders and eyebrows like their dad. No wonder those two were no-fail buds.

Alianna was his only ally—no, that wasn't true. He also had Natalie. They'd been together since the eighth grade science fair. She'd been right there when his parents' divorce broke through his house like an earthquake, and Tyler descended into what Natalie referred to as his "debauchery degree." Natalie had never judged Zach for not being able to sleep. Or when he came too early, which was pretty much every single time. Not for crying either. He cried way too much, and she never said a damn word against him.

"I want her back," he said to Alianna.

"No, you don't." She scowled at his thumb. "Why are your nails so freakin' huge? I can never get enough paint for the whole thing in one swipe." She wiped the paint off his thumb with a paper towel and started over again. "You just don't want to be alone, Zatch. That's no reason to be with someone. That's not love."

"It's something like love," he said, because he was certain of it. When he was in the depths of his insomnia, awake for the third night in a row, his eyes burning from staring at the TV, Natalie was the one who crawled through the basement window and curled up with her head on his lap. It didn't always help Zach knock out, but it sure as hell made him feel better about not being able to sleep.

"What happens when she goes to college?" Alianna asked, and Zach ignored her and the question just like he had when Jaycee was asking.

"Will you help me get her back?"

"I'll think about it." She sighed and moved on to painting his other hand. "And only if you start to stand up to her."

After church, Zach was relieved to find Tyler heading to his frat house uptown and not coming back with his dad and Alianna. Zach kept the overhead lights off and descended into his basement bedroom. His old room had been tucked beside his parents', and sometime around the second year of their nocturnal screaming matches, he'd blearily moved downstairs. He'd even become the coolest guy in seventh grade because of his lair.

That was the upside.

The downside was that he never relearned how to sleep. Whenever Zach closed his eyes, he heard his mother crying and his father telling her that she was stupid. Whenever Zach closed his eyes, he felt like he was a little kid again, praying for Jesus or the boogeyman to come get him. Whoever was faster.

The small rectangular window by the ceiling was propped

open, the curtain pushed aside. By the early afternoon light, Zach could make out Natalie's outline in his bed. He kicked off his shoes and crawled under the covers beside her. She'd wept all over his pillow, and the sogginess smelled of booze. She was also wearing some guy's old shirt.

"What happened?"

"I'm sorry," she said, her voice tiny and wounded. "I went to Kolenski's after The Ridges. I thought you'd be there. I wanted to make up, see if you were okay, but you weren't there, and I…got drunk." She started to cry so hard that the mattress shook beneath them.

"It wasn't cheating," he said, because he knew her that well. "We were broken up. If you made out with someone…" He sighed. "It's okay. I'm not mad."

And he wasn't mad, which was weird. He was just glad that she had come here. To him.

"I slept at Jaycee's house. She…oh my God, Zach, she hates me."

"I didn't get that impression. It's more like she's mad at you. If she's mad, you can do something to make her…not mad. You know?"

"Like what?" Natalie said, a sliver of hope in her pillow-muffled voice.

"Let's just sleep for now," he said. "You'll feel better when you're not hungover." He pulled her into his arms and his whole body slumped. Maybe if he was the most supportive, wonderful boyfriend this summer, they'd stay together when she left. They could do the long-distance thing, and he'd even drive up to New York every couple of weekends. That would make for some unbelievable missing-you sex…

He still had two months. He could do this.

She was shaking, so he leaned over her shoulder to kiss her. She pulled away after a brief moment, her lips bumping on his as she spoke. "Did Bishop make it home okay last night?"

"Yeah, he texted. He wants to go hiking around man-made ruins again. That's the first thing he's cared about since Marrakesh. Go fig." Zach bowed to a huge yawn. "He's going to the Columbus Museum of Art today to look at some statues or something. He'll be back tonight. Hey, maybe Jaycee could take us out again, and you two could talk."

"Maybe." Natalie seemed deep in thought, and he wondered if she was thinking about Jaycee or the other guy—whoever she'd kissed. Who was it? Kolenski? Zach felt himself dropping into sleep before he could get too worked up. Natalie's emotions were always unbelievably tiring. The essential cure for an insomniac.

CHAPTER 14

JAYCEE

I SAT AT THE EDGE OF THE DRIVEWAY, ARMS CIRCLING MY legs, head resting on my knees.

Waiting for Mik.

I'd finally gotten a text from him during dinner—if you wanted to call it a text. The message was an empty bubble, but I'd fired back a dare that I thought would work. Especially if Zach was right about Mik's, uh, interest.

Moonville Tunnel. Pick me up at sunset.

I pulled at my shirt. I really needed to stop sweating. This was one of the first summer days not to bow to the chill of dusk. I closed my eyes and tried to remember how we cooled down in the past: a cannonball in the overchlorinated city pool, followed by a challenge from Jake to drink the whole gallon of lime-green Kool-Aid. Summer didn't taste like that anymore. It hadn't for years, but I still reached back to that place where things were simpler. Paper airplanes and lightning bugs and so many bonfires that my memories glowed with the stick-skinny shadows of Jake and Mik leaping over flames.

Every time my mom caught us, she would line up the boys, sometimes with Natalie and me, and lecture us on safety and responsibility. Natalie would say that she agreed, that she had warned us. Then Jake would call her a snitch, and she'd cry.

I burned when I thought about my mom. How long would she stay at Stanwood this time? Would she even want to come back when she was released? The last two times she'd been sent home, her doctor had said she was ready, not her. And she told us that over and over.

Would you like more coffee, Laura? my dad would ask.

I wasn't ready to come back, she'd say.

Or *Would you like to go to Jaycee's first track meet?*

I wasn't ready to come back.

My head hurt. My eyes smarted. I didn't want to think about my mom.

I checked my phone, but there was nothing besides Mik's empty text. Would he show? No clue. And why in hell was I so uneasy about it? It wasn't a date, no matter what Natalie and Zach had implied via all those liking and kissing comments. That stuff made me uncomfortable. Made me itch. It also made me check my phone a thousand times per hour and trade out my sports bra for a real bra, which made my shirt snug in the right spots.

Of course that felt weirdly obvious, and I pulled on one of Jake's button-down shirts like a security blanket. I had to admit that I'd never changed three times in one evening before. Is this what Natalie's life was like? Terrible.

Mik's old blue car appeared down the street, and I stood, hugging Jake's urbex journal to my chest. Mik pulled in the driveway, and I tried to jump in, but I wasn't fast enough. My dad must have been watching. He was already halfway down the driveway, nearly running toward Mik's car.

"Drive," I told Mik, but he only took a quick look at me—long enough for me to see that he had recently showered and wasn't in his trench coat—and got out. They shook hands before the hood of the car. Then my dad put his arms around Mik as fast as he had gone after Natalie. I couldn't hear what my dad was saying to him, but I just about died when he patted the side of Mik's face like some sort of mobster godfather giving his blessing. And then Mik's lips moved.

Mik *said something.*

Natalie's speech that morning about him talking to *some people* came back like a bug bite, and I wanted to scratch the words into oblivion. So Mik really did talk to some people. I just wasn't one of them. He couldn't even text words to me, apparently, although he had gone to a party and saved Natalie like some kind of superhero. Speaking of, why had he even been at that party? That didn't seem like his scene, but then, what the hell was his scene?

Mik and my dad both looked back at me in the car. I waved. Not sweetly. More like *what the hell, guys?* Mik slid back into the driver's seat while my dad came around to the passenger window. I rolled it down, and my dad's face leaned through the square.

"Should I give you a curfew?" he asked. "Midnight?"

"I'm eighteen. I don't have a curfew," I said, tucking Jake's urbex journal under my knees and hoping that my dad didn't see it.

He looked at Mik. "I suppose I should say something about having a shotgun and a shovel, but I really don't have either, so just bring her back safe."

Mik nodded.

"I love you, Jayce."

It was an unspoken, iron law in my family; you never left without saying *I love you*, because what if you never came back? What if Mik wrapped his car around a tree or aliens descended in a blue flare of abducting light beams?

"I love you too," I said, not looking up.

My dad walked to the front door, and we watched him go.

"It appears," I said into the awkwardness, "that my dad thinks we're going on a date."

Mik had no response. Not even a sideways look. He kept his hand on the gearshift as though he had no idea where to go.

"Moonville," I said a little too bossily. "Please. You know how to get there?"

Mik's answer was to pop the car in reverse and drive. I hadn't been in a manual transmission for a long time, and the way he maneuvered the stick from gear to gear was mildly hypnotic. I could also feel the engine rev up in my legs in a way that I hadn't ever thought about before. All of which put me on edge, which meant that my mouth started running.

"Thanks for the two a.m. Natalie Cheng home delivery. I was up to my eyeballs in puke." *Holy crap, Jayce. Say something nongross.* "I guess it's good. We got to have a long overdue heart-to-heart, even though she kind of poisoned me. You know what she actually said? 'You're a day past graduation now. You already made it further than Jake ever did.' Who points out that someone's made it further in life than their dead brother?"

I brought out Jake's journal from under my knees and hugged it to my chest. "Now I'm going to be gauging my life events off that. When I turn twenty-one, I'll be sitting there thinking, 'Three years older than Jake ever got to be.' When I hit eighty? 'Sixty-two years past Jake's allotment.' What happens if I get married or have kids? 'This is my son. He's the kid my brother never got to have.' Damn."

I stopped talking about five years too late. Mik gave me a really strange look, and I felt warm all over. "Sorry. Sometimes I think you only get to see my morose side." I wanted to have something better to say, but all I thought about was Jake. What else was there to tell Mik? All I could scrounge up was what had kept me excited all day.

"I got into Jake's urbex journal today. And I found this map." I dug into my pocket and held up the little paper football. Just holding it brought back hints of the vibe I'd gotten while standing on that chimney stack—the sensation that Jake was not far away at all. That he was actually really close. I'd do anything for that feeling again. "I'm going to go to all the places on this map this summer. Do the things that Jake did. You could come with me…if you wanted."

Mik didn't respond, not even to nod. We were headed down a twisty stretch, and I stared at him, knowing that he wouldn't be able to look away from the road and catch me. He seemed younger than usual. How old was he after all? Twenty? Twenty-one? Jake would have turned twenty-three this year, and Mik was exactly in the middle of the five-year age difference between my brother and me.

Perhaps it was the absence of the trench coat that made Mik seem young, or the fact that he must have shaved his face, like, five minutes ago. Either way, I spent a little too long looking over his black T-shirt and cargo pants, at his boots that seemed as large as shoes could be without being built for snowboarding. By the time I looked back up, we were at a stoplight, and he was doing the same thing to me that I was doing to him.

Taking inventory.

I flipped Jake's journal open, sweating even worse now. "So Moonville is on Jake's map. The TB ward is too, along with the marker we found on the porch. Jake was leaving messages—dares—in all these places and taking notes. He wanted to have his own danger-hunting reality show. Do you remember that?"

Mik nodded.

"I'd kind of forgotten until Natalie reminded me. That girl remembers everything. But there's something weird here. I've been reading Jake's journal, and you're…not in it," I said, angling my question as a statement to avoid the weird pause of his silence. "You didn't go on any of these trips with him. And I kind of remember that you and Jake didn't hang out a lot in high school." I paused, feeling a strange twist in my chest that probably had something to do with heartburn. "That sort of makes me feel better about Natalie. Maybe all childhood friends grow apart. Maybe that's just part of the deal."

I flipped to the Moonville Tunnel entry that Jake had left-hand scribbled across one page. "The writing is warped like he wrote it when he was wet," I said. "Is there a lake or river out there?"

Mik shook his head. Did he not know? Or was he saying that there wasn't a body of water? My next words flew out like a sneeze. "I saw you talk to my dad."

This time when he looked at me, there was pure panic in his

dark eyes. He opened his mouth a fraction, closed it. Pressed his lips.

My pulse slammed a warning, and my sudden guilt was weirdly stressful. "Sorry. I just don't understand when you talk. When you don't." I buried my face in the journal. "So anyway, Jake was hanging out with two guys. Heberman and Ferris. Ferris," I repeated like an idiot. "Zach's older brother?"

Mik's hands went tight on the steering wheel, and he nodded. He did more than nod, really. His face seemed to take on a shadow.

"Okay…" I cleared my throat. "So you and Jake drifted apart for a few years, but then you guys were hanging out again when he graduated. You were there when Jake…"

When Jake…

"Hell." I pressed my hands over my eyes. "You know what? I'm going to stop talking for a little while."

Mik pulled off the main highway and onto a tight, twisting back road. In a few places, the incline was so steep that he had to downshift into second, the engine striving. I'd never been in Mik's car before, but I already kind of loved it. It was old and lived in. It had a pep to its forward surge and a vanilla scent that was doing an amiable job at masking the smoke smell. If I'd never met Mik, I'd probably be able to tell several things about him from this car. That he was laid-back, clean but disorganized. That he had a somewhat problematic Subway addiction from the wrappers in the back and that he wasn't on the MP3 player bandwagon. "May I?" I asked, holding up a folder of CDs.

He nodded, and I flipped through them. "Ryan Mikivikious, you have an eighties addiction," I said. "Oh, wicked." I pulled out a disc, popping it into the player. The Cure's "Lullaby" filled the car, and embracing the way Zach had blazed music through my stereo last night, I turned the volume way up.

The dirt road continued to narrow. The surrounding woods were thick and dense, spinning a kaleidoscope of twilight greens. We soared past a few swampy areas, and I let the music fill me up with something that was equally creepy and, well, sexy. I hadn't anticipated that angle, and by the time we pulled over, my mouth was dry and my pulse seemed to have confused this drive with a walk on a tightrope.

The dark had come on fast, and there were no other cars. Mik's headlights illuminated a flat hiking path. The train tracks had been removed years ago, leaving a platform-type walkway, and yet trees were crowding in, disrupting the memory of the wood crossbeams and iron rails.

We got out, and despite the heat, Mik grabbed his trench coat out of the back. He threw it over his shoulders, and the worn cloth snapped. Instantly he looked more like the boy I was used to. More like the boy I didn't feel like a silly girl around. I breathed easier, and we walked toward the creek and the cement supports leftover from the now-missing train trestle. It was getting darker by the moment, and I had the weirdest feeling that we were being watched.

We stood on the blocks, avoiding the raised spines of metal rods. "This place is supposedly really haunted," I said, looking into the gathering shadows of the woods. The last trickle of dusk was leaving everything blurrily edged. "Jake wrote about a prank he and his friends played on some hikers. They pretended to be the ghost that haunts the tunnel."

We climbed the rocks that made a walking path over the creek. Halfway across, I heard a crashing sound and froze.

I felt Mik's hand on my shoulder, and I reached back to grab his wrist. We dashed the rest of the way across the water, soaking my left shoe before we reached the other bank. When I looked back at the other side of the river, I gasped. A dark figure stood on the concrete block where we had just been.

Stood and stared.

"Do you see that, Mik?"

The whole woods went too quiet. And something huge splashed in the river beside us.

I whipped around to find another ghostly person on our side of the river. It released a demonic cry, and Mik and I ran up the gravel embankment, colliding. We slid toward the water, landing in a pile of old leaves and poking pine branches.

Two figures stepped out of the woods, and I recognized them painfully slowly.

"Vengeance!" Zach crowed. "How does it feel to have the piss scared out of you, huh?"

Natalie leaned over Mik and me while I made sense of Bishop's silhouette on the piling. She flicked on a headlamp, illuminating her altered appearance. She looked like she'd gotten dressed in my closet, her hair in an all-business pony-tail. "Greetings," she said. "A nice night for a hike, don't you think?"

Her tone reminded me that I was all over Mik. Or he was all over me. In trying to get up, I got seriously familiar with his thigh, and he totally grabbed my under-boob area. By the time we were both standing, I couldn't look at him.

"Well, well, well," Zach said. "Isn't this a romantic spot? Hey, where's my ice cream?"

I scowled at him. "What are you doing here?"

"You're as predictable as a Thanksgiving table spread. I knew you'd come as soon as I saw that map," Natalie said. "And now we're coming with you."

"You're not invited."

"We're already here." She shrugged, completely unaffected.

Bishop joined us. "Sorry about the scare," he said. "Zach was so determined."

"It's fine," I forced. "I managed not to pee my pants, although I can't speak for Mik."

Mik shrugged, and Bishop laughed.

"This way to the tunnel." Natalie started through the woods, down a path marked by gray rock chips. Bishop followed, and Zach jogged to catch up with Natalie, taking her hand.

I supposed they were back together. *How possibly wonderful*, I snarked.

Mik cleared his throat, and it was the loudest sound I'd heard from him in years. I looked over, realizing that it had gotten doubly dark over the last few minutes. It would be pitch-black soon. Mik held out a green apple like he was presenting me with a bunch of flowers.

I rubbed it on my jeans. "Cheers," I said, hoping that the lack of light hid my scorching blush. Reality was doing that hellish thing that it always did—it was sneaking up on me. To Mik, this really was something like a date.

CHAPTER

15

Natalie

NATALIE STILL TASTED SOMETHING HORRIBLE IN HER MOUTH from last night, but she smiled. This could work. It would work. It had to work.

After making up with Zach, she'd done research on Moonville, packed supplies for the outing, and got Bishop and Zach ready to go like toddlers for a picnic. She'd even let Zach orchestrate his little shock-the-hell-out-of-Mik-and-Jaycee prank, which, she had to admit, had worked fairly well. Now Natalie just had to muster the courage to be cool. Relaxed. Chill. Whatever people called it. A cool, relaxed, chilled person didn't implode under pressure.

And didn't hook up with the worst person on the planet and then get psychotically drunk to cover it up.

Natalie stomped up the embankment beside the river, passing the cement pilings and heaving each breath. She thought about her amended two-step plan over and over.

1. I am Natalie. Which means a lot of things, and that's okay.

2. I can do this. Which means I can also fail while trying to do this, and that's okay.

Natalie knew only one thing for sure: she had to start living now. No more waiting for New York. No more being terrified of how everything could go wrong in the blink of an eye.

Natalie swallowed back that awful taste. Was it the vomit or the liquor that stayed with her like that? Or was it just the memory of *that guy*. She couldn't even think his name, because it made her body go cold and her mind freeze. *Clothes off. His laughter. His pinching fingers…*

Slumping over with her hands on her knees, she nearly retched into the undergrowth.

Zach stopped beside her and rubbed her back. "You all right?"

She stood up and pressed her face to his T-shirt. If Zach ever found out what had happened, he'd never speak to her again. Hands down. "I'm fine," she lied.

Zach gave her a sweet kiss on the temple, and they walked on until they beheld the Moonville Tunnel. Her head craned back to see the top; it was easily twice the height she'd thought it'd be. By the silver-clear light of the moon, she read the jutting bricks over the mantel of the tunnel. The first letter had long since fallen.

O O N V I L L E

"Holy shit." That was Bishop, but Natalie had to echo the sentiment. He held up his arm. "Goose bumps. Anyone else?"

Natalie felt the prickles on her own arms. "Yes," she whispered. "There's something old and angry in that stonework. It feels like we've time-traveled."

Bishop looked over at her and flashed a smile. "Cool. Yeah."

Zach's mouth had fallen open as he stared up. "How tall is that?"

"Easily two stories," Bishop said. "The other side comes out in the underworld."

Zach snapped his head toward his friend. "Huh?"

Bishop laughed. "No, but really, if anyplace leads to the River Styx, my money is on that path." He pointed into the black.

They walked closer to the strange, looming relic. It felt ancient in a way that nothing in America seemed to muster— European old or true old. Forgotten old. It didn't help that the trees crowded out any sense of history and the whole shebang was frosted by a lunar glow. The end result was that Natalie felt more creeped out than she had in the dense, dust-coated silence of the TB ward.

"Where are all the ties and tracks?" Zach asked, firmly holding Natalie's hand.

"Removed. Like the trestles," she said. "The railway stopped running in the seventies, and then hikers kept getting hurt, so they dismantled the tracks and turned it into a state park."

"Strange that everything is gone except the tunnel, which still looks rather...imposing." Bishop's voice held awe as he stepped beneath the archway.

Jaycee and Mik brought up the rear, and Jaycee let out a string of wonder curses that almost sounded like poetry. Natalie wondered if she'd catch them holding hands, but Jaycee's were firmly in her pockets.

Natalie did what Natalie did best: she whipped up the history into a picture. "Moonville isn't just the tunnel. It was a town that popped up around a small coal-mining settlement from about 1860 to the 1940s. The railway gave the area life, but it didn't last long."

"It's pretty damn spooky," Zach said. "How many people died here?"

"A few. Including a ten-year-old-girl who was fooling around on the tracks." Natalie risked a look at Jaycee, remembering her fascination with Margaret Schilling's death. "There's also a rather infamous ghost known as the Brakeman. He's supposedly seen at the other end of the tunnel, with a long, white beard and holding a lantern."

Everyone stared into the dark, seemingly endless tunnel. Natalie felt like she was peering into a black mirror, briefly remembering a childish game she used to play with Jaycee.

"We have to see the other side. Come on." Bishop held out a flashlight while Mik used his Zippo. Zach left Natalie's hand and entered with the guys.

Natalie was rooted to the spot, and she wasn't alone. Jaycee stared up at the missing M.

"You were here," Natalie heard Jaycee murmur. The boys had become small dots, their voices fading into the hushed echo of the tunnel's acoustics.

"Do you...talk to Jake?" Natalie asked. "Do you think he hears you?"

Jaycee's glare was sharp by the small beam of Natalie's headlamp. "Why did you bring them here?"

Natalie picked her words carefully. "Bishop needs to get his mind off his heartbreak. Zach needs to do something that doesn't land him at the bottom of a bottle every evening. And I...it's like you said. I need to climb the roof or whatever."

"This is you climbing the roof?" Jaycee flicked Natalie's headlamp.

"There's nothing wrong with being prepared."

"Sure, except it takes a little of the fun out of it." Jaycee smiled. There was something familiar in this back and forth, reminiscent of the personality brawling they'd done as kids.

Jaycee took a few steps into the tunnel, and Natalie moved next to her. The brick walls were covered in names, dates, and swears. Most of the graffiti was rough and slapdash, but some of it was pure art.

"Bishop must be in heaven," Natalie said. "Look at that!"

They paused before a gray-and-black stenciled image of a huge train. Painted railroad tracks reached out in front of the image and a dress-clad woman stood in its onrushing path.

"It's a picture of the girl who died." Natalie's mouth felt dry. "She was ten, but lots of people tell the story incorrectly. They say that she was a young woman on her way to see her lover. Stories always fracture over time."

"That's why you love history," Jaycee said. "You love the cracks."

"You remember that?" Natalie looked at Jaycee, blinding her with her headlamp.

"Watch it!" Jaycee yelled, effectively killing the moment. They walked slowly, toward the distant light of Mik's flame and Bishop's flashlight at the other end. When Jaycee tripped over a rock, they grabbed hold of each other.

"Mik looks like he got dressed up tonight," Natalie said. The dead air of the tunnel was messing with her nerves. "His clothes are extra black. He might even have combed his hair."

"Quit swinging your head around. It makes the light spaz," Jaycee said. "And I'm not going to girl talk with you about Mik. Oh, and thanks for eating pancakes with my dad. He went on and on about how nice it was to see you."

"I like your dad." Natalie looked down, illuminating an old fire pit that they'd almost walked through. "Where was your mom this morning? I saw her at graduation. She looks…different."

"She looks crazy," Jaycee spat. "Because she is. She lives at Stanwood Behavioral Hospital for most of the year. Addicted to happy pills and crying about Jake."

"Jesus, Jayce!"

"You asked." Jaycee sighed. "It's actually a lot easier when she's not around. For her. For us. It is what it is. You know she was never the soundest boat in the marina to begin with." Jaycee's snark was rolling downhill fast. "Speaking of crazy, how'd you get Zach back?"

"It's more like we never broke up than that we made up." Natalie felt a feverish flash of what had happened in that frat boy's bedroom. "Zach is better than I deserve."

"I don't know about that," Jaycee said. "You seem made for each other in a weird, 'it's a small world' kind of way."

"If you knew what I…" Natalie was desperate to talk to someone, but Jaycee? Jaycee would not hold back her judgment. She would definitely not make Natalie feel better about what had happened or almost happened. That was the worst part. Natalie couldn't actually remember how far she'd gone in that bedroom, but outside of asking the guy in question, what could she do? Ask Mik?

Could she ask Mik? What had he seen when he busted into that room?

No. She didn't want to know. She didn't.

"Knew what, Natalie?" Jaycee's tone implied that she already suspected Natalie was hiding something ugly. "What *did* you

do last night? Or perhaps more importantly, *who* did you do?"
Her voice dropped. "Was it something you wanted or…"

Natalie's emotions flared. "Look. You're innocent, so I'll
break it down for you. There are *not* two types of sex in this
world. It's not all black and white. It's not all perfect or a crime.
There's another kind. And it's gray and miserable and right in
the middle."

Jaycee snorted. "And those hookups are called…what exactly?"

"*Mistakes*," Natalie said affirmatively, exactly like she'd been
telling herself all day. If Natalie had in fact slept with that guy,
it *was* a mistake. Mistakes were part of the human experience.
Natalie remembered ever-so-damn-clearly how much she'd
gone after him. Singled him out. That was before she'd gotten
drunk, but she still couldn't remember why she'd done it.

God, why?

Natalie's chest went tight, her head spinning. Jaycee backed
up instinctively.

"You're having a panic attack," Jaycee said, taking Natalie's
bag off her back. "Breathe."

"I'm trying!" Natalie pressed her face against the brick of the
tunnel and bit back a sob.

Jaycee grabbed the water bottle and squirted it down the
back of Natalie's neck. The coolness hit her like a slap, and she
inhaled in a rush.

Natalie came out of the attack feeling old. "I suppose I
should thank you for that." She took the bottle and drank most
of it. "Don't say anything. I don't want Zach to know."

"About the panic attack or the guy you boinked?"

"Both!" Natalie cried out so loud that the tunnel bounced
her desperate voice back at her.

"I'm trying to get you to relax," Jaycee said. "You're worrying me. A lot."

Natalie sat down with her back to the brick and flicked her headlamp off. The instant dark helped despite the tunnel's creepiness. "Do you remember when we used to talk to our shadow selves, Jayce? When we'd turn the lights off and whisper to the dim reflections in the mirror?"

"Yes."

"That's how I see myself. All the lights are off. I'm not always sure I'm there."

"Sometimes I feel that way," Jaycee said, her voice dead serious. "Maybe you should shed some light on things." She switched on Natalie's headlamp. "The truth always helps me. I throw open the curtains and look in the mirror and say, 'Jake's dead.'"

Natalie somehow managed not to point out that that seemed to be the very root of Jaycee's problem, not the solution. She shuffled to her feet, tucked her water bottle back into its assigned pocket, and tried not to growl. "Thanks anyway."

Jaycee was quiet as they walked toward the far side of the tunnel. "Do you really not let Zach know when you're having a panic attack?"

"It's none of his business."

"Your mental state is none of your boyfriend's business? Isn't that a bit weird?" Natalie flashed a look at Jaycee that appropriately blinded the girl with the headlamp, but then after a minute, Jaycee added, "Hey, Nat, I've got a question for you."

"*What?*"

"Why are you still wearing my shirt?"

Natalie gave a small, surprised laugh. "We're hiking. I

wanted to wear something comfortable and old." Natalie looked down, the beam highlighting the ripped holes in the knees of her jeans. Despite the look, they were brand-new—from her purposefully laid-back wardrobe she'd been compiling for Cornell.

"Oh, right." Jaycee was smiling again, her teeth extra white in the dark. "This is a perfect place to wear old stuff."

Natalie turned to greet the boys, and Jaycee snapped a tag off Natalie's back pocket. Natalie flashed her a warning look, but Jaycee just laughed, her voice echoing through the tunnel.

"What's happening here? Were you guys kissing?" Zach asked. "Please tell me you were kissing." Bishop punched his shoulder. "Well, it's not out of the question. Right, Natalie? Remember what you told me about when you guys were kids and you wanted to practice—"

Natalie punched his other shoulder. Jaycee laughed harder. It made her look even more beautiful, and it was a rare glimpse at the girl Natalie remembered from childhood. All the boys noticed. Especially Mik. He smiled and glanced away. Yep, Mik was totally in love with Jaycee. Natalie would have to do some serious work to get them together. No doubt Jaycee would be against the idea like a brick wall, but Natalie knew all her tricks. Maybe this was how she'd win Jaycee's forgiveness…

Natalie launched into the campaign. "Where do you go to school? What do you study?" There was a static pause while everyone realized that she was talking to Mik. "Do you still live in Athens?"

"He doesn't talk," Bishop pointed out.

"*Selective* mute. That means he talks sometimes. I'm simply giving him the opportunity, should he be interested."

Jaycee moved between Natalie and Mik. "She's harmless," she told Mik, glaring Natalie's way. "Most of the time."

Natalie felt Zach's hand on her lower back, and she left the rest alone. At least she'd gotten Jaycee to stand closer to Mik. Better than nothing.

Jaycee opened the Mead journal she'd been carrying and tried to use her cell phone to read the pages. "Can I borrow that headlamp?" she asked after a moment.

"You mean the headlamp you made fun of?" Natalie asked.

"Yes. May I borrow the headlamp I made fun of?"

Natalie gave it to her, and Jaycee beckoned Mik back through the tunnel. The two of them began a thorough search of the walls.

"What're they looking for?" Zach asked.

"A marker from Jaycee's brother," Natalie said. "Like they found last night. If they find it, expect something stupid to happen next."

Bishop looked around like he was in love with the walls. He touched the graffiti.

"I brought you something," she said, pulling out two cans of spray paint from her bag.

Bishop took them with a huge grin. "You completely read my mind. Thanks." He went to find a spot for his art, muttering something about letter stencils.

Zach wrapped an arm around her waist. "Jaycee seems kinda happy with you. At least, she's not *unhappy* with you. You feel better?"

"Maybe." Jaycee and Natalie had actually talked—really

talked. Natalie had even admitted that thing about her shadow self. And Jaycee didn't tell Natalie that she was being imprecise like her therapist did—or melodramatic like her mom.

Natalie touched Zach's hair, pushing it to the side of his face. Why, why, why had she gone after that other guy? How could she? "I love you," she said. "*You.*"

He put his arms around her and kissed her neck. "I love you too."

I am Natalie. I can make this right.

She took his mouth with hers, and the kiss was much deeper than Zach was ready for. He leaned out of it. "Hey. You can't just kiss me like that. Do you know what you've started?"

She kissed him again and tugged on his belt. "Let's go down the path. Out of sight."

"But you never...you said no way would you do it outside *ever.*" Zach blinked at her. "Is this a trick? This is a trick, isn't it?"

She shook her head and led him farther into the woods. Finding the right spot without poison ivy or problematic rocks took forever, but then she was on her back, all their clothes laid out like a blanket beneath her. She was nearly breathless from watching the contrast of the moon on the sky while Zach pressed into her. He was always gentle.

The branches of oaks and buckeye trees reached over them like shadowy hands, and the wretched half memory of the previous night made her cling to the thrill of what she was doing. *Zach, Zach, Zach,* she thought to remove the other guy from her thoughts.

She hoped and prayed that her daring would line

everything up. Maybe shed some light, like Jaycee had said. Natalie even picked the brightest star in the black night above and made a wish.

Please let me feel brave.

CHAPTER

16

MIKIVIKIOUS

WHAT'S *THAT?*

DID *YOU* DO THAT?

NO.

MIK AND I HAVE BEEN ON THIS SIDE THE WHOLE TIME.

ASK BISHOP.

THEY HAVEN'T WALKED PAST ME.

CHAPTER 17

JAYCEE

NATALIE KIND OF ATTACKED ME, BUT IT WAS WORTH IT. ZACH pulled her off, and I kept laughing until my stomach clenched. I fell to my knees and couldn't catch my breath. Laughing felt foreign. New. Beautiful.

"Not funny. Go get my headlamp," Natalie threatened before adjusting her glasses. "I'm going to the old town cemetery across the road. I saw pictures of it on Google. Who's coming with me?"

Zach shook his head. "I want to go swimming in the river. I saw a rope swing, and I'm all…sweaty." Natalie blinked at him like she couldn't believe he was admitting that.

"I'll go to the cemetery with you," Bishop said. "Sounds cool."

Zach scurried down the embankment to the water. Natalie and Bishop crossed the creek, jumping stone to stone, before heading back up to the road.

A new quiet left me with Mik's still-smiling face in the night's glow. I suspected that Natalie had *meant* to take everyone away from us via her excursion to the cemetery. She wanted Mik and me to be alone. Subtle, Natalie Cheng. Very subtle.

Mik's eyes were on me in a permanent sort of way, and I could barely hold his gaze.

I motioned to Bishop's picture on the wall. "Quite the masterpiece. I think love broke off a piece of him and threw it away." I stared at the image of a gorgeous woman, the words in her hair striking a rather strong chord. "It is a fair question. What *is* the opposite of lonely?"

Mik took a step toward me, and I stumbled back. "Let's get that headlamp," I said, fleeing into the tunnel.

It was freakier this time. Mik didn't ignite his Zippo, and we walked through the dark, toward the swinging light at the far end. I tripped and swore. I felt Mik at my elbow, but I walked faster, wanting to put some distance between us.

It wasn't that I didn't like him. No, that couldn't be it; I did like him. I just didn't know what was happening. What was he hoping for exactly? I couldn't ask him because he didn't talk, and what if he wanted something like Natalie and Zach's relationship with all the hand-holding and codependency? If I couldn't be off on my own when my emotions went nuclear, I'd destroy whoever was in my way.

Like my poor dad. I blasted him apart way too often, and these days, I had to nearly tell him that I hated him to keep him from crowding in.

There had to be some way to explain this to Mik. Some simple and straightforward way. I even found myself curious about Natalie's opinion; she was good at factoring in people's feelings. She was good at being careful, with the large exception of how she'd handled me during my brother's death. I, for one, didn't have anything close to this skill set.

I shoved my hands in my pockets, my fingers closing tightly

around the triangle of Jake's map. For all my hesitation, I had to admit that I wanted Mik in my life. I wanted to see him every year in The Ridges while we remembered Jake together. But more than that, he had been there—*right there*—when Jake died. He probably even knew things about Jake that I didn't. I wanted to ask him. Come to think of it, I really wanted to talk to Mik, or at the very least, for him to text me. Man, that was a lot of wanting…

Maybe he could feel my energy, or maybe I'd slowed down without knowing it, but all of a sudden, Mik's hand was on my lower back. I stopped walking, and I was suddenly hyperaware. The air prickled with deep cold in the tunnel, and my eyes caught on the bright water stains trickling down the curved wall. Mik moved even closer, his other hand now on my waist, and I could feel the inch between us.

His fingers were asking a question, turning me around, and I let them. The only light shone in from Natalie's headlamp on the far stump, and Mik's face was mostly shadow and dark eyes. His intensity made me stumble even though I wasn't moving, and now we were chest to chest. I was nearly dizzy from how he was looking at me, and it made me wonder why I didn't want him like that, and then it made me wonder if maybe I did.

But regardless, something was between us.

He leaned toward me, and I turned my face away.

"Mik, this isn't really…I mean, I can't…" The truth flew out as fast as a snuffed match. "Every time I look at your mouth, I think about the playground. About you giving Jake CPR."

He stepped back, all his desire extinguished.

And then Natalie's headlamp flicked off. *By itself.*

I gasped. Total blackness.

I fumbled in my pocket to find my cell phone, and when I hit the power button, the weird brilliance of the screen lit up Mik's back. He was halfway gone down the other end of the tunnel.

I'd ruined something that I didn't even know I wanted, but what was I supposed to do? Not tell him how I felt? Wouldn't that be worse? Wouldn't that be just as bad as Natalie hiding her panic attacks from her freakin' boyfriend?

I reached the headlamp at the other end, suddenly furious. I kicked the stump. "Come and get me you fucker Brakeman's ghost." I smacked at the headlamp until it flicked back on. "Every day of my life is worse than whatever you got."

Moments ago, I'd been laughing so hard that I couldn't stand up straight. And then I'd been nearly kissed. My first kiss. From Mik.

Hell on fire. Truth was supposed to work. It was supposed to be hard and fast and freeing, but for the first time in my life, I wondered if telling the truth could make you a liar.

CHAPTER
18

BISHOP

CHAPTER 19

ZACH

ZACH COULD NEVER REALLY TELL HOW A NIGHT WAS GOING to go. Sometimes events got epic in the woods with your buds. Sometimes they wound up with a make-out session in the backseat that heated the car up like an oven. And sometimes you ended up all by yourself in the woods because your friends were too busy thinking deep thoughts or pontificating or some shit.

Zach splashed in the creek because he needed to piss again, and he didn't want to be the guy who had peed twice since they'd got there. *Tiny, female bladder*, Tyler always taunted.

When Zach was a kid, crying because of his big brother's crap, his mom would gather Zach on her lap and explain that Tyler just wanted Zach to be like him. To do what he did. She said this like it wasn't a bad thing, but when Tyler broke his Stomp Rocket, he broke Zach's too. When he spilled his milk into his spaghetti, he'd pour some into Zach's bowl as well. Being like Tyler had been the worst part of Zach's life so far. Worse than his parents' flame-torch of a marriage and all the fights he'd endured with Natalie put together.

And this was all still happening. When Tyler became a drunken undergrad Lothario, he'd dragged Zach into that scene by the hair and told him to be a man. Zach had run crying to Natalie, which only escalated Tyler's cruelty from a six to an eleven.

Besides Zach's bladder, there were other reasons he wanted to be alone. First off, he just felt weird. He walked farther down the creek thinking about Bishop, who had talked about their trip inside The Ridges like they had gone backpacking through Europe. Granted it had been cool, but life changing? Not quite. Then there was Hottie Snarktart Jaycee and her "too cool for words" boy toy.

Zach snorted. Those nicknames were pretty solid, although if he were being honest, he'd have to admit that they scared him. He was pretty sure that although Jaycee had warmed up to him the night before, she could turn on him at any moment. And Mikivikious? There had to be knives concealed in that trench coat. Didn't the *Bowling for Columbine* assholes wear trench coats? That was a good point; he should tell Bishop and Natalie that one.

And Natalie…Natalie had definitely cheated on him.

Zach kept surprising himself by turning this thought over. Technically it wasn't cheating. Technically they weren't even together for those hours. Besides, he'd kissed a girl two years ago when he was in LA visiting his cousins. That was his big, black secret, and he kept it in the back of his mind like a Christmas present he'd never opened.

Natalie had definitely done something bad enough to shake up her whole personality. Maybe whatever it was would be her secret, and they'd match one another even better than before…

Crueler thoughts snuck into his head, but he smacked at his ears, pulled his hair, and told himself that *that* was impossible. Natalie loathed Tyler. *Loathed.* That's the word she always used, like her hatred of his brother was so advanced that she needed an SAT word for it.

He pissed and then looked around at the towering trees. Unlike The Ridges, this place didn't scare him. Not one bit. This was just like some of his longer treks into Wayne National Forest, and he often went by himself, finding his peace out in nature.

Another dark thought revved up as he took off his shoes and put his sweaty feet in the cool water. Why did this have to be the only place—outside of his basement—that he was comfortable? And why wasn't there a damn major in geocaching?

"Fuck me!" he yelled at the night sky.

"What's got your hackles up?"

He jerked and nearly fell in the creek. Jaycee was above him, crouching on the cement block of the missing train trestle. A hot gargoyle in a black tank top. He was going to have nightmares about this.

"What're hackles?" he asked.

"That bit of fur at the back of a dog's neck that swells up when it's angry."

"I don't look like that."

Jaycee placed a purposeful elbow on her knee and rested her chin in her palm. The gesture would have driven Natalie mad, and Zach could kind of imagine how they had grown up together, egging each other on left and right.

"What're you majoring in?" he asked finally, sounding angrier than he thought he would.

"Nothing. I didn't apply to college."

Zach's mouth fell open. "How is that allowed?"

"I'll get to college when I get to college. I'm not interested yet," she said.

"Well, that is…fascinating." A muscle jumped in Zach's jaw and made him want to bite something. "I wish my parents were as cool as yours."

"My parents have very low hopes for me. They want me to stay alive." Jaycee dropped down from the piling, landing at the edge of the creek. "You're telling me that Natalie hasn't told you what to major in yet? She'll happily pick out the rest of your life for you."

"She has to get in line for that job." Zach glanced up toward the road, hoping that Natalie couldn't hear him. "Besides, the only subject I'm interested in, everyone has dismissed."

Jaycee scooped her hands in the water and spread cool drops along her arms. "Which is?"

"This. Hiking. I like to geocache. Apparently there's no major for that."

"That's not true. You could go into natural sciences or park management. Become a ranger."

"That's not a stable career choice in today's economy," he said automatically.

"God, Natalie's mom has mad talent."

"What?"

"Nothing." Jaycee stood and faced the moon, and he realized she was crying. Epically silent tears left shiny streaks down her face.

"What're you…you okay?"

"This?" She wiped her face with the back of her hand. "Sometimes I leak. Not a real problem."

He toed the water's edge, reaching for something else to say. "So…what were you and Mik doing with that journal?"

"Looking for my brother."

"Did you find him?"

Before she could respond, footsteps crunched behind him, and he swung around. Mik was watching, and he was spookily close. He had his keys in his hand.

"You leaving?" Zach asked. Mik nodded and then looked at Jaycee. "Are you going too?" he asked.

She shook her head. "I'll ride back with you guys. I still haven't found Jake's marker."

"What if it's painted over?" Zach said. Jaycee and Mik exchanged pained looks, and Zach realized that he was smack in the middle of a conversation that had nothing to do with him. "You know what? I'm going to go rub elbows with the Brakeman's ghost. Have a blast, kids."

Zach disrupted a nest of small creatures that scurried over his bare feet. He climbed the incline and grumbled, "Just talk to her, dude," when he passed Mik.

He could have sworn that the guy muttered, "Not ready," but when Zach swung around, Mik was already halfway across the river rocks, heading toward his car.

Zach left it alone. He wasn't going to push them like Natalie was probably already planning. And oh man, if she somehow succeeded to hook Jaycee up with Mik, it would mean a summer of doubling with Athens' misfit couple. Then again, Mik and Jaycee would be better than all those double dates with Bishop and Marrakesh. Damn make-out monsters.

Zach came face-to-face with Bishop's graffiti art at the entrance of the tunnel. He'd left his phone in Natalie's bag, but the moonlight illuminated the whole thing: a glorious-looking woman as well as a very stupid question.

"Togetherness," Zach answered, but that wasn't really true, was it? You could be with a bunch of people and still feel lonely. Sometimes Natalie would be having sex with him, and she'd have that look like she couldn't wait to get back to studying, and he'd feel so damn lonely that he couldn't see straight. Of course, this poem wasn't about Natalie. It was about Marrakesh. To Bishop, everything was about Marrakesh, which was why Zach had been so surprised by Bishop's interest in urban exploring. Zach had tried everything to get Bishop out of the funk from that horrible British girl—concerts, camping, college visits. His attempts had only weakened their already strained friendship.

Zach returned to the river, wondering if he'd find Jaycee lip-locked with Mik, but she was hunched on a distant piling, and Mik's car was gone. Zach stripped down to his boxers and jumped in the little pond. The cool water hit his balls like a punch, but it was kind of refreshing. He splashed around until his feet slipped on decades of mucky leaves at the bottom, and he started to worry about snapping turtles.

The opposite of loneliness had to be something inside you. He thought about lying in his bed at night, his mind tortured by the nonstop syndication of his worst memories. Sometimes— *sometimes*—his own voice would rise up and tell the images to fuck off. Those were the only times he really fell asleep.

CHAPTER 20

Natalie

BISHOP AND NATALIE CLIMBED A WINDING HILL THAT NEVER seemed to stop. The incline was good though. It burned her calves and kept both of them huffing too much too talk. Natalie knew that, at some point, Bishop was going to ask what happened last night, and she didn't have an excuse ready yet.

Then again, maybe he wouldn't ask. Maybe he'd leave it alone, and she could go on feeling like she'd glued herself back together after such a monumental screwup.

At the top of the hill, they came to a clearing, a small plateau of graves. The moon lit up a few broken headstones.

"Wow, look at that!" Natalie whispered. Someone had been drinking out here, and shot glasses were arranged in the grass along with an empty collection of liquor bottles. When were those people here? An hour ago? Last night? Last year?

"There're only a handful of graves," Bishop said. "Where are the rest?"

"You're looking past them. We're so used to headstones, but in poorer places, people just used rocks." She pointed Bishop's flashlight arm toward the mounds of stones that told the sad history of the people who once lived here. "We're surrounded."

"Wicked." Bishop's grin was beautiful in the dark. "You're pretty chill tonight, you know that?"

Natalie managed a smile. This was one of those sideways compliments that she hated. "Oh, you look hot," someone might say, but what they really meant was, "You don't usually look hot." Her hands clenched and went limp. *At Cornell, no one will say that because no one will know what I used to be like.*

Bishop popped his knuckles. "Natalie, Zach told me you were out last night after The Ridges and—"

"I saw your portrait of Marrakesh in the tunnel. Striking."

"I hate it when you say her name like that," he said, turning away.

"Like what?"

"Like she's a circus act."

Natalie took a deep breath. "Bishop, come on. She wasn't that great, especially to Zach and me. At some point, you're going to have to accept that fact. Besides, I'm sure you'll find a new goddess the week you start in Michigan." Holy God, Jaycee's honest streak was already rubbing off on her.

Bishop's shoulders hunched. "Guess I spoke too soon about you being chill."

"I'm going to be how I'm going to be," she said, and she was shockingly proud of herself. She tucked her hair behind her ears just as Zach's phone beeped loudly in her bag, making both of them jump.

"I take it by your sudden interest in Marrakesh that you don't want to tell me what happened last night, so can I ask you a different question? Why did you get back together with

Zach? I thought we talked about you giving him some space so he can process our leaving."

"Bishop, I know you think you're making it easier on Zach by being distant, but I think…I think you're just mad at him. I think you two need to make up before you leave."

"Zach has a problem with Marrakesh, which means that he has a problem with me."

"Yes, that would be true if you and Marrakesh were the same person, but news flash, Bishop, you're not." Natalie had never spoken to anyone but Jaycee like this. It felt sort of brilliant. Briefly. "You're his best friend," she added quietly. "And you don't really care about what he thinks. You haven't since the day Marrakesh came around, and that's eating him."

Zach's phone beeped again. They jumped again.

"You didn't answer my question. Why did you take Zach back?"

Natalie didn't have an answer. Because she had no one else? Because he was there? The plan was to stay with Zach until she left for New York, and it was a good plan, wasn't it?

Another beep.

"Christ," Bishop said. "Turn that thing off. It's freaking me out."

"It's Zach's stupid, old broken phone. It's going to keep beeping until you clear the new text notification." She turned her back to Bishop so that he could get the phone out. "I didn't have any service down there. Zach must have a bar or two up on this hill."

Bishop pulled the phone out, and even though Natalie had her back turned, the eerie cemetery glowed from the screen's light.

"Oh, this is sick. Tyler texted a picture of one of his drunken conquests again."

"Just delete it," Natalie said before processing the words.

She whipped around and reached for the phone, but Bishop pulled it away.

"Hey." He looked at the image more closely. "That's you."

"No."

"Hell, Natalie. This is *you*." Bishop held out the screen. The girl in the picture had her face turned away, and the image was mostly bra and an open mouth.

But it was definitely Natalie Cheng.

"Delete it," she whispered.

"Oh, holy shit! *Holy shit!* You hooked up with Tyler last night?" He threw his hands in the air like he couldn't believe it. "But you hate Tyler! Everyone hates Tyler!"

"No, I didn't!" Natalie's voice was small but determined to stay in check. "Well, I don't know exactly. I got drunk. I don't remember if we actually did anything."

"Guess what, Natalie?" He held out the phone's cruel image again. "You definitely did *something*. Did Tyler force you to—"

"No! Why does everyone keep asking me that?"

"Because he's *Tyler*. Your boyfriend's evil whore of a brother. Goddamn, Natalie! This is insane!"

"I know!" She was screaming, and it suddenly felt like she'd been screaming since last night. "I know! FUCK! You don't think I know how bad this is?" As fast as the truth had come out, it left her empty. She folded into herself on the grass, arms grasping her legs, head tucked between her knees. When the anxiety came on, it felt permanent. Not an attack, but a state of being. *I am Natalie, and I am broken.*

Bishop sat in the grass beside her. "Hey," he said calmly. "Hey, talk to me."

She peered at him through the tangle of her hair. "It was

my idea, but I don't know why I did it. I wasn't even drinking. My brain felt sort of...fried, and I jumped him, and then I was in his bed, and I didn't want to be there, so I grabbed this bottle and started chugging. Then I woke up at Jaycee's." She clenched her teeth and then forced the rest. "I don't want to know if anything else happened."

Bishop was staring at the picture on the phone. "Zach thinks you made out with someone from our class. He says he isn't upset, but I think he's deluding himself."

"Zach doesn't need to know. Delete it," she whispered. "Please."

Silence stretched between them until Natalie couldn't stand it. "It was just a mistake. I don't know why I did it. It was a mistake!"

"I'm only agreeing with you because Zach can't see this. Ever," Bishop said like he needed to justify his action. "He'd be destroyed."

Natalie watched him delete the picture like the world had slipped into slow motion.

Bishop dropped the phone on the ground and took her shoulders in both hands. Up close, he smelled like the high school art room, and his eyes were the sort of brown that seemed velvety. "I know why you did it, Natalie. You don't want to be with Zach. Not really. So you snapped and sabotaged your relationship with him."

"No, I didn't! I love him."

"Natalie, you hooked up with the only guy on the planet who Zach could never forgive you for hooking up with. *And* you can't even tell me why you took him back because you don't know. Admit it."

She didn't know, but she couldn't say those words.

"I feel sorry for you," he said, and then he hugged her tightly. "But not as sorry as I feel for Zach."

She pulled out of the hug, wiping back tears. "What?"

"He deserves to know. You have to find out what happened and tell him."

"But then I'll have to know what happened," she whispered. The words terrified her more than the surrounding cemetery of expired souls. No matter what sect of Honesty to Death religion Jaycee believed in, Natalie knew deep down that the truth did not set you free.

It just didn't.

She stared at where Zach's phone was shining screen-up in the grass beside her brand-new sneakers with the black accents. The ones she'd hoped would make her look like a girl who sometimes hiked and sweated, a girl who knew how to let loose without completely devastating her carefully arranged life. Sabotage? Had she really *sabotaged* her four-year relationship with Zach? Why? He'd never been anything but nice to her. Was she even capable of that? Her thoughts skipped to how she'd avoided Jaycee after Jake's death, and she put her hands over her face. She honestly didn't know what she was capable of.

"I can't...I can't tell him, Bishop. It would destroy him."

"Not as much as finding out about all this from Tyler. Don't play games with his feelings, Natalie." Bishop stood up, and although his nearness had felt strange, the sudden distance was bleak. "Figure out what happened. Then tell Zach," he said. "Or I will."

He started to leave, and she ran after him. "Wait, I need time. I don't know how to find out what happened. How to tell him!"

Bishop nodded. "I'll give you two weeks."

THE GATES OF HELL

CHAPTER 21

JAYCEE

TWO WEEKS LATER. WELL, NOT REALLY. THIRTEEN DAYS.

Was I actually counting the days since Moonville? Insane, but then, I *was* in the family session room at Stanwood Behavioral Hospital, a.k.a. The New Ridges. Maybe the crazy was rubbing off.

"She nearly *died*," my dad said.

The walls were carpeted. Sound absorbing, maybe, or possibly just a little safer to smack your forehead against in frustration. I'd certainly thought about it in the past. Although this time I wasn't thinking about rhino-ing the wall, and I certainly wasn't considering my dad's semihysterical words. I was picturing Jake's map.

Moonville had been a bust, but there were three more places where I might feel Jake alive in the air like his spirit is just hanging around, climbing stuff.

"And the worst part? She doesn't even seem to care."

I pulled myself away from the safety of the map, blinking back to my parents and my mom's therapist, Dr. Donaldson. "Nearly died? Come on, Dad. My car skidded out in the little valley next to the highway. It didn't roll or combust or do anything that would require Bruce Willis moves."

"This is a big deal, Jaycee. You've lost your license for reckless driving." My dad was literally on the edge of his seat. I worried that he might topple over at any moment. "The cop said he clocked you at ninety-seven miles per hour!"

I shrugged. "Not exactly my record." Wrong move. My dad's face got splotchy, exactly like it did every time he was trying not to cry.

My mom touched my arm with the sort of calm that was prescription inspired. "I want to know how Jaycee got poison ivy all over herself."

"Oh, come on. That was weeks ago!"

I flashed back to driving away from Moonville in Natalie's aptly named Oldsmobile. Zach and Bishop had seemed so gung ho about going urban exploring with me again. Not Natalie. She stayed as silent and slumped as a wet blanket. I had no doubt that she was the reason no one had texted. My face burned like my dad's, and I looked at my lap. Bishop and Zach might not know how important this was to me, but Natalie knew. I'd thought she was actually trying to be friends again. I'd even started to think that maybe I wanted that too.

Wrong, Jayce. Always wrong.

Yesterday I'd wrestled down my brushed-off feelings and headed to Jake's urbex location in Columbus on my own, only to end up getting pulled over. Well, not really "pulled over" as I jerk-skidded into the breakdown lane when I saw the flashing red-and-blue lights…before careening down the hill. I remembered the scream-swears and my chest going so tight. I remembered thinking that my car was about to flip or smack into a tree—and how, at the same time, I'd sort of wanted it to.

Dr. Donaldson sat forward, clasping his lanky fingers together. "We know there have been instances of danger in Jaycee's recent life. Situations that she has sought out—"

"I'm not suicidal!"

He acted as though I hadn't said a word. I suspected that he didn't like me, which meant that my mom had been bad-mouthing me—or that they were sleeping together, an idea that seemed more likely every time I was here. He continued. "I want us to try to see beyond. What are the good things that Jaycee has to look forward to in her life?"

"Hemorrhoids," I said. "Oh, I know. Becoming the old lady who works in the bookstore and scares the undergrads!"

My dad ignored me as well. They always ignored me when Dr. Donaldson was in the room. "Well, she did hang out with her old best friend, Natalie, after graduation. And oh, Jaycee went on a date with Ryan Mikivikious a few weeks ago." He beamed.

My hand twitched toward my cell phone. I'd heard nothing since Mik drove off in Moonville. There had been no response to the apology-excuse I'd texted to him. Not even another empty message bubble. My fingers curled tightly around my cell, and I imagined the glass cracking and going to crystal splinters in my hand.

"No phones, JC," Dr. Donaldson said in that passive-aggressive way he had of abbreviating my name.

"*Jaycee.*" I highlighted the flow of the word with a wave of my hand. "Six letters, not two. It's not nice to cut someone's name short, Dr. Donald."

He nodded, strangling me in his thoughts, no doubt. "And who is Ryan Mikivikious?"

"A nice boy," my mom said through a sigh. "He's had a crush on Jaycee since they were both playing with LEGOs. It's sweet."

"He has not!" I said. "Mik was Jake's best friend when we were kids." Considering the fact that my mom was at Stanwood *because* of Jake, I was always annoyed by how little my brother came up in conversation. The phrase *avoided like the plague* sprung to mind. "Besides, it was not a date."

Shame rained down my face, making my whole expression dampen. I glanced at my phone, praying for a message from Mik. Something to prove that he understood.

"JC…"

"I'm checking the time." I turned the phone to show Dr. Donaldson the screen. "And look at that. It's up." I stood, and my mom pulled me back onto the couch, hip to hip. She held on to me, and I let her. It was the best I could do.

"I don't like Natalie," my mom said, surprising me. "She was not there for you when she should have been."

No shit.

"She didn't know what to do, Mom. What to say," I added, somewhat shocked that I was defending Natalie. "No one does. There're only two kinds of people. Those who saw Jake crack his neck"—I looked over the blank faces of my parents—"and those who didn't." I swallowed hard. "Natalie didn't see. She doesn't get it. End of story."

"You don't think we 'get it'?" my mom asked, her words sparking with something I referred to as Dead Son Momma Rage, which would be a really sweet band name, come to think of it. "You're telling me that I don't *understand*?"

"It's time to go," my dad said, standing up. "Jaycee has to get to work."

My mom let go of me with something like a mild shove. I managed not to say, *Oh yes, Mom, sorry. I forgot that your feelings trump everyone else's.* Instead, I kissed her forehead like she was the kid and I was the parent. It was an arrangement that worked best for us these days. I said nothing to Dr. Donaldson, but as I shut the door, I heard the sound of my mom getting off the couch. Undoubtedly to move a heck of a lot closer to her therapist.

I glanced at my dad. Did he have any idea? Probably not.

In the car, my dad did a bunch of heavy sighing. Pure provoking behavior.

"What?" I finally asked.

My dad held the steering wheel with both hands. The perfect ten and two. "Why wasn't it a date, Jaycee?"

"With Mik? Because I'm not…you know. I'm too busy." Yes. That sounded good. I was too busy with this Jake stuff to completely switch directions and head down Happily Ever After Road with Mik. Not too busy, however, to stop thinking about him.

I fiddled with my phone, turned it on and then back off. On. Off. Maybe it was broken. Maybe Dobby had magically stolen all of my friends' messages. I snorted. Wow, that Harry Potter stuff really gets into your psyche, but isn't that what kid experiences are supposed to do? Give you a safe way to interpret all the sharp edges of adulthood? Then again, even childhood has a few razors in the sandbox. Hell, poor Dobby got a knife to the chest.

"Jaycee, have you told Ryan that you're not interested in him?"

"Not in so many words," I said, thinking of Mik's face so close to mine in the tunnel. "Keep in mind, he doesn't talk to me." I turned in my seat to face my dad straight on. "But he talks to you."

"Of course he talks to me. I've known him since he was learning to talk."

"Well, so have I. Why won't he talk to me?"

"Because you make him nervous." My dad glanced over, his grip slipping on the wheel. "You know you intimidate people, Jayce. You do it on purpose. There are very few of us who know that there's a lot more going on beneath that cement surface."

"I'm not cement. I'm a peach," I said.

"Be a peach to Dr. Donaldson next time. It'll make your mom happy."

"Dr. Donaldson makes mom happy," I muttered.

"What was that?"

I slapped the dashboard. "They're sleeping together. Don't you see it?"

"No, I don't." His expression hardened. "Don't be paranoid on your way to being mean."

"That doesn't make sense."

"You don't make sense. You press yourself into my business and your mother's business and then you hide and pretend like you were never there." His voice sent shock waves through the car, effectively shorting out any comebacks.

I strapped my hair into its ponytail. My mom liked it when I wore it down, so I did that for her. A peach, indeed. Although suddenly, all I could picture was Natalie and her band of lost boys hanging out in a café, making anecdotal jokes about the one weekend they'd spent with Jaycee the sad, off-putting, morbid girl.

When we were back in uptown Athens, my dad pulled up outside the bookstore.

"Jaycee."

I waited, but he didn't have anything more than my name. It was accusation, plea, and affection, all rolled into one. "I know, I know," I said. "I'll be a peach."

"I love you, sweetie." He waited for my mandatory response with his eyebrows slightly raised. Some impatient jerk honked behind us.

"Every time you say *I love you* like that instead of just saying goodbye, I imagine myself dying. Every single time. It's like you think I might never come home again, and so I go ahead and imagine that I won't."

My dad's eyes glassed with tears. "Jayce…"

"Never mind. I love you, Dad."

I got out of the car and raced into the store. I clocked in before slipping behind the stockroom boxes. Why did it always feel like only *my* honesty was unwelcome? My mom was allowed to act destroyed. My dad was allowed to act peppy, and yet they both treated me like I needed to be…something else.

"Jaycee?" my boss called out from the stockroom door. "You back here?"

"Yes," I croaked, hiding behind a stack of cookbooks.

"Are you all right?"

I heard my dad's voice like he was trying to take over my thoughts. *Say you're fine. Say that you miss him, but don't say how much. Don't make everyone else feel bad. It's not their fault he's gone.*

So whose fault is it? I argued back. *Whichever one of Jake's brainless friends dared him up there? The guy who built the swing set or hammered down the blacktop? Or hey, how about the jackass who bought him the beer?*

"Jaycee?"

"I'm crying, Mrs. Munson. Be done soon, and then I'll fix the window display."

Tears leaked down my face while I dug Jake's map out of my pocket. I spread it out on a box of children's books. My brother felt close to me through his scribbles. He felt real. Alive. Maybe I could hitchhike to these places. How long would it take to walk to Cleveland?

Don't even think about it. My dad's voice was back. *If we lost you too, we couldn't go on.*

Oh yeah, right. I forgot. My parents had me and I had them, whether we liked it or not.

I folded up my brother's map and slipped it in my pocket. Jake wasn't here, so he couldn't be disappointing. Couldn't let me down like everyone else. He got a free pass. Apparently dying was the easiest way to turn into a peach.

CHAPTER 22

Natalie

NATALIE WATCHED JAYCEE THROUGH THE GLASS FRONT OF the bookstore. She was clearly supposed to be setting up books in the case, but instead she was the display: a girl sitting cross-legged on the floor, hunched over a text exchange on her phone.

Natalie's own phone buzzed in her pocket, making her jump and pull it out.

Tell Zach tonight. Time's up.

She cleared Bishop's latest message and dropped her phone in her bag, suddenly swearing in a way that would have made Jaycee proud. She walked away from the window and leaned on the brick. Her breath cut in fast, and she pressed her hands over her eyes. Goddamn it, Bishop, she was trying! She'd texted Tyler. Even cornered him on the street. Zach's brother was avoiding her like it was a game, and Natalie felt toyed with, cat-and-mouse style.

At least Tyler hadn't sent any more half-naked pictures to

Zach—although she knew they were on his phone, lying in wait.

Natalie tried to focus, but her thoughts zoomed to something even worse. The day Jake hit the blacktop like a meteorite. Natalie had run home in the middle of the hysterics and crawled into her bed. When her mother came in and asked if she knew what had happened on the playground, Natalie had said *no* out of some strange, self-preservation instinct. *No, I've been here all afternoon. I have a stomachache.* The lie had felt so good that she'd made it into a lifeline. Nope, Natalie hadn't been there. She hadn't seen. She wasn't horribly scarred like all those other kids.

Her heart suddenly raced as she stepped forward and knocked on the glass. Jaycee looked up with an intense scowl. "See? That's your first problem," Natalie said loudly. "Why is your initial reaction always so hostile?"

"How about my secondary reaction?" Jaycee held up her middle finger.

Natalie ignored it and walked into the store. The clerk behind the counter greeted her and was in the middle of asking Natalie if she needed help finding anything when Jaycee crawled out of the display stage.

"My customer," Jaycee said. "She's my Ghost of Christmas Past."

The clerk smirked, muttered, and walked toward the back.

"How do you get to talk to everyone like that?" Natalie asked.

"It's a dead brother thing. Everyone feels bad for me."

"It isn't," Natalie said. "You've been like this forever. How were we ever compatible?"

"Oh, I have something to show you!" Jaycee ran to the door and held it open. "It's the exit. Why don't you use it?"

Natalie leaned on the front counter and checked her nails. *Don't let her get to you.* "Bishop wants to go urban hiking again. Zach too."

"Urban *exploring*," Jaycee corrected before pausing to lift an eyebrow. "You did that on purpose. You never mess things up. You trying to rile me, Cheng?"

"I think you came pre-riled today."

Jaycee's face twitched with several conflicting emotions. "Well, if you guys were so into it, how come you disappeared for two weeks?"

Natalie had anticipated the anger, but there was more. A twitch on Jaycee's cheek belied that she was, well, *hurt*. Unbelievable. Jaycee Strangelove had missed her.

"We were all busy, I guess. Sorry."

"Whatever. I don't need you guys." Jaycee's hostility was shrinking into an earthworm, tiny and easily squished. Natalie worried she might step on it.

"You know, I didn't even think you were here. Why isn't your car out front?"

Jaycee moved behind the counter. "Lost my license," she mumbled.

"What?"

"I lost my license!" she yelled. "For reckless driving."

Natalie twisted a finger in her ear. "Well, *that* was bound to happen, wasn't it?"

"When you gloat, you look like a toad."

Natalie glared. "I'm trying to ask if you want to go to another one of the places on your brother's map, Jayce. *With us.* So do you?"

"What map?"

Jaycee lied so poorly. Natalie leaned over the counter and snagged the paper sticking out of Jaycee's pocket.

"Hey! That's mine! You'll just mess it all up like last time."

Natalie unfolded the map and smoothed it down on the counter. "These places in Cleveland will have to be a solid weekend trip, so…" She pointed at Columbus. "There. The Gates of Hell. We'll go tonight. I'll drive. Meet at Zach's house. You text Mik."

Jaycee took the map back. "No way."

"Why not? Have you even seen him since you gave him the cold shoulder?"

Jaycee looked up, and anxiety lined each word. "First off, he doesn't text me, so I'm not going to text him. Secondly, I *see him* all the time because he's borderline stalking." She pointed out the window. "He walks back forth on the green at least twice a day."

"Eww," Natalie said. "That's a problem."

"It looks like he's going to Alden Library, but I don't know what he'd be doing there."

"Studying?"

"Studying what?" Jaycee asked, and Natalie knew the question wasn't for her. It was a huge, dangling, *who the hell is he* kind of question.

"Maybe he's in college. There's a strong correlation between selective mutism and high intelligence."

"Look who's been googling."

"Well, it is my superpower."

Jaycee pulled out her phone. She opened a text conversation and turned it over to Natalie. "See. He doesn't text me. He sent me one message with nothing in it. And I saw him talk to my dad. So apparently he talks, just not to me. Not even to text."

Natalie read the conversation. A blank bubble, followed by Jaycee's demand that Mik pick her up and go to Moonville. And then? "'You freaked me out'?" she read aloud. "What's that supposed to mean?"

"That he scared me. It's an apology for…what I said."

"What did you say?"

Jaycee stared at the floor. "Nothing that wasn't true."

Natalie sighed. "An apology is an apology, Jayce. This sounds like an accusation."

Jaycee looked like she might be sick, and then her face went even paler. "Devil," she said, pointing out the window. "Speaking of."

Natalie caught sight of Mik. He was walking under the arch toward the green, his all-black clothes like a heavy line against the redbrick walkway. "I'm going to talk to him."

"No! Don't!" Jaycee yelled.

Natalie was already out the door. She jaywalked across Court Street, making for the green. Mik was easy to find, sitting on the stairs before the rather idiotically designed veterans statue that looked like a penis with a soldier on top. He was reading a huge textbook, and perhaps she was wrong, but it did actually look like he was studying. She sat down beside him and crossed her legs.

"Hey there, Mikivikious."

He closed his book and shoved it in his bag. Then he checked her from shoe to hair like she might be armed. Natalie's reaction was so different. So *strong*. Her heart started to tear itself up as she looked at Mik and memories of that night two weeks ago sprang forward. Her mouth started running, and she didn't try to stop it. "I've worked it out. Maybe you thought Jaycee would be at that party. After all, she'd taken Zach home, and God knows he probably tried to get her to go out drinking with him."

Mik blinked at her. He was not as mysterious in the daylight as he was in the dark of the woods or the creepy confines of The Ridges. He actually looked fairly normal apart from the trench coat. One of her top priorities would be to help him lose it.

Natalie bit her lip before returning to her line of explanations. "*Or* maybe you were invited to that party. You went to school with most of those guys, I bet. Like…Tyler Ferris. He was a grade older than you."

Mik made a fist and his knuckles went starkly white.

"Clearly you *do* know him." Natalie took a deep breath. "I think I know why you took me to Jaycee's after you found me. We used to be friends. Maybe you thought she'd help me. But whatever, you took me to her house, and Jaycee's filled me in on the rest."

Mik looked across the street toward the bookstore, and Natalie followed his gaze.

"She thinks you're stalking her," Natalie admitted.

Mik's face sunk into his hands, and Natalie might have imagined it, but she was pretty sure his muffled groan was a swear.

"Look, Jaycee's completely backward, and I'm not sure how anyone is going to turn on her love engine, but I'm willing to help." Natalie paused. "First you have to trust me."

She took out a small notebook and a pencil. Her hands were shaking, and her mouth just kept on running. "I've done some research on people with your condition. I know that it's based on social anxiety and shyness, and that given enough time, you'll just relax and talk to us. I get that. But I can't wait for an answer." She scribbled her question. "I'm not trying to make you talk. I was blackout drunk, and I can't remember. Knowing is better than not knowing. Please."

She didn't want to tell Mik about Bishop, but that reason—*knowing is better than not knowing*—where had that come from? The words seemed to throw a spotlight on her insecurities, and Natalie felt naked, hands trembling as she held out the notebook. "I love Zach," she said. "I don't know how I could do something so horrible."

Sabotage.

"I need to know if…I really did it." If she knew, she could make a plan. If she made a plan, she could understand. Hopefully.

Mik took the notebook, read the question. And then he made eye contact with her, which he'd never done before. Full-on eye contact. His expression was so miserable that she almost didn't need his answer anymore.

"Jaycee," Natalie said, setting her sights on a problem she could solve. "She's obsessed with Jake. I doubt she's ever thought about going on a date with anyone. But what if you just hang out with her? Come over to Zach's tonight. The guys will be playing Nintendo in the basement." She fielded his questioning look with a nod. "Zach likes old-school video games. He's a purist, or a simpleton, depending on how you look at it. But anyway, they'll just be guys being guys. I'll get Jaycee there. I told her we could go to Columbus to the next spot on Jake's map, so she's likely to show."

Mik stared at the notebook. At Natalie's awful question about whether or not she'd slept with Tyler.

"You better be good enough for her," Natalie said, still too nervous to stop talking. "For example, let's hope you've gotten over the thrill of pouring glue into girls' hair."

Mik closed the pencil in the binding without writing anything. He leaned back on the statue and shut his eyes.

"So you won't help me?"

Mik was still for a long moment. Finally he opened his eyes, stared up, and folded his long fingers together. When he started talking, Natalie didn't stop him, although she wanted to. Oh God, she wanted to.

"I thought Jaycee would be at that party. I found you— jumping on a couch and waving your sweater around—and I took it as confirmation that Jaycee was probably nearby and in a similar state. I searched the house. The backyard. When I came inside again, you were gone. I had...a bad feeling."

Natalie pictured Mik's words as though she were remembering a movie she'd seen, not her own life.

"It took me a while to find you upstairs in his room. He'd locked the door, so I pushed it in. You were crying. Half-dressed and hugging a bottle of liquor. His pants were open, and I couldn't tell if he was in the process of taking them off or putting them on. He was pissed. Most likely because you did not sleep with him. I drove you to Jaycee's house, and you cried the entire way."

It was so much worse aloud than it had been in her head. So. Much.

"So you don't know if I slept with him?"

"I don't know." He looked at her, and again, the depth of his eyes blew her away. This guy understood misery. No one could fake that. "The only part you're wrong about is the reason I brought you to Jaycee's house. It's not because you used to be friends. It's because I saw her unleash on you when we were at the TB ward. That's not Jaycee. That's Jake."

He cracked his knuckles. "Jake used to unload on me like that. Wanted me to talk more and hang out with people like Tyler. We were friends when we were kids, but we weren't friends in the end." He turned his face toward the tree line again. "I want you to remind Jaycee that she's not Jake. I know you can."

Natalie was nodding, unsure of when she'd started. "I think the real problem is that she doesn't remember. When I talk to her about old times, it's like her head is underwater."

"But you'll help her?"

"Of course." Natalie felt stronger instantly. Nothing cleared her mind like problem solving.

"I'll see if I can help you as well." He got up.

"How?" she asked, but he kept walking. "For the love of God, text Jaycee something," she called after him. "Anything!"

Natalie watched him go and took three practice breaths. "Nothing is so bad that it can beat three practice breaths," her mom had promised when Natalie was really young. She'd believed it then. That was before Jake's neck pulled a right angle. And before she'd learned that the worst things in life weren't horrific accidents, but the things you did to the people you loved. Things that could make you unrecognizable to yourself.

CHAPTER 23

JAYCEE

Descending the stairs into Zach's basement room was like a time warp to middle school. His posters were all yellowing and curled, and on a strictly Zelda/Mario/*Dragon Ball Z* theme. A neon party sign hung from one wall, while a majority of the room was taken up by a TV, couch, huge bed, and shelving unit full of movies.

I'd been here once before for Natalie's surprise fourteenth birthday party, nearly six months after Jake's accident. Zach had invited me, possibly thinking that he could get us back together as a sort of present to Natalie. It hadn't gone down like that though.

Zach looked up from the couch. He was playing a video game with Bishop, who was seated on the floor by his feet. Natalie had her legs across Zach's lap while she read a book.

"You came," Zach said. "Huzzah!"

"Against all odds," I muttered. "Didn't I drink a bottle of Tabasco in this basement?"

"And puked it up on the Oriental rug," Zach finished. "We don't have to do that this time."

I stood behind the couch, feeling so very out of place. Exactly like I had four years ago.

Bishop glanced over his shoulder with a good smile. He had a sort of model beauty to his cheekbones and dark skin. It didn't do anything for me, but it sure as hell was nice to look at. "Why would you drink a bottle of Tabasco?" he asked.

"Because someone dared her," Natalie said, flipping a page in her book. "And if anyone starts truth or dare tonight, I'll nail them with my pepper spray. You've been warned."

"Still, Tabasco?" Bishop asked. "A whole bottle?"

"She just likes to act like Jake," Natalie said caustically. "He was into stupid stuff."

My frown tightened. "When people feel awkward about something, they avoid it," I said. "And when they can't avoid the topic, they avoid the person."

Bishop nodded and sighed, his expression telling me that he understood.

"No one knew how to talk to me after my brother died. So no one talked to me. Not even my closest friends." I glanced at Natalie and was happy to see that her face was glowing red. "I went to Natalie's birthday party because my parents wanted me to be social. And I took everyone's dares because it was the easiest way to distract from the awkwardness of my sorry family history. The easiest way to get people to talk to me."

"Is that what those dares are about?" Zach asked without taking an eye off his game. The boy had a phenomenal ability to be unaffected by personal talk. I kind of loved it. "I was in the woods with Kolenski and that crowd when you rolled half-naked in the poison ivy."

"You're lucky I wasn't there," Natalie muttered.

Bishop leaned over the back of the couch. "Natalie says we're heading to Columbus."

I nodded. "The Gates of Hell. Also called the Blood Bowl because of all the skateboarders who've wiped out there." I snuggled my backpack closer to my chest. Jake's prized possession, his skateboard, peeked out of the top. His urbex journal chronicled his skating at the Gates of Hell, and I was ready to bet the $3,489 in my savings account that getting the Jake Albany Strangelove experience was going to involve some skinned knees.

Natalie swung her legs over the side of the couch and led me across the basement to a king-size bed with anime sheets. Porcupine-haired, vaguely Asian characters screamed up at me with huge, blue eyes and tight fists.

"These sheets are awesome," I said. "Where do you even find *Dragon Ball Z* sheets for a bed this big?"

"Don't be mean."

"No, really. I'm genuinely curious."

"eBay," Natalie said. She held open a bag of supplies, showing off the spray paint she'd collected for Bishop, a first aid kit, flashlights, headlamps, snacks, and bottles of water. "I've packed a little something for everyone."

I picked up a brand-new Swiss Army knife still in the package. "Remind me to come find you during the apocalypse."

"I'm going to take that as the first compliment you've given me in five years."

I gave my blessing, waving my hand like a pharaoh. My phone vibrated in my pocket, and I pulled it out, ready to reassure my dad once again that I would return in one piece. But the text wasn't from my dad.

It was from Mik.

Do you want me to come?

I froze.

"Say yes," Natalie hissed from where she'd magically appeared over my shoulder.

"What're you, a ninja?" I said, batting her out of my breathing space. I typed *yes* but couldn't hit send right away. This wasn't as simple as Natalie seemed to think. If I invited Mik along, I might get distracted from my mission to find Jake's marker. To *really* remember him like I ached to do.

There were other aches, surprisingly deep ones that wanted me to press send.

I did, and Natalie held both arms up like I'd scored a goal. I slipped my phone into my pocket like nothing happened, which was a lie, because my pulse was banging like I'd sprinted around the room.

I pressed on the mattress. "So, did you lose your virginity on these awesome sheets?"

Natalie's mouth fell open. "See? *That.* That's what you have got to work on. You can't just say everything that pops into your head around Mik. You'll drive him away."

"Why not? He likes me—at least everyone seems to think so—and I've always been this way. How would I drive him away by being myself when myself is what interested him in the first place?"

"She's got a point," Bishop yelled over.

"This is *real* girl talk," Natalie snapped at him. "Go back to your digital boobs." She looked at me very seriously. "It's good you're finally admitting that he likes you."

I shrugged. "Jake used to tease him about having a crush

on me when we were kids, and then Mik would turn bright red and stop talking in my presence for a month." My mom had reminded me of that earlier today, and now I had an odd, old flash of Mik standing up for me when Jake tried to make me jump off the garage roof. After which Jake wrote MIK + JAYCEE on the *outside* of his tree house so that every kid in the neighborhood could mock us. "Jake hated when we hung out."

Natalie was watching me with that calculating expression she did so well. "Come on, Jayce. You've got to read between the lines. He likes you *a lot*. Remember back at The Ridges when you bugged him about his cigarettes? I have not seen that boy smoke since that night. Have you?" Natalie folded her arms, possibly trying to keep all that know-it-all inside. "You've got to tell him how you feel. No playing games. If you just want to be friends, you have to say that. If you're curious about—"

"I thought all you girls set out to play games," Bishop yelled.

Natalie shook her head and spoke quietly, although I had no doubt that her voice carried to the couch. "Marrakesh did a number on him. She was cruel."

"That girl scared me," I admitted. "She sang show tunes in the girls' locker room. Something about the worst pies in London."

"Drama queen," Natalie muttered. "'Suffered' for her art." She stepped even closer. "You know how she broke up with him? She had him drop her off at the airport, and then right before she walked through security, she said, 'We're done forever,' and handed him a backpack containing everything he'd ever given her. Every card and poem. Even ticket stubs from the movies they'd gone to together."

"That sounds psychotic."

Natalie nodded solemnly, and I glanced at Bishop. He was pretending not to listen.

"So Mik is coming?" Zach asked conspicuously from the couch. "I think I like that guy."

"Yes," Natalie called back.

I was slightly shocked when my phone buzzed again.

Here.

Natalie looked at it. "Tell Mik to come down. Or wait, let's just go now." She grabbed Zach's controller and turned off the game. Both Bishop and Zach swore at her.

"Zatch!" a small voice called down the stairs.

Natalie grabbed Zach by the shirt before he could run up. "Don't tell Alianna where we're going," Natalie said.

Zach issued a few groans and went upstairs to help his little sister with something. I used the free second to reread Mik's messages on my phone. How many times had I stared at this screen, willing him to send me a text? Now I had two. By the time I glanced up again, I'd almost missed a rather gruff exchange between Bishop and Natalie.

"I'm…trying. Give me a chance," she said.

"Do it tonight," he said. "This isn't going to be like my breakup with Marrakesh. I'm not going to let him smack into the truth all by himself." He elbowed past her and up the stairs.

"What was that about?" I asked when he was gone.

Natalie smoothed her hair behind her ears nervously. "Bishop thinks Zach and I hate Marrakesh. I guess we do. Or did. She got too intense. We tried to warn him. Well, Zach did. It didn't go so well. Bishop accused Zach of all kinds of nasty things, and they haven't been the same since." She dug through her bag and produced a neatly folded pile of clothes. "I brought you something to wear. Hurry up and change."

"Not a chance." I looked down at my beat-up shirt and jeans. "These are perfect for draining, which is what we're going to be doing if you don't remember."

"*Draining?*"

"Yes. An urbex subset involving drainage ditches and sewers—a.k.a., draining. You remember?" I longed to see some spark of recognition in my old friend's eyes. When we were eight, we'd found an open sewer hatch behind the elementary school.

"The portal," she said, smiling.

It made me grin and feel entirely too happy.

"You remember how we thought we'd end up in Narnia?"

"Yeah, but we just came out at the far end of the block."

"Still, it was magical," I pushed.

Natalie looked away. "We're lucky we didn't get lost and die, or pick up some disease."

My smile folded in on itself, and I poked at the V-neck navy shirt and the jeans that were more spandex than denim. "I'm not wearing clubbing clothes."

"You've never been clubbing," Natalie said, "so how would you know? Besides, these stretchy jeans are surprisingly comfortable."

"For a Barbie." I dropped the clothes on the bed. "I'll wear these if you wear my clothes."

I really thought I'd won. There was no way that the Natalie from my childhood—or the girl who'd growled *You're*

embarrassing me in my ear while I was puking up Tabasco—
would wear my baggy, beat-up Jake hand-me-downs. But a
few moments later, Natalie and I stepped outside of Zach's
house so altered in appearance that the boys would have
stared—if they weren't busy watching Mik throw Zach's
brother up against a car.

CHAPTER

24

ZACH

ZACH WAS STOKED. A NIGHT OUT DOING MILDLY ILLEGAL things with his girl and his best bud? This was what he had been hoping his summer after graduation would be like. Bingo. Yes. Let's do this.

Zach waved at Mik, who had just parked along the street. He even slapped Bishop on the shoulder, and when his friend gave him a *Don't* look, Zach didn't even feel bad. He just clapped his hands together and jumped down the front steps.

And then goddamn Tyler pulled up.

His brother got out of his car like he owned the world, the driveway, and Zach—in that order. "What's up, dicktart?" Tyler yelled across the yard.

Zach's words came out tired. "Fuck off, Tyler."

Tyler walked toward him, and Zach readied himself for an arm around the neck, a forceful poke to the ribs, and some bullshit whispered into his ear about how hot Zach's girlfriend was. But that never happened.

Mik intercepted Tyler. He grabbed Tyler by the shirt, swung him around, and knocked him against Natalie's ancient

Oldsmobile. Zach couldn't hear anything, but he blinked hard because he was pretty sure that Mik was *arguing* with Tyler.

"What is *that* about?" Bishop asked.

"Old history?" Zach tried. "They were in high school together."

The girls stepped out of the house, and Zach felt Natalie's arms reach around him.

"What's happening?" Jaycee asked. Zach looked over at her and almost fell down. Boobs. Her boobs were smiling up at him from the top of a V-neck shirt. "Well?"

"No clue," he said.

The four of them stepped closer to the near-fight, and Mik released Tyler with a shove.

Tyler recovered fast. Too fast. He flashed a slick smile at Jaycee and Natalie. "Hey, ladies. What're you up to tonight? Ditch these dicks. Come out with me."

Ordinarily, Natalie would mouth off something fierce at Tyler, and that's what Zach was waiting for. Only Natalie said nothing and stepped farther behind him. Tyler came closer, and what happened next was so swift that Zach almost missed it.

Mik scooped Alianna's basketball off the end of the drive-way and threw it at Tyler's head. Zach's brother never saw it coming. It nailed him so hard that Tyler bit into that stupid, grin, nearly falling over.

Zach rushed with joy.

"What the…" Tyler yelled. He'd bitten his tongue, and his words were a mess. He dared a glare at Mik, but then backed away and into the house.

Zach was practically sending out rays of sunshine as he slapped hands with Mik. "I knew I liked you! I knew it! Oh man, I'm going to wish I had that on video for the rest of my life."

Mik's smile was a little sheepish from the attention.

"That really was priceless," Bishop admitted.

Zach turned back to Natalie, finding her gripping onto Bishop's arm, her face white.

"Hey, you okay?" Zach asked. She nodded, and Zach kissed her, still dancing inside from the sight of Tyler's embarrassment. "Of course you're okay. You look adorable. Like you're going on a mission trip to build houses in Chile."

"Hey," Jaycee said. "Those are my clothes."

Bishop cocked his head at the girls. "What happened here? Jaycee, you look...hot. I'm not coming on to you. It's an observation," he added in Mik's direction.

Mik didn't seem to notice. He still looked pretty keyed up from dealing with Tyler, and Zach didn't blame him; he always felt that way around his big brother.

"Let's go," Natalie said. "Bishop, you're driving." She got in the passenger side and slammed the door.

A half hour later, on the long, black stretch of Route 33, Zach was still unpacking the rapid-fire events that happened in his driveway. Why was his brother so determined to embarrass him these days? It was like Tyler was extra bored this summer, and what was going on with Natalie? She never passed up an opportunity to insult Tyler with confusingly large words.

Zach had more current problems as well. He was stuck in the backseat beside hostile hottie Jaycee with Mik on the far end. To top it off, Bishop and Natalie were having some sort of existential, drag-out argument in the front.

"A civilized society shouldn't allow its citizens to have guns," Natalie snapped. "It's common sense."

"Depends on your definition of civilization," Bishop threw back. "Is a civilization defined by a self-sustaining society? Because our society has developed weapons powerful enough to destroy the world thirty times over, which is hardly civilized."

"So you're saying we should have guns because we're *not* civilized?" Natalie snapped back. The stabbing tones in their discussion reminded Zach of his parents and made him want to change the subject. He had to think of something, and to his luck, something came driving along on the other side of the highway.

"Padiddle!" Zach crowed.

Natalie took off her shirt without a word—really Jaycee's shirt—and kept debating.

"You have to take off your shirt," Zach said to Jaycee. "Those are the rules."

"The rules of what?" she asked, looking at him like she might have a concealed knife and was thinking about using it.

"Strip padiddle." Zach pointed to the other side of the highway where the line of headlights stretched east for a few miles. "Boys versus girls. One headlight out, you hit the ceiling, call 'padiddle,' and the boys have to take off some clothes. One headlight out on a semi, you say 'big ass padiddle,' and the boys have to get naked. If you accidentally call a padiddle for a motorcycle, you have to get naked. The driver is exempt. And all the same rules apply if a boy calls the padiddle on the girls like I just did. Got it?"

"I think I'd rather discuss civilization," Jaycee said. Mik chuckled, and she glanced at him like she'd forgotten he was on the other side of her. Man, if that girl really wanted to hook up with him, she'd have to stop treating him like an alien.

"Natalie," Jaycee called up. "I'm not taking my clothes off for your boyfriend."

Natalie looked back, and her eyes definitely flicked to Mik before she narrowed her sights on Jaycee. "Zach's right. Those are the rules in the Bonemobile."

"The what-mobile?"

"Bonemobile," Zach said. "I named it."

"You don't say." Jaycee got another small laugh from Mik, which seemed to make her smile against her will.

"It's like this," Zach said. "Oldsmobile. *Bonemobile.* Because it's the color of bone, and because Natalie and I…"

"All right," Natalie and Jaycee said at the same time. Natalie continued. "It's a regular teenage thing, Jaycee. The stuff you always miss out on." Then she threw down the hammer. "Just think of it as a dare, and you won't have a problem."

Jaycee took off her shirt with an angry flourish that was pretty hot. "This is so much worse than the Tabasco," she muttered. "Although the heartburn is similar."

Zach leaned back to give her a once-over with his peripheral vision, but Mik was fast with a warning look that said, *Think about it and I'll bounce a basketball off your face.*

Zach sighed, ready for them to get there already. But before that could happen, Jaycee hit the ceiling and yelled, "Big ass padiddle!"

"No way. Those are so rare! Illegal! Nonexistent!" Zach yelled. But there it was. A big fat semi with one headlight out.

Zach stripped and tossed his shirt up to Natalie, but she didn't even complain. Mik stripped too. Jaycee suddenly leaned all the way against the bench seat in front as though she was determined not to look at the boys even though their clothes were piled strategically on their laps. Which really took the fun out of it.

They pulled up in the Tim Horton's parking lot on High Street. The Gates of Hell were apparently hidden in the wooded ravine behind it, and yet Zach felt damp with disappointment. How could things change without changing? He wasn't in high school anymore, but he was still hanging out with the same people, still playing dare games and drinking secret booze in his basement. Only it felt weird all of a sudden. Slightly dated.

Bishop and Natalie weren't the same, of course, but even Zach was changing against his will. He wasn't ready to be done with the mindless thrill of strip padiddle or making out with Natalie in the backseat or besting Bishop at *Mario Kart* for three hours straight. Was all their forced maturity rubbing off on him? Was he going to end up debating politics in a coffee shop?

Those bastards…

Zach was the first one out of the Bonemobile, pulling on his clothes as he skipped through the edge of the trees. A party was *happening* inside the football field–sized cement drainage ditch. Dozens of teenagers were drinking, listening to music, and skateboarding. A bonfire burned in an old metal trash can.

"My people!" Zach ran down the slope and into the crowd to make some new friends.

CHAPTER

25

Natalie

EVERYTHING WAS GOING ACCORDING TO PLAN. MIK WAS here, Jaycee was in girl clothes, Bishop was already looking for a place to make his graffiti art, and Zach? Zach had made friends with a pack of Columbus boys, chugging some sort of pink vodka drink out of a gallon jug.

She'd worry about that later.

First she had to find out what happened between Mik and Tyler on the driveway. Mik was pulling his shirt back on, so she tried to get close without being too obvious. Before she could say anything, he thrust a scrap of paper in her hand and took off. She jammed it in her back pocket, but she wasn't fast enough. When Natalie looked up, Jaycee was scowling from where she was seated on the cement edge, hugging that Mead notebook.

Natalie sat next to her. "Was it such a party when Jake was here?"

"No," Jaycee snapped. "It's supposed to be abandoned. I can't picture Jake here. And I'll never find his marker with all these idiots around."

Natalie wasn't going to get anywhere with this line of questioning. She switched gears. "So what do you think about Mik?"

"What do I think about Mik passing notes with you?"

Natalie's cheeks went hot. "No. That's not what I meant. That's about…nothing."

"How do you know that, Natalie?" Jaycee asked. "You haven't read it yet. Does this have anything to do with you ending up half-naked over his shoulder two weeks ago?"

Natalie fought for a comeback. "No. No, I was asking about Mik being shirtless. Just now. When we all got out of the car and the boys were getting dressed. What did you think of Mik's chest?"

Jaycee looked down fast. "I didn't look. That's pervy."

"Seriously? You missed it?"

"I don't oversexualize men physically in the good faith that they don't do that to me." Jaycee stared at the journal. "Speaking of, if your boyfriend ogles my boobs one more time, I'm going to hand him his balls in a Ziploc bag."

"While I appreciate your moral standard, you are *hopeless*. And just for the Zach threat, I'm not going to tell you what I saw on Mik's naked chest."

Natalie had her now. Jaycee glanced down at where Mik was investigating the massive, wedge-styled gates that surrounded the huge open drain that the place was named for.

When Jaycee noticed that Natalie was watching her, she dug into her bag and placed the skateboard next to her, her fingers running over the stickers and the stencil of Jake's name.

"I remember the Christmas when Jake got that board," Natalie said. "You slept over that night. We were so excited because we didn't have to do traditional family holiday stuff."

Jaycee was suddenly pleased. "I remember this one. I slept over because my parents had to take Jake to the hospital after he tried to skateboard on some black ice and broke his arm." Jaycee paused, her eyes glassy. "My mom hated this board. She said he'd break his neck." Her voice was so eerily smooth. "Isn't that funny?"

"I'm not laughing," Natalie managed.

Jaycee bent over the journal as Mik appeared, hovering in the vicinity while still giving them space. Natalie had to hand it to him; he knew how to orbit Jaycee without ticking her off. He rocked the skateboard with his foot as gently as Jaycee had rested it on the cement.

Natalie glanced at Jake's notebook. "How can you read that? Looks like gibberish."

Jaycee turned a page. "He was left-handed, ADHD, and more than a little dyslexic. Give him a break."

"Oh, that makes sense," Natalie said, crossing her legs and checking on Zach, who was laughing super hard at something one of the Columbus guys had said. "Kids with learning disabilities often act out because of their frustration."

Mik touched the skateboard with his foot again.

"Mik wants to use the board," Natalie said.

Jaycee shoved the skateboard toward Mik, and a moment later, he was trench coat–free, sailing down the cement with ease. Jaycee watched him before turning to Natalie. "So you speak for Mik now?"

"He was being obvious. And you're being obviously weird with him. Why?"

Jaycee folded the journal. "Was Mik the guy you hooked up with when you drunk?"

Natalie ground her teeth. "I already told you no."

"I don't believe you. And you *really* wanted me to tell him to come with us. And you were acting weird on Zach's driveway. Plus you're passing notes. He barely even texts me."

Natalie took a long time to find the right explanation. Pointing out Jaycee's subtle jealousy wasn't going to go well, although that's what she really wanted to do. "Would I be trying to get you two together if I had hooked up with him?"

"I don't honestly know. Would you?" Jaycee was looking entirely too smug by the light of the trash can fire. "What did you tell me about Mik? I have to tell him how I feel. No playing games. So how about you practice what you preach. What do you want from me, Nat?"

"Don't call me that. I'm not a bug."

"Did you hear a *g*?"

"It's silent."

"Like the worst kind of bugs."

Natalie almost laughed. So did Jaycee. The exchange was entirely too reminiscent of their childhood bantering. After a quiet moment, Natalie managed, "I want to be friends again."

"Why?"

Natalie didn't have an answer. Not one she could give Jaycee anyway. *I feel profoundly guilty? I've never found another person I can be myself with?* Or how about, *I think I'm cracking up and you're the only person who's ever made me feel strong?*

All pathetic reasons. They probably weren't even true.

Who is Natalie? What is she capable of?

"I don't know who I am," she murmured.

"You're Zach's girlfriend," Jaycee said, turning a page. "You're your mother's puppet." She turned another page.

"You're a Cornell freshman." She shut the book. "You're my ex-best friend."

Natalie stared at her, aghast. "You've rotted, Jayce. I've no idea what he sees in you."

Jaycee had the decency to look stricken. She glanced at the far side of the drainage plane where Mik held the edge of the skateboard. He dropped onto it, looping into the bowl with a twisting turn that took him out of sight around another group of skaters.

"Mik's good. He's showing off for you."

"He should be good after the endless years he and Jake spent glued to those boards."

"So you're still angry that Jake wouldn't let you join in, huh?" Natalie said.

Jaycee ignored her, wiping her hand across her face before pointing at the notebook. "What I want to know is why Mik and Jake weren't friends in high school. Why didn't Mik do all this stuff with him? He's not in here at all. And all of his other buddies are. Even Zach's disgusting brother is in here."

Natalie was so thrown off by the mention of Tyler that she didn't realize that Jaycee was waiting for her to answer. "You think I know why they weren't friends in high school?"

"I think you know about ditching your childhood best friend for shiny, new friends."

"You *know* it wasn't like that with us." Natalie stood up, and it only sort of slowed her down to see that Jaycee had very silent tears working their way down her cheeks. "I was scared of you. How about that? You were frightening when you were upset. Remember the afternoon after the funeral when you told me you wanted to drink gasoline and then you threw Jake's hatchet at the wall over and over?"

"That's not exactly what happened." Jaycee tightened her ponytail with a yank.

"Tell me flat out if you're never going to forgive me. I'd rather not waste my time."

Jaycee shoved the journal in her bag and stood up. She was taller than Natalie, and when she stared down in Natalie's face, Natalie felt like a shrimp. "Hmmm, will I forgive you for running away when I needed you the most? Let me think on that, *Nat*."

Mik skated up and jumped off the board. His arm shot out between them like a safety bar.

Jaycee grabbed the skateboard out of his other hand and set it down. "Watch my bag." Before Natalie could stop her, Jaycee sent herself flying over the edge.

Natalie sat down so hard that she nailed her tailbone, but the pain that spiked up her spine was nothing compared to deeper hurts. "This is Sisyphean." Mik sat beside her. "She doesn't *want* to forgive me. She likes being mad, the old coward."

Natalie gathered her own courage slowly and took Mik's note out of her back pocket. She held it up to the bonfire light.

TYLER SAID HE HAD SEX WITH YOU. HE COULD BE LYING.

"Thanks for trying," she said hollowly. The words etched themselves in her mind until all she could see was the word *sex* in bold, crimson font. "Wait, did you ask him? Like you talked to him?"

Mik rubbed the back of his neck, which felt like a confirmation.

"Well, it was sweet of you." She crumpled the piece of paper and shoved it back into her—really Jaycee's—baggy jeans. "I guess I have to get used to not knowing."

Fuck. What would she say to Bishop? Would he still make her tell Zach if she didn't even know what happened?

Mik and Natalie watched Jaycee roll up the other side of the drainage ditch, turning jerkily and heading back down. It was nothing like the poetry Mik had wielded when he'd flashed around on the skateboard.

"She's going to wipe out," Natalie warned before putting her hands over her face. *Zach's girlfriend…her mom's puppet?* This is what Jaycee thought of her, and Jaycee didn't even know the whole truth about why they were no longer friends. If she did know…

"I can't tell him," she said suddenly. "I can't tell Zach. I'll have to make Bishop understand. This can only hurt people. We have to pretend like it never happened." Mik shook his head slowly. "I know what I'm doing," she lied. "I've been down this road before."

At least that part was true.

CHAPTER

26

MIKIVIKIOUS

DO YOU HAVE ANY SHOOTING PAIN?

WHAT?

CAN YOU ROTATE IT?

YOU *TALKED.*

IT'S A MILD SPRAIN.

YOU'LL BE FINE.

CHAPTER 27

ZACH

ZACH'S NEW BUD WAS DARREN. DARREN HAD MADE THE PINK vodka drink that was currently turning Zach's stomach into a fire dance.

Zach was planning on ignoring everyone he'd come with for the rest of the night, and the booze made this seem like a brilliant idea. He could ignore them like they were so good at ignoring him. But then, he couldn't ignore Jaycee standing there, screaming in the middle of the party.

"What the hell's her problem?" Darren asked.

"Everything," Zach said.

"She should quit screaming. The cops don't really like us down here. If we give them a reason, they flash their search lights and make everyone scatter."

"Hold on. I'll get her." Zach quick-stepped through the crowd, wondering where Natalie and Mik were. Weren't they supposed to babysit loco Jaycee? "Hey!" he yelled, grabbing her arms. "What's going on?"

"Some fucker stole my bag!" There were tears in her eyes that made Zach's face sting. Man, he was so bad at not feeling what everyone else felt. "My brother's notebook was in there."

"Okay, so we'll find it. I'll help you. I'll ask my new BFF." Zach took her by the hand, but Jaycee pulled away sharply, wincing.

"Hurt my wrist," she said. She offered her other hand, and Zach was surprised that she held onto his fingers sweetly like Alianna used to before she turned twenty-five, a.k.a. twelve. He led Jaycee to Darren, who began to inspect her boobs with fierce admiration. Zach felt oddly protective in that moment, especially because Jaycee's usual fire and contempt were missing. She looked like she was about to start sobbing.

"Someone stole her bag. Do you know who'd do that?"

Darren glanced over the crowd. "Yeah, fucking bored middle schoolers. They steal our stuff and throw bottles and cans at us from up there." He pointed to the top of the iron wedge gate that stood before the massive drain opening.

"Where do they take it?" Jaycee asked.

Darren pointed into the drain. "They have a little hideout. About thirty minutes' walk."

"Thirty minutes!" Zach said. Jaycee was already off, slipping through the iron gate and heading into the black hole of the huge sewer. "Wait! I'm coming with you!" He ran and tripped. "Should we go get Natalie and her thingy?" He tapped his forehead to indicate the headlamp.

"They stole her bag too. But we have this." She held up Mik's Zippo.

"Where's the trench coat that comes with it?"

"Probably making out with Natalie."

Zach froze, imagining Natalie and Mik all hot 'n' heavy. Was he the guy she'd hooked up with weeks ago?

"I'm not serious," Jaycee said. "They're being pals and looking at me like I'm overreacting. Like this is my fault. It's Natalie's fault. She was supposed to watch my bag."

Zach pushed his hair out of his eyes. "Okay, so we go after the kids. We'll get your stuff. Don't stress." She cradled her injured wrist against her chest.

The drain was huge. Zach reached his hands up and touched the cool, damp cement. "Heeeellllloooo?" he called into the dark.

Bishop appeared, stepping forward out of the black with a large Sharpie in his hand. "Zach. Are you drunk?"

"No."

Jaycee pushed around Zach. "Did you see some idiot kids come in here?"

Bishop nodded. "Little punks. They ruined something I was trying to draw."

"Which way did they go?" she asked. Bishop pointed into the tunnel, and Jaycee started off on her own.

Zach looked to Bishop. "We've got to get Jaycee's bag back. Want to come?"

Bishop shook his head. "I'm working on something."

"Yeah, of course." Zach walked after Jaycee, his thoughts stinging with unsaid words. Within a few minutes, the low light from the partiers and their fire was gone. Jaycee held up Mik's Zippo with the hand that wasn't bandaged. It illuminated the graffiti outline of a black man with triangles on his chest—a sentinel of sorts.

"Shit. This is spooky." Zach imagined what it would be like to get lost down here, all alone in the cement cold. The pink vodka tossed around in his chest. "If Mik jumps out at us like he did in The Ridges, I'll kick his nuts."

"He won't." Jaycee snorted. "He's pouting because he accidentally talked to me."

"Say what?" Zach asked. "I thought you wanted him to talk to you or that he wanted to talk to you or something more…mutual?"

"Ask Natalie," Jaycee said. "She claims to have all the answers."

"But she's not like you. She won't show her cards. Not for anything. You're honest."

"Keep in mind that Natalie refers to my brand of honesty as 'brutal.'"

"Exactly." They pushed farther into the drain, and Zach couldn't hold back anymore. "Do you know who Natalie hooked up with after graduation? She said she went to your house."

Jaycee scowled. "You should just ask her who she slept with."

"Slept with? Whoa, no. She made out with someone." He burped and felt the burn of the liquor in his throat. "She's been weird about it. Do you think she…hooked up with Bishop?"

The quiet in the drain became too loud, even their footsteps were silent.

"That seems possible," Jaycee said. "She's definitely acting weird. Oh…hey, I did overhear her and Bishop arguing about something personal."

Zach's face crashed into his palm. As much as he had run his thoughts through the idea of Natalie and Bishop, he couldn't actually stomach it. "I don't know what she's capable of," he said miserably. "She's getting ready to dump everyone before taking off to New York. That stupid place. I swear its tagline is 'Where all Natalie Cheng's dreams come true.'"

"Are you sure she wants to go there?" Jaycee was walking faster. "Seems like she's just running away. And majoring in psychology? That's got her mother stamped all over it."

"I don't really know where her mom ends and she begins," Zach admitted.

"How could you spend four years with her and not know that?"

He shrugged. "We don't do a lot of talking."

"Ew."

"No, really. Our relationship is more about physical support. There's stuff that she's going through…stuff she says I can't understand. And vice versa. We tend to hug it out instead of talk it out. Not that that's been happening lately."

Jaycee was quiet. And unfortunately, her silence invited more of Zach's insecurities.

"Maybe you can help me with something. I've been thinking about how you don't have to go to college. How you said you're not interested, and your parents *listened* to you. I…want to do that too. How do I do it?"

Jaycee's face looked pretty stark by the light of Mik's Zippo. "I played the dead brother card. Don't think that'll help you much."

"Oh. Right." Zach could picture the next five years like they were a movie he was being forced to watch. His mother would end up needling him until he studied something she approved of; his father would hound him into a job with security. Alianna would come over when she was in high school and steal his booze, pointing out that his girlfriend didn't respect him. And then to top it all off, Tyler would stop by and make him feel eternally like the nine-year-old who'd found condoms in his mom's glove compartment.

Jaycee kept speeding up. Their steps were now echoing loudly along with the sound of water trickling deep. "So these are storm sewers?" he asked, because he was starting to imagine never getting back out to face the moon again.

"Sure. At any moment, these drains could flood, and we would be swept to our deaths."

"Hey, Creeperson, don't freak out the person who's helping you! You think about these things a lot?"

"You don't?" she asked. He shook his head. "I guess that makes sense. When I saw my brother die, my whole perspective on things changed. Life has borders all over the place. I like looking for them. Feeling them out. It gets you close to the other side."

Zach imagined Jaycee standing right on the edge of nothing. "Are we talking heaven or *The X-Files*?"

Jaycee smirked. "A mash-up of both, I think." She continued after a moment. "Natalie thinks I'm damaged. That's why we can't be friends. She wasn't there. She didn't see Jake. She can't understand."

"I get that. Bishop acts like I can't possibly understand his heartbreak but—"

Jaycee shushed Zach. At the same time, footsteps began to pound toward them, getting louder and faster. Zach flattened himself against the tunnel wall, but Jaycee stood in the way, closing the Zippo so that they were in the pitch-black.

When the middle schoolers came rushing through, they hit Jaycee, colliding into a mess of limbs on the damp ground. A few of them yelled, but Jaycee snagged one by the collar. Zach used his phone to illuminate the kid's petrified face while the rest of them bugged off. "Your friends ditched you. Ouch."

"You stole my bag. Where is it?" Jaycee said.

"Lemmego!"

"My. Bag."

The kid pointed in the direction he'd come, and Jaycee hauled him to his feet by the back of his shirt. She marched him through the tunnel until they found the hideout, which consisted of a pile of milk crates and boxes. Green glow sticks had been snapped and strung on a wire overhead.

Zach tapped one of them, making it swing, while the kid pointed to a pile of bags and purses. Jaycee dug, tossing Natalie's survival gear bag at Zach. She pulled her beaten canvas bag out of the bottom and yanked it open—but then her face went even more sickly green than the glow sticks.

"Where is the notebook?" She grabbed at the kid, and Zach instinctively held Jaycee back before she throttled the boy.

The kid fell on his butt, and yet he laughed. "We burned it in the fire pit."

Jaycee went to nothing in Zach's arms. One minute she was there, and the next she was empty. She made no sound. No movement. The kid stopped laughing after a few seconds, perhaps figuring out that he'd done something *really* wrong. He got up and sprinted past them.

Zach slid down the tunnel wall with Jaycee's weight crushing him. She started to shake hard, and fear spiked through him. They were a long way away from help.

"I'm going to…we're going to go now," he said. "Come on."

Jaycee was way heavier than Natalie, and they fell many times, getting grimy in the runoff water. He fought the feeling that he was in his own coffin by rebuilding the scene in his mind, LEGO brick by LEGO brick. They weren't in the sewers beneath Columbus. They were in a snapped-together plastic-block world…

When he could finally see the distant opening of the drain, Zach leaned against the wall, breathing hard. "Say something, Strangelove. You're freaking me out."

"I hadn't even read the whole thing yet," she whispered. "This is all Natalie's fault."

"Maybe it didn't burn all the way," he said. "Maybe it's on the edge of the fire. Or someone pulled it out."

Jaycee was up in a flash, sprinting. Zach could barely keep up with her as she ran out of the drain, through the crowd to the rusted metal trash bin holding the fire. Zach realized immediately how cruel it was to give Jaycee hope. Anything that went into that trash can went up in a blink. Game over.

CHAPTER 28

Natalie

NATALIE SEARCHED FOR JAYCEE. THE GIRL WAS PROBABLY IN the depths of the drainage system now…or wandering the streets of Columbus…or in Zach's arms?

The fire illuminated quite possibly the weirdest thing Natalie had ever seen—Jaycee wrapped up in Zach's hold, staring longingly at the fire pit.

"Zach!"

Zach let go of Jaycee, and she stumbled as if he had been keeping her from diving into the trash bin. Jaycee's gaze reached across the fire to meet Natalie. The girl's eyes were unbelievably black.

"Natalie," Zach started. "Something happened and—"

"You did this," Jaycee said.

"Did what? What did I do now?" Natalie yelled, furious. "And what did *you* do? Seduce my boyfriend to get back at me? That's ridiculous even for you!"

Mik appeared behind Natalie, touching her shoulder in restraint.

"Looks like we've traded," Jaycee said hotly.

Natalie threw Mik's hand off. "I can't believe you'd think I'd—"

Jaycee walked away. She left the light of the bonfire and the riot of the partiers, heading up the side of the cement ditch. Natalie had to follow. Her brain was so fed up that she couldn't see anything other than Jaycee's back. "Get Bishop," she snapped at Mik. "We're leaving."

Natalie told herself that she was going to have it out with Jaycee right now come hell or high water. And considering she was standing at the "gates of hell," which were built for high water, that couldn't be more apropos. But before she could move, Zach's voice stopped her.

"Natalie. Those kids burned her brother's journal."

Natalie's anger flatlined. Mik swore. And then they were all heading up the incline, beating back trees to find Jaycee in the parking lot. Natalie was the fastest one. "Jayce—"

Jaycee moved in so fast that Natalie braced for a punch, but instead Jaycee hugged her. *Really* hugged her.

Natalie held on tight. "Oh God, I'm so sorry. I'm so, so sorry, Jayce."

All three boys came up the incline, and Natalie waved them back while she held on to Jaycee. The girl's whole body was trembling.

"Every time I trust you, I get burned," Jaycee whispered.

"What?"

"I can't trust you." Jaycee's hand slunk into Natalie's back pocket. "You shouldn't trust me either." Jaycee stepped away, already reading Mik's note about Tyler.

"Don't say anything," Natalie breathed.

Jaycee looked from the scrap of paper. "I thought you slept with Mik. Or possibly Bishop."

Natalie glanced at the boys. She could tell two things

instantly. One, Mik and Bishop knew exactly what was happening. Two, Zach had no clue. Until Jaycee held the note out
to him.

"Jaycee!" Natalie cried.

"What's this?" Zach took it.

"Truth," Jaycee said to him. "Natalie slept with your brother."

There was a dead moment.

And strangely enough, the first person to act was Mik. He
moved forward, caught Jaycee by the upper arm, and hauled her
back toward Natalie's car. Bishop touched Zach's shoulder and
looked like he was going to say something, but then he left too.

"I don't understand," Zach finally said. He held out the
note. "What does this mean?"

"Wait, Zach. Hear me out. That's not the whole story.
That's just what—"

"What does this mean?" He threw the piece of paper.
"WHAT'S HAPPENING?" Natalie stepped back. Zach
tugged his hair until it flared crazily. "You slept with Tyler?"

"No. Well, not really. I don't know if I—"

"Don't lie! You were at his frat? In his *bed*?"

Natalie couldn't answer. The look on Zach's face was killing
her. It made her heart beat miserably loud and her ears ring
with her own voice. "Zach, let's go home. We'll talk."

"You were either in his bed or you weren't. Answer."

"I…I was."

He fell backward like she'd hit him. She grabbed his hand
and tried to help him up, but he flung her away. "Don't fucking touch me!" He got to his feet, started toward the partiers,
and then whipped around. "Why?" He was crying. "Do you
hate me? Did I do something wrong?"

"No, I love you. I was upset, but not with you. I don't really know why I did it."

"I know why. It's because I'm the village idiot, and you're sick of being brought down."

She reached for him again. "Let's go home, Zach."

"Leave. I'm not getting in a car with you."

She called his name, but he was gone. Bishop appeared at her shoulder while she stood there, shaking and tearing at her arms with her nails. He sighed. "This is exactly what I didn't want to happen."

"Bishop?" she whispered.

"Yeah?"

"Fuck off."

CHAPTER
29

BISHOP

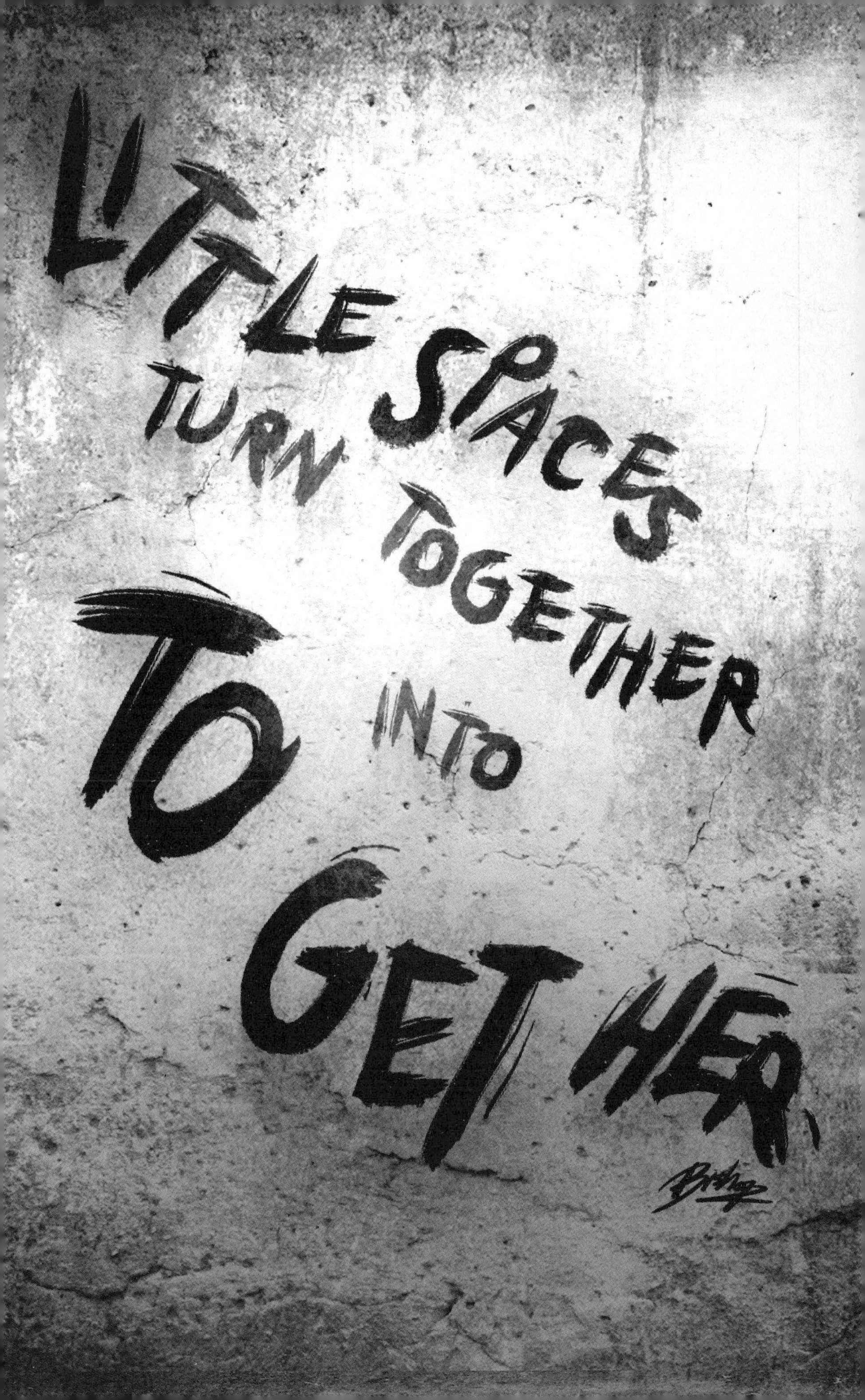
LITTLE SPACES
TURN TOGETHER
INTO
TO
GET HER.

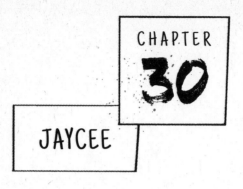

CHAPTER
30

JAYCEE

TWO A.M. MAYBE LATER. NATALIE WAS DRIVING, WHICH probably wasn't a good idea. Not because she was so upset that she was going too fast—nope. Quite the opposite. She was driving at least ten miles under the speed limit. No one said a word about it.

No one said a word period, and yet the silence was deafening. In the backseat, I forced my fingers in my ears, unable to stop the sounds of what had happened. That thunderclap look on Zach's face…Natalie's shrieking, pleading. Mik shoving me into the car and slamming the door.

I tried to focus on Jake, on his journal, but I couldn't hold on to it. Not its image. Not my anger at its destruction. Jake's death had always been a void, bleak and bottomless, but ultimately safe. I could scream into that black hole and not even hear myself, but all this? It was deafening. Poor fucking Zach. How would he get home? What if something happened to him?

My voice broke with a drowning sort of gasp. Mik looked across the expanse of the huge backseat. Did he hate me? He'd been so angry…or hurt…or…I don't know.

I grabbed my phone and sent him a text.

What do you want from me?

I stared him down until I knew he felt his pocket vibrate. Until I knew that he was ignoring it on purpose. After all, he'd seen me type it.

These trips were supposed to bring me back to Jake, but now all I could feel was the distance. The mounting miles between Natalie and Zach. The impossible gap between Mik and me. My lungs burned like I was trying to breathe water. What was this? Guilt waterboarding? I started to laugh. Couldn't stop myself. Natalie glanced at me through the rearview mirror like I was a bomb that had snuck into her Oldsmobile.

"You all right?" Bishop glanced over his shoulder.

All right? All right was not in my vocabulary. I turned toward the window, pressed my face to the pane, and kept laughing. If I stopped, I'd start to cry and drown, and they'd all see just how ugly my feelings could get. My phone buzzed, giving me Mik's one-word answer.

You.

I laughed harder, and Mik scooted next to me. Hip to hip. I had half a mind to open the car door, duck, and roll, but he took my arm. I calmed enough to let him unwrap the bandage. He rotated my hand, watched me wince, and then held the back of my wrist to his cheek like he was checking the temperature. He wrapped it back up and kept my fingers cradled in his. We weren't holding hands. We were somewhere in that gray area—touching but not touching. I spent so long trying to figure out what our hands were doing that before I knew it, we were back in Athens.

Natalie pulled the car in front of Bishop's huge mock-palatial house, and he left without a goodbye. Mik's thumb started to draw small circles on my palm, and when Natalie *slammed* to a stop in front of Zach's house, I almost wanted her to keep driving.

"Get out," she said.

"You're not going to take me home?" I had assumed that she would drop everyone off and then take me home the long way so that she could berate me into oblivion for giving Zach that note. This felt worse.

"Mik will take you."

We got out, and I stood on Zach's driveway where a thousand hours prior, Mik had thrown a basketball at Tyler Ferris's face and made us all laugh. I watched Natalie's out-of-fashion rectangular taillights disappear, the sudden lack of humor deafening.

Mik was busy cleaning out his front seat. He dumped an armful of things in the back and then went to the driver's side. I got in, sitting awkwardly on a few items that had missed his sweep.

I held up a small, plastic BIC razor. "How often do you have to shave?" His stubble was creeping up like a shadow around his jaw. He didn't answer, and I felt newly wounded by the wall I was talking to. The one I couldn't see over. I yanked a deodorant stick out from under my leg. "Old Spice? Isn't that a grandpa thing?"

Mik tossed it into the back, expressionless.

He drove me home, and with each street, I grew heavier again. I tasted water. Sipped at the air. I saw the surface slip farther away, turning the world into a blurry mosaic. I remembered all the kids and teenagers on the playground that day. At least a dozen people from Jake's graduating class. And Mik. I remembered how the paramedics took one look at Jake and shook their heads. Then there were the cops who roped everyone off from the scene and the black tarp they dropped over his body...

The digital clock on Mik's dashboard read 3:83.

"How can you have eighty-three minutes in an hour?" I asked. "Is it broken?"

Mik nodded.

I eyed his mouth—the same mouth that had tried to breathe for Jake while I stood by unmoving. "Say something."

Give me something else to think about.

Mik pulled into my driveway. He killed the engine, and his face held too much anxiety. I could tell that he was working himself up to speak, and now I hated myself for making him.

"Don't worry about it." I released my seat belt, needing to get out of this car before I said something I'd really regret.

What do you want from me?

You.

"Natalie said I should be clear about my intentions, and I agree with her for once. I don't want dates or anniversaries or anything that's going to confuse me with the promise of normality. So that's it for us. Sorry." But that wasn't *really* it, and this was the first time I'd ever struggled to brandish the whole truth. "You can't trust me. You saw what I did to Natalie and Zach."

Disappointment flickered on his face, and I remembered

that he'd hero-hauled Natalie out of that drunken hookup *and* threatened Tyler. "I'm sorry I ruined…" I shook my head. It wasn't ruining anything to tell the truth. Zach needed to know, didn't he?

"Whatever, I wish you luck, and thanks for fixing my wrist." I·left the car in a rush, but Mik followed me to the front door, and for a radical second, I hoped he was there for me. Instead he held out Jake's skateboard like it was sacred and fragile. Like I had been holding it earlier.

I took it by one wheel, and the wood banged on my knee as I let it dangle between us. "Do you ever picture what it'd be like if Jake were here?" I blurted. "Do you remember how much he hated it when we hung out? He would *never* let us date."

Mik didn't move, and I stared at his chest, roughly at the spot where his heart was beating beneath a black T-shirt and skin and ribs and blood. Natalie had insisted that there was something notable about his chest. What was it? Muscles? Chest hair? Scars?

I was suddenly desperate to know what I was missing, and I touched him. He reached into my hair, around the back of my neck in a way that made me lean into his fingers and want to moan, and for a whirl of a second, I thought he was saying my name.

"Jay…" He cleared his throat, his voice raw. "Jake *isn't* here."

Wrong answer.

I pulled away. "I hope I see you next June 26."

I shut the front door behind me. In the living room, I turned off the TV and tossed a blanket over my dad's bare feet. They looked exactly like Jake's. Second biggest toe popped up. I took the stairs to my brother's room like usual, but I couldn't lie down. Instead I stared at the shrine of Jake's things until my insides felt like they were morphing.

Suddenly I was furious I'd found that journal. That it had existed, period. My fists clenched as I knelt on the carpet. I wanted to beat something. Anything. I dragged the toolbox out from beneath the bed.

The skateboard rocked and creaked while a wrench took care of the wheels and my thoughts blazed against Jake. He was to blame for everything. For my dad's personality change and my mom's psychosis. I went back to the toolbox and found a hammer to take out the trucks. One knocked off for Natalie's broken friendship. One for my frozen life.

It wasn't enough. Jake's stenciled name peered up at me, and I scratched a screwdriver through every letter, thinking about how good Mik's hand had felt in my hair and how I'd probably never find the courage to let him touch me like that again.

Breathing swears, I sat back on my heels and surveyed the damage. It could still be fixed. Put back together and re-drawn—unlike Jake. He was a rotted mess by now.

I took out Jake's hatchet. Held it high with two hands.

The first blow bounced away with little more than a notch, but the rest of them bit in. Searing words poured out faster than tears ever could as my arms swung down over and over until the skateboard was nothing but a pile of shredded grip tape and hardwood splinters.

CHAPTER 31

ZACH

WHEN TYLER PULLED UP IN THE TIM HORTON'S PARKING lot, Zach almost didn't get in the car.

He'd called Tyler because he was going to have it out with his brother. Maybe beat him to a bloody pulp. Also because he was drunk. Very, very drunk. So drunk that Darren had to get on the phone and give Tyler the address, because Zach was in the background puking.

But how could he beat up his brother when there was a pretty, college-aged girl in Tyler's passenger seat?

Zach got in the back, slamming the door. "Who's this chick?" he slurred.

"My brother is *real* mature," Tyler said to the girl before turning back to glare at Zach. "She's my date. From the date you interrupted when you demanded I come pick you up in motherfucking Columbus, you dickweed."

"You, you ass! You slept with—"

Tyler cranked the volume in the backseat. Zach fell over on the stiff and stained upholstery. He clasped his hands over his ears and cried out because the noise *hurt*. Or maybe that was just his heart exploding. He tried to imagine himself as Mario in overalls and a plumber's hat, but this wasn't a game. Not even close.

Zach passed out with his chest rumbling along with the car's souped-up bass, and when he woke, he was on his huge bed in the basement with Alianna next to him. She was reading one of his comic books. "How bad is it?" she asked.

Zach screamed into his pillow. She touched his shoulder, and he nearly punched his little sister. Instead he jumped off the bed and slammed his fist into the cinderblock wall again and again until his knuckles were as mashed as raw, ground meat.

NO MAN'S LAND

CHAPTER 32

Natalie

THIRTEEN DAYS AND SHE'D BE GONE.

Natalie tried to keep her mind on that fact, but her resolve kept falling to pieces. She hadn't been out of her room in a week except to see her therapist, and even then, the woman had said she was just suffering from transition nerves. Of course she'd say that, because Natalie never really told her what was going on. Natalie never told anyone.

She could feel a panic attack coming a mile away, and she dropped onto the floor on her back, waiting for her chest to spasm and her mind to roll black. It didn't. Even her anxiety was broken. She felt blank. Was Zach okay? Was Jaycee destroyed without Jake's journal? Were they all hanging out without her?

She dragged herself upright and touched her three matching suitcases. Each one was filled with precision that was embarrassing. She'd picked out her outfits and even labeled them for the first few weeks of classes. Glancing down at her stiff clothes, she longed to dig out some of her laid-back wardrobe. But those outfits were for Future Natalie. And she was still Old Natalie.

The Natalie who was strung so tight that she might have slept with the worst human on the planet. God, not knowing was hell.

Thirteen more days, and she could pretend like this summer never happened. In the meantime, she stared at her phone and willed it to ring. Ring!

The phone began to buzz, and Natalie jumped backward. She picked it up and checked the caller ID: Jaycee.

Jaycee?

Natalie paced while the phone hummed in her hands. They had to fight, of course, about Jaycee busting the Tyler news so cruelly on Zach. Natalie wouldn't win, but who cared about winning anyway? Natalie did, especially when it came to Jaycee. She slid the bar to answer and slammed the phone against her ear. "We need to talk."

"Ah, hello! Is that you, Miss Natalie?"

"Mr. Strangelove?"

"Yes, it's me!" He was whispering, kind of. "Jaycee jumped in the shower, and I stole her phone. I feel like a villain in one of the Muppet movies." Natalie couldn't stop a smile. "I'm calling because I need…help. With Jaycee. She's a bit off her rocker."

"You don't say."

"Oh, it's not *too* bad. She's been breaking Jake's stuff. Even his old toys that were in the attic." He paused. "She nearly burnt down the shed this morning trying to torch his G.I. Joes. And I think, yeah, I think I need backup."

He was trying so hard to be cheerful. Natalie wanted to hug the man for his commitment to optimism in the face of all things Jaycee. She dropped into her desk chair. "I'm not really qualified for that anymore," she admitted.

"But you guys seemed like you were getting back together."

"That didn't go so hot." Natalie accidentally imagined Jaycee in a burning shed with all that long, dirty-blond hair dangling like a ready fuse. "Have you talked to Mik?" Natalie remembered Jaycee laughing psychotically in the backseat while Natalie's heart burst apart over Zach, only to catch Mik and Jaycee holding hands. "He's better with her than I am."

"I don't know how to get in touch with him. Do you have his number?"

Natalie frowned. "His number is on Jaycee's phone. I've seen it there."

"She must've deleted it," he said. Natalie put her hand over the mouthpiece and groaned. *Jaycee, how did you ruin it this time?* "I thought maybe they were dating, but when I asked her about it, her eyes started gleaming like Jack Nicholson's in *The Shining*. I'm really on Wit's End Road over here, Miss Natalie. If I get her to the coffee shop next to her work around five, would you meet us there? Maybe talk with her?"

"Yes." The word flew out so fast that she was shocked.

"Oh, great!" Mr. Strangelove said. "I always thought you two were yin and yang. Perfectly matched. That being said, you might need to bring your boxing gloves." He paused. "Oh boy, the shower shut off. You're the best and brightest, young lady. I'm proud of you."

He hung up so fast that Natalie didn't get a chance to tell him that he deserved Dad of the Year. Her own dad was either on a business trip or jet-lagged. Their connection had waned ever since she'd grown up too much to be excited about presents hidden in his suitcase.

Natalie put her phone down, feeling suddenly ill-equipped to handle Jaycee. It was too bad she couldn't call Bishop...or

Zach. He was sort of shockingly good with Jaycee. Mik was the answer, of course, but where would she find him? Did he really spend his days at the library?

Natalie ran out the door, jumped in her car, and in a few minutes, she was trekking up the brick path to Alden Library. The air-conditioning *whooshed* in her face as she pushed through the revolving door. The summer kept getting hotter, especially at night, and Natalie missed the cool of Zach's basement. If she was being honest, she missed the ease of being with Zach in general.

Like Jaycee, he wanted to make every afternoon an adventure. Just a few months ago, he'd insisted that they make a fort out of the couch cushions, and when they were crouched inside, laughing, he'd told her that pretending to be a kid was more fun than pretending to be an adult. After that, he'd shook his lovely blond hair and added, "You probably don't have to pretend to be anything."

Oh, Zach. She should have told him the truth then and about everything since. About her broken-necked night terrors and constant panic attacks and Tyler—maybe even about Jake. Natalie headed downstairs to the study rooms and nearly glanced right past her quarry. She doubled back, stepped around the chairs, and sat down across from Mik. He was alone with a serious stack of books, and Natalie hadn't recognized him because he wasn't wearing the trench coat.

"So you don't always wear that abomination. That's good," she said. "I worried about you in such heat."

He didn't look up. "I wear it for Jaycee. She warms up to me faster when I look like the boy she used to know."

Natalie opened her mouth to comment on the fact that Mik

was talking but thought better of it. "Have you seen her over the last two weeks?"

"No." Mik turned a page. He was reading an anatomy book, and the image before him was all veins and arteries. "She dismissed me until next year. I now walk the long way around the green so that she can't see me from her bookstore." Mik looked up, and Natalie read pain and hints of anger in his expression. "You had something to do with it," he said. "You and Zach."

"Well, no one will talk to me. Not even Bishop. So don't think I got off light."

Mik closed his book. "What do you want, Natalie?"

"Closure," she said. "I want to tell Zach how sorry I am, and I want Jaycee's forgiveness. I have thirteen days, and you're going to help me."

"Should I be writing this down?"

"Oh, you're sarcastic. What a sweet match you make for her."

Mik scooped up his pile of books and started toward the stacks. "There's no point. I'm pretty sure that if Jaycee sees me again before she wants to, she'll act like she can't. Like I physically don't register. Invisible." His words faltered. "She's done it before."

"Jaycee's always been pretty powerful." Natalie imagined the Jaycee that Mik was probably seeing. Headstrong, gorgeous. Intense. Jaycee had always been as daring as Jake but smarter, and therefore more infectious. "Niagara Falls, am I right?"

He glanced around. "If she ever hears you make that joke, we'll all be dead."

Natalie crossed her arms. "That only makes me want to go yell it at her and see if she gives chase. I want her back. Not the girl who's married to her grief. The real Jaycee."

"If she's still in there," he said. "I'm beginning to doubt that."

Natalie felt a sharp jab in his words. She followed him out of the library, trying to find something to say to keep him from leaving. "Mik, can I ask you a question without ruining this whole conversation?"

"You want to know why I'm talking," he said. Natalie nodded. "Because you were right. You kept speaking like I might respond. Now I feel like I can." He stopped walking by the outdoor amphitheater. "Why are you here now, Natalie? It's been weeks."

"Jaycee's dad called me. She's completely malfunctioning."

"She hurt herself?" His voice sounded scraped.

"She's okay." Natalie took a deep breath. "Apparently she's been breaking Jake's things. Her dad is freaked out, and that's saying something. He's seen a lot from her, you know?"

"So she's *not* okay." Mik sat on the grass incline and put his hands over his face.

Natalie understood that look. "Guess I'm not the only one terrified for the day she finally kills herself."

There was a strange peace in sitting next to Mik, talking to him openly. "I missed you," she said. He looked at her strangely, and she added, "I miss all of you guys. A lot." She pretended to adjust her glasses and shoved away a few tears. "Give me your phone. Please." Mik handed her his cell, and she dialed Bishop's number. "He won't answer if I call on my phone," she explained. She pressed the screen to her ear, waiting for him to answer. "Bishop, we're getting the band back together."

Bishop sighed. "No, Natalie. Just…no. I think I'm done with you forever."

"I'm calling bullshit. You say you're done with Zach and

me, but then how many texts did you send about telling Zach the truth? Admit it, you do care about him. About all of us."

Bishop was silent on the other end. "He shouldn't have to go through what I did."

"Well, he is. Right now. Have you been hanging out with him? Or has he been all alone since everything blew up?"

More silence and then, "What do you want me to do?"

"Go to his house tonight. We'll come over. Make sure he lets us in."

"Us?"

"Mik and me."

"If you two are dating, don't come within a mile of Zach, Natalie," Bishop said.

Natalie warmed to hear such protection in his voice. "Ew, no. I'm not going out with Mik." Mik gave her a *Hey, how am I that bad?* look, and she rolled her eyes. "We're going to bring Jaycee even if I have to throw a pillowcase over her head and haul her on my shoulder."

Natalie hung up and stood, amped.

"Pillowcase?" Mik asked. "That's how we handle her?"

"Yes, but we throw her over *your* shoulder. She's turned into a giant since we were kids." *Oh my God, this could work.* Natalie felt so much stronger all of a sudden. "I'm dropping in on her at the coffee shop tonight. You wait outside, and then we'll just sort of...take her."

"Settle down, Liam Neeson." Mik chuckled, but then his expression settled. "Do you still want me to talk to Tyler about what happened?"

Natalie's shoulders deflated. "No. I mean, no thanks. I think that ship has sailed."

CHAPTER

33

JAYCEE

FOR THE FIRST TIME IN FOREVER, I HAD PLANS. AND YET, I'D
been shanghaied to the café that reeked of toaster-burned bagels.

"I only have ten minutes before I have to go," I told my dad,
staring at the muddy swirl of coffee in my cup. "And I'm pretty
sure this is just water dyed brown. My taste buds will never
think this is a good idea."

"Caffeine will convince them. Until then..." He opened a
pack of Sugar in the Raw and dumped it into my cup. "You'll
get there," he added. "And now we talk futures."

"Noooo."

"Yessss." My dad sat forward. "Jaycee, you have no plans.
No goals."

"I knew this was a trap." I should have suspected something
when my dad picked me up from work, only to drag me across
the street and force me to drink brown. "You said you were
going to be cool about college. You said you'd let me think
about it."

"*Are* you thinking about it?"

I've always been a terrible liar, so I didn't even try.

"You're not looking forward to anything," he said. "It saddens me and your mother."

I used the little spoon to excavate a few granules from the bottom and sipped on those, crunching in the aftermath. "Who 'looks forward' to things? That's old-timey. Anyway, it's not even true." I'd woken up the other night with a scheme inbound. A road trip down the old Route 66. I'd gotten up and searched out campsites and urban exploring places along the way, but then I'd realized that I didn't have anyone to go with me. I didn't even have anyone to tell my idea to.

My dad cradled his cup. "Natalie Cheng looks forward to things. She's planning for college *and* graduate school. She even has several career options in mind."

"You mean her mother has several career options in mind for Natalie."

"Why don't you talk to her? She could help you find a school, a major. Lots of things," he said. "Jaycee, I'm worried about you. So are your mother and Dr. Donaldson."

I snapped a look at him. "You talked to Donald Duck about me?"

"We had a family meeting."

"And *he's* in the family? Why are you just now telling me this?"

"I'm telling you now because it happened this afternoon. I had to tell them about your behavior. Dr. Donaldson believes"—my dad ran a hand over his forehead—"that maybe you should stay at Stanwood. Maybe just for a few weeks. We should think about it."

His words sent a thousand volts through me, and I wondered if my skin was smoking.

"Please don't get upset, Jayce, but you've become really... destructive." He leaned forward. "You can still talk to me, you know. Or you could talk to Natalie. She wants to help."

"Dad, I'm upset *about* Natalie!" I put my hands over my face to muffle a cursing stream.

My dad sat back. "Well, I didn't know that you were upset with her when I...called her this morning."

"What?"

"You nearly burned down the shed. It was high time I talked to your friends."

"Dad, she's not my friend, especially not after what I did to her."

"What did you do?" My dad looked horrified, like maybe I'd tied Natalie up in the shed with the rest of Jake's stupid, old toys and sprinkled her with gasoline as well. The truth was worse. The murdered look on Zach's face when he read that note was going to stay with me forever, trumped only by Natalie begging him to listen, crying that she didn't even know if she'd slept with Tyler. "What did you do, Jayce?" my dad repeated.

"I told her boyfriend that she cheated on him with his brother."

My dad blinked. Then he blinked again. "Was that a lie?"

"No. I don't lie. Natalie is the liar."

"Okay." My dad's words came slow and careful. "Natalie didn't seem angry when I spoke with her. She seemed genuinely concerned, and you know, deep down, we're all liars, Jaycee, but we don't all have the courage to admit it."

At the table beside ours, a dread-headed guy reading Nietzsche looked up at my dad. "Truth, dude. Lying is part of the human experience." He nodded at me. "You should try it some time. It's good for the soul. A little fiction to balance out all the facts."

"People lie when something they love is at stake," my dad threw in. "Believe it or not, that's good."

"That's not what I hear," I said. "Wait, what do you lie about?" I was asking my dad, but our second-party friend answered first.

"I tell my fat cat that she's not so fat. It makes her meow all happy-like."

"I lie on my taxes." My dad smiled.

"No, you don't." I paused. "Oh, so you just lied to me about lying on your taxes. Classy."

"I'm not asking you to spread falsehoods, Jaycee. I just want you to imagine life beyond Athens—beyond Jake—even if it *feels* like a lie."

The hippie opened his mouth again, and I stopped him with a glare. He got up and left.

I held on to the table and repeated my question. "What do you lie to me about?"

"Sometimes I say that I understand what you and your mother are going through." He stared through the window. "But I don't understand. I *want* to be happy again. I don't want to forget Jake, but I want to keep living. I can't understand why you don't."

I was quiet for a moment, but then my answer poured out of me, surprising us both. "You sometimes go a whole week without mentioning Jake. Did you know that? And you're rewriting history. The other day, you said something about him being 'a pretty good student.' No, he wasn't. He barely graduated. You're losing him, trading him in for this happiness that seems more important than remembering your son."

I was afraid to look up and find tears, but he didn't respond, and eventually I had to check his expression. He didn't look sad; he looked confused.

"What are you doing, Jaycee?" He set his coffee down. "If I'm rewriting Jake's history, what are you doing when you burn and break his things?"

I didn't really know what I was doing. I was angry with Jake, and I couldn't blast open his bedroom door and pelt him with a peach pit like before. And I couldn't even say why I was angry. Because he was dead? That was stupid. Who gets mad at dead people? Or maybe because he left me behind in this mess? Too pathetic. I pictured the space I'd made by throwing all Jake's clothes in the basement and putting the ones I liked in the bureau. I'd even filled one of his drawers with my bras. Take that, Jake. "I'm making room," I finally said.

"For what?"

Again, I had nothing. I tried to sip my coffee, but I couldn't.

After a few moments of god-awful silence, he glanced at his watch. "I…I want you to think about it, and then we can decide about Stanwood. For now, I have to go to the bathroom."

"Thanks for the warning."

He left, and I found out about half a minute later why he'd run away. Natalie sat down in his seat.

"Are you going to drink that?" She sipped my coffee. "Eh! Too much sugar, Jayce."

"Wow, so my dad brought in the big guns," I said.

"We need to talk. I have a feeling that Zach is really messed up. We all need to help him."

"I know."

"You know because you've been talking to him?"

"Because I was there." I crossed my arms. I couldn't tell her the truth—that I had plans for Zach. Plans that had taken me a week to nail down and that were already in motion. Maybe I should have shared that with my dad. Something like, "Well, I might not be signing up for classes, but I am getting to the bottom of this Tyler Ferris bullshit tonight."

I glanced at my watch-free arm. "Look at the time. I've got a date!" Natalie made an epically disbelieving face. "Is it so impossible to think that I have date?" I pointed to my clothes. I'd dressed up in my best tank top and my jeans that were actually designed to be worn by girls.

"Yes, it is impossible."

"Let my dad know that I had to go." I got up. "Peace out, homeslice." I had no idea why I'd said that except that I was unnerved by this whole Dad and Natalie tag team.

I headed for the door, and Natalie called out, "Do us all a favor and say hi!"

"What?" I yelled.

"Don't act like he doesn't exist. It really bothers him." She went back to downing my coffee. I shelved my curiosity and hauled butt out the door—and right into a pacing Mik. It was a car crash on the sidewalk. He bumped into a table, and I stepped on his foot, and then we did that terrible thing that you do when you try to walk around someone and they go the same way.

My face burned, and I grabbed his arms and steered him right while I went left.

Natalie's words hit me like a brick to the face. *Say hi.*

"Hi," I said—and kept walking.

CHAPTER 34

ZACH

Zach was in his basement lair. The little pixilated mushroom guy on the screen jumped from cloud to cloud, and Zach's eyes fuzzed. He was going insane. Natalie always said you could go insane from not sleeping, and it'd been five days. It was happening now.

He could even hear a tapping sound. "Nevermore," he muttered. Then he laughed because that was a lame joke. But the tap continued, and he paused his game.

Was Natalie at his window? He couldn't bring himself to turn around and look.

The tapping got louder.

"Hey," a voice called out—a not-Natalie voice. "Unlock it or I'll break it in."

Zach crossed the room and unlatched the small, squat window. Jaycee pushed the curtain out of her way and came in legs first. She would have done all right if Zach hadn't moved the desk from beneath the window—the one Natalie always used to climb down onto. Without it, Jaycee was left dangling. He grabbed her by the waist and helped her the rest of the way.

When he didn't let go of her hips, Jaycee took the sides of his face in two firm hands. "Get a single romantic thought about me, and I'll be forced to kick you in the dick."

Zach jumped back. "What the…"

"I find it's best to get stuff like that out in the open." Jaycee looked like a girl for once, not dressed in tomboy clothes. She held up a grocery bag. Whatever was inside had the right size and shape to be a pint of Ben and Jerry's. "I come bearing reparations."

"I don't know what that means, but I just so happen to be hungry." Zach grabbed the bag and dropped onto the couch. He popped open the ice cream and dug his fingers in. After a few shoveled bites, he looked up at her. "Don't judge. I'm not walking upstairs for a spoon."

She held her hands up. "No judgment. I'd do the same."

Zach took a few more bites before getting to the crap talk. "Come to stomp on my heart again?" Jaycee looked through the graphic novels on his bedside table. Was she shame-blushing? She was. Good. "You don't just spring horrible things on people. You've got to have…tact."

"Who gave you that word?"

"My little sister," he admitted. Jaycee nodded. "And if you're here to tell me to take Natalie back, I'll have to refer you to Alianna. And *she* will punch you in the tit."

"Sounds like a good girl, but why would I want you to get back together with the devil?"

Zach was so tired. Maybe Jaycee wasn't even there. Maybe he was imagining this whole conversation. "Is Natalie really evil? None of this makes any sense. She hates Tyler."

Jaycee sat forward. "I don't necessarily think she's evil, but she's mismanaging her life, which is very un-Natalie. I think the key to what's wrong is your louse of a brother."

"Louse?"

"Scoundrel. Not Han Solo scoundrel either. Real scoundrel. Think Goebbels."

Zach stretched, stiff from not sleeping. "So what is it that you want to do about my gerbil of a brother?"

"Mess with him. Find out the truth about what happened that night."

"I'm in."

"But you don't even know what I want to do to him," Jaycee said with a small smile.

"Don't care. What do I have to do?"

"Be up at The Ridges tonight at eleven. Can you find that window where I led you guys in at the beginning of the summer?"

"I think so. Can I bring Bishop? He sent me an email and said he's coming over tonight."

"That's fine. I'll meet you guys there." Jaycee glanced at the window and then walked upstairs. Zach watched her butt all the way. It was a good butt. Natalie's was better.

He dragged himself into the bathroom and opened the back of the toilet. Inside, he removed a fifth of whiskey from a plastic bag. If he was going up to The Ridges with Jaycee Fucking Strangelove, he was going to need some liquid gold.

Hours later, the whiskey was down about six inches between him and Bishop, but the booze did nothing about the tension. They climbed the hill to The Ridges slowly.

"Wish you'd tell me what's going on."

"Jaycee said we were going to rough up Tyler." Zach squinted at the moon.

"That's interesting. Natalie and Mik had plans to kidnap Jaycee tonight. To make us all meet up in the basement. Guess Jaycee has her own mission."

"You were going to trick me into hanging out with Natalie tonight? That's why you emailed?" Zach couldn't hide his hurt. He sat down hard in the grass beneath one of the red-brick towers. "What the fuck, man?"

Bishop sat down beside him. "Look, I know I haven't been around lately, but I—"

"Oh, I get it. You wanted me to know what it felt like when Marrakesh left and you were all alone. You wanted me to know how shitty that feels." Zach touched his nose and pointed at Bishop. "Bingo. Got it. Point made."

"That's not what I wanted, Zach."

"Well, who cares. When do you leave for Michigan anyway?"

"Next weekend."

Zach started to laugh and sipped his whiskey, but really he wanted to cry. Bishop was here because Natalie had sent him. "Do you know what Alianna says? She says that guys are bad at being friends. That I'm expecting you to be, like, my best bud as if we were still boys, but we're both eighteen now, and all we care about is women." He glanced at Bishop's shadowy face. "You believe that?"

"Yeah. Unfortunately, I do."

"Hmph. Women." Zach wasn't really mad. He was dumb-founded. "I never thought Natalie would be capable of hook-ing up with Tyler. Or almost hooking up with him, but you know what? Sex or no sex, she voluntarily made out with him. Went to his room." Zach handed the bottle to Bishop and caught sight of two people walking up the hill toward them. "Holy shit. Look at that."

Tyler's arm was around Jaycee's waist, and her hair was down and long and beautiful, *and* she was laughing sweetly.

"I have a bad feeling about this," Bishop said.

"Yeah. Call for backup. We need the trench coat."

"I don't have Mik's number. Text Natalie."

"I don't have her number anymore." Zach wrestled his new phone out and sent a spastic text to his sister. "Well, if they really do drop by my house, Alianna will send them up here, right after she takes out Natalie's kneecaps."

They stood up as Jaycee and Tyler approached.

Tyler glared at Zach through the dark. "What is the crybaby doing here?"

Jaycee hauled the bars off the brick and yanked up the window. "I told them they could come." She crawled through the opening, and Zach found himself chest-to-chest with his big brother.

"Do anything to screw this up," Tyler said as he pinched Zach's cheek super hard, "and I'll piss on your bed. Make no mistake. I'm going to fuck her." Tyler ducked through the window, leaving Zach to look at Bishop.

"I no longer have a bad feeling about this," Bishop said. "He deserves whatever he gets."

Zach grabbed Bishop's shoulder in agreement, and they entered The Ridges. Zach would be lying if he didn't admit that his heart was beating hard, that he was hoping that Natalie really did stop at his house and end up here. That he was longing to look her in the eyes and ask, "What happened to us?" The question had kept him awake for five days now, and if he didn't find the answer soon, he was going to lose it.

On the creaky, old stairwell, Tyler caught sight of Zach's whiskey and stole it. He drank quite a bit and handed it to Jaycee. She eyed the bottle and then took a long, deep swig— the kind of swig that only a person who'd never drunk before would take. She gasped, and Tyler smacked her butt. Jaycee wiped her mouth with the back of her hand and gave Bishop the bottle.

"This is so fucking kinky. I've never done it in an abandoned building," Tyler said to Jaycee as they climbed to the top floor. "Jake only wanted to explore. I told him this place would make for an epic party."

"My brother respected the ghosts," Jaycee said. "Don't you feel their energy in the air?"

"Hell no. I don't feel anything."

Zach snorted. "Ain't that the truth."

Tyler shot him a warning look.

Jaycee spoke all too happily. "Plenty of people have been up here and not had an incident, but then there's the story about that OU student. The one who touched Margaret Schilling's body stain and claimed that good old Marge followed her home that night. The girl ended up killing herself in Wilson Hall, but not before writing satanic symbols all over the walls in her own blood."

"Oh for fuck's sake," Tyler said, tripping over a bit of broken chair. "You better be an amazing lay."

"I am."

Zach and Bishop exchanged glances.

At the corner of two hallways, Tyler turned on Zach. "You two homos go that way. We're going this way. Got it, baby brother?" He flicked Zach in the forehead.

Zach watched them walk away, biting back the cannon fire of a thousand insults. "So what do we do now?"

Bishop shrugged. "Wait, I guess."

"For what? She didn't even tell us what she was going to do with him."

Zach's phone beeped, and he looked down at a text from an unknown number.

2 min come running

He showed it to Bishop. "Must be Jaycee." He turned to his phone. "Siri, set a timer for two minutes."

"You got an iPhone?" Bishop asked. "The new one?"

"Yeah, and I decided not to transfer my numbers, just to save the ones that came in."

"That's a good idea. It's a fresh start."

Zach glared at him. "This is the first text I've gotten all week."

Bishop looked like he had been expecting this. "I was out of town on your birthday. I sent you an email about it."

Zach tensed. He didn't want excuses or goddamn emails. And he definitely didn't want to tell Bishop that he'd spent his eighteenth birthday in the basement with Alianna, listening to his parents try to set up a "party" for him upstairs that neither one of them wanted to throw. His dad had been on his best behavior because his girlfriend was there, and his mom had made 101 veiled comments about domestic abuse. Good times.

Zach took a large swig from his whiskey, really feeling it this time. His phone alarm went off just as he heard his brother yell. Bishop and Zach ran down the hallway, finding Jaycee holding a door shut with all her strength. Bishop threw himself against the old wood, and Zach managed to get the rusty lock engaged.

Tyler banged on the door. "Let me out, you stupid fucking whore!"

"Hey, that's not nice!" Zach was officially drunk. "You be nice to my friend!"

"We have some questions for you," Jaycee yelled over the noise of his thrashing.

"Is he going to hurt himself in there?" Bishop asked.

"Padded-walled room. No way out." Jaycee kicked a pile of Tyler's clothes, and Tyler's phone flew across the dusty floor. "And bonus? He's pretty much naked."

"How'd you manage that?" Bishop asked.

"With my mad skills," Jaycee deadpanned. Then she laughed. "I told him to take his clothes off. He did."

Zach slid open the peek slot on the door, and Tyler peered through. In only seeing a little of his face, Zach recognized the bully he'd grown up with.

"Spooky in there, isn't it, Tyler?" Jaycee grabbed the whiskey from Zach and took another long swig. The alcohol seemed to be bolstering her to new heights. "Here's the deal, Tyler. You answer truthfully. You don't get colorful or nasty, and we'll let you out of there. But if you can't behave yourself and play along, you'll have to wait for the security guards who come through at nine a.m. Got it?"

"Okay," Tyler whimpered.

"This is awesome." Zach was practically dancing. Bishop picked up Tyler's phone off the ground and was busy going through it.

Jaycee elbowed Zach. "Ask him."

"Okay. What really happened with Natalie at the beginning of the summer?"

"She wanted it, so I gave it to her," Tyler said.

"Now see? That's nasty." Jaycee slammed the peek slot, nearly clipping off Tyler's nose.

"Okay, okay," he yelled from the other side of the door. "She showed up at my frat. She was with your stupid high school friends, and she went after me. I even offered to find her a ride home, and she asked to go up to my room. She was begging for it."

"Strike two," Bishop yelled.

Tyler's voice strained to answer. "She said that she'd never done anything wild. Never let loose. She said that she was the 'New Natalie' or some shit, but after we'd made out and got semi-naked, she started crying and drinking everything in sight."

"You made her cry!" Zach said.

"She was crying about you, idiot," he yelled. "I didn't do anything to her. Call me old-school, but I don't sleep with crying girls. I was getting ready to head back to the party when that asshole Mikivikious busted into my room."

Mik's name made Jaycee stumble backward.

"You all right?" Zach asked. "You drunk?"

"I don't know," she said. "I don't have a whole lot of experience with alcohol."

Zach heard a strange, disembodied cheering, and he started to wonder if he was drunker than he knew as well. But it was just Bishop watching something on Tyler's phone.

Jaycee whipped around. "What was that?"

"Nothing."

Whatever Bishop had been watching was already over, and

the phone disappeared behind his back. Zach had never seen him move so fast. Zach stared, wondering if he should press the issue, but then Bishop stepped forward, suddenly boiling.

"You're fucking sick, Tyler. Fucking sick!" Bishop stomped down the hallway, and Zach looked at Jaycee. She was standing there as though she'd been frozen in carbonite.

"Hey, hey, Jayce." He shook her shoulders until she blinked back slowly.

"My dad's right. I'm losing my mind." She took the whiskey from Zach and hit it hard, then she scrubbed her hands over her face. When she resurfaced, she seemed so fierce that Zach backed away. "So to clarify, you did not have sex with Natalie Cheng?"

"Yes. I mean, no. I definitely didn't," Tyler said. "Now let me out!"

Zach punched the door, making it jump in its frame and hit his brother's face. Tyler's howl of pain echoed loudly in the padded room.

"I think we're done here," Jaycee said.

"Now let me out so I can motherfucking kill you, Zachary!"

Jaycee blasted the peek slot closed. "Well, that's an oversight."

Zach slumped against the door. "Oh God, Jayce. He really is going to kill me as soon as we unlock that door."

Jaycee slumped to the floor next to him. "We need Natalie to plan these things. I'm only the idea person."

Zach slung an arm around her. "You're all right, Strangelove. Let's have another drink."

CHAPTER 35

Natalie

"So the new plan is that we get Zach and Bishop, and then we go find Jaycee. Wherever she is."

Mik was driving Natalie's car, and they were almost to Zach's house. She was so nervous to face Zach that she couldn't stop talking, let alone steer.

"What if she really is on a date?" Mik's tone was cool, but she could sense his anxiety.

"That's such bullshit," Natalie said. "She's up to something." They passed the elementary school. In a few moments, they'd be at Zach's house, and then Bishop would let them into the basement. What would happen? And then how would they find Jaycee and get her all tangled up with Mik where she clearly belonged?

"What if, when we're all together again, I rope her into a truth or dare game and dare her to kiss you." Natalie sat up taller. "Oh, or I could dare you to talk to her."

"Please don't, and that's not really funny considering how hard it is to open my mouth in her presence."

"Why is it so specifically hard? You've known her your

whole life. I mean, I know she's stunning, but she's also just Jaycee." They pulled to a stop in front of Zach's house. Natalie rubbed the back of her neck, feeling sweaty and twitchy. Would he scream at her? Ignore her?

Mik parked on the street before Zach's house, and then his voice seemed to come from a mile away. "I have to tell Jaycee the truth. Then…we'll see how she feels."

"Huh? What truth?"

Mik stared her down. "About Jake's accident."

"Oh. That." Natalie's stomach bottomed out. "So you know I was…that I've been…"

"I saw you. And I'm pretty sure you saw me," Mik said.

Natalie could suddenly feel the bright sunlight on the playground that day. She remembered giving Jaycee the slip and hiding under the slide, spying on the boys who were drinking. She was going to rat them out before one of them got behind the wheel, because hey, if Jake was going to call her a snitch her whole life, she was going to be a snitch.

But then the whole world…flipped.

"Wow," Natalie murmured. "What a pair we make."

"I need to come clean," he said, gripping the steering wheel. "It's killing me."

Natalie shook her head, and her glasses slid down her nose. "Not me. The truth will only make everything worse." He raised an eyebrow at her. "I realize I'm playing with fire, but this is how it has to be. Trust me. She'd never understand why…why I had to lie about it."

Mik didn't respond, and Natalie had to hand it to him. He was skilled at the empty response. They headed for Zach's front door, and all of a sudden, she didn't feel so awful about facing Zach. What she'd lied to Zach about was pretty small compared to what she held back from Jaycee. Perspective was a bitch.

Alianna answered the door in her princess pajamas. "Zach's out with another girl," she said instead of hello. "She's hotter than you."

"Where's Bishop?"

"Come and gone." Alianna tried to close the door, but Mik held it open.

"Are they with Jaycee? A tall girl with dark-blond hair?" Natalie asked.

"Why would I tell you that?" the twelve-year-old threw back. "You broke him."

Natalie's body folded in, and Mik surprised her by putting his arm around her shoulder.

Alianna looked at both of them appraisingly. "This is your new piece of meat? You bring your new boy toy over to your old boyfriend's house? What a lowlife bi—"

"You sound an awful lot like Tyler," Mik said, his voice sharp. "You must be related."

"Only by blood." Alianna scowled and dug her phone out of her pajama pants' pocket. "I only care about Zach. He sent me this text about twenty minutes ago." She held out her phone.

Tell Nat @ Ridges Tyler w/ JC Hurry

"Jesus." Natalie showed the text to Mik, and they were back in her car so fast that she barely knew how they'd gotten there. "What is wrong with Jaycee?"

Mik was driving fast. "It's for you. She's finding out the truth."

"Yes, but she's with that psycho! Why are you smiling? Aren't you worried?"

"Jake would sell your darkest secret for an Oreo," he said. "Not Jaycee."

"True. Jaycee always was fiercely loyal." Could Jaycee actually be doing something to Tyler *for* Natalie? Her heart spun tight. "Mik, drive faster. She has no idea how horrible he can be."

Mik parked at the playground lot, and they sprinted up the hill. They found the bars removed outside of Jaycee's secret window and hauled themselves inside. They never even had a chance to wonder where to go, because Tyler's yells led them straight to him.

Zach was collapsed on the floor before a locked door. He was covered in gray dust and incredibly drunk.

"Zach," Natalie said, kneeling beside him. He grabbed hold of her and didn't let go.

"Natalie bear," he muttered.

She looked over his shoulder to a pair of eyes peering through the door's peep slot.

"Let me out!" Tyler yelled.

Natalie ignored him and cradled Zach's face in her hands. "Are you all right?"

"No. I'm not." Zach tried to stand and fell. Mik grabbed him by the shoulders and got him to his feet. "He"—Zach pointed to Tyler's eyes—"didn't have sex with you." Zach kicked the door. "Tell her!"

"I didn't. Now let me out!" he shouted.

Natalie slipped to her knees, her pulse drilling through her. So he didn't...they didn't... "Why did you say that we did?" she whispered through the slot.

Tyler looked away. "I was fucking with Zach and Mik. It had nothing to do with you."

"It has everything to do with me!"

"Don't you spin this like I forced you into my room. I was drunk. You led the way. You told me you wanted to have sex."

"I know. I remember that part." She sighed. "You're a waste of space, Tyler Ferris."

"Fuck off on your high horse," he said, looking away again.

Natalie had a strong flash of kissing Tyler—how it'd been like kissing a warped Zach. They'd grown up together, had so many of the same experiences, and yet Tyler seemed like someone had cut up Zach and pasted him back together. Same sad childhood, but a much more deranged outcome. Natalie wondered if Zach would ever know how lucky he was not to end up like Tyler.

She popped the lock open, and Tyler came flying through. He might have killed Zach, except that Mik intercepted him and slammed him against the wall.

Tyler wriggled, naked but for his boxers. "Give me my clothes," he managed despite Mik's forearm pressed to his throat.

"Let him go, Mik." Natalie held on to Zach. She had hoped that in learning she hadn't actually slept with Tyler, she could forgive herself. Wrong. The regret was still there, still taxing and exhausting, and yet it didn't have the same sting. She'd made a huge mistake, so...so what?

So what now?

Mik released Tyler, and the guy grabbed his pile of clothes. "Where's my phone?" he snapped. Mik stepped forward threateningly, and Tyler took off at a sprint.

"Do you think he knows how to get out?" Natalie asked.

"Who cares," Zach said, sniffling. He rested his head on

Natalie's shoulder, and she slipped her arms around his waist. It felt like old times. Like the last few weeks hadn't happened.

"Where are Bishop and Jaycee?" Natalie asked.

"Gone. Bishop's all fired up about something." He sniffed harder. "Jaycee drank all my whiskey. That girl's a hurricane when she's drunk. She wrecked that stain room too. Will Margaret's ghost make Jaycee kill herself?"

"Wait, *drunk* Jaycee?" Natalie asked, stunned. "Oh Christ, where'd she go?"

"I think she went down to the playground."

Mik started jogging, running. He turned a corner and was gone.

"Let's get you out of here." Natalie led him through the creaking quiet of The Ridges until they passed into the renovated section and out the window.

"I'm sorry," Zach said when they were under the silver shine of the moon. The clouds were fiercely backlit, great big puffs of things that hung over their heads in wait. "He's such a dick. I'm so sorry he weaseled his way into your life."

"Don't." Natalie sighed. "I went after him for something. I tried to use him to make my choices for me. Choices I was too afraid to make." She waited for Zach to ask what she meant, but he was too far gone.

"I kissed a girl in LA. That time when I went with my family for the holidays."

"I know," she said. "You tell me that almost every time you're blackout drunk."

"I need to throw up," he said in the second before he fell in the grass and heaved. She rubbed his back while he retched, then pressed her face against his shirt.

Zach was so good for her, had been so good to her for four

years, and yet, they weren't going to get married and have babies, let alone make it through this summer. How could she hold on to him while letting him go? What would she be like all on her own up in New York? Would she snap back into controlling mode despite all her brilliant plans to chill out? What could she even do to make sure that she never made decisions purely out of fear again?

I'm Natalie, and that means what exactly?

When she heard the smash of glass, she looked up to see Tyler jumping through a broken window. He hit the ground hard, and he was still only half-dressed.

Natalie smiled. "Zach, don't miss this. Look. Look at that idiot."

Zach watched his brother flee down the hill. He laughed and wiped his mouth. "Nat, it was kinda amazing...locking him in and hearing him freak out."

"Jaycee's idea?" Natalie asked without doubting for a second that it had been.

"Yeah."

"Is she still mad at me?"

"She called you the devil."

Natalie smiled again, wider this time. "Coming from Jaycee Strangelove, that's halfway to a compliment." She helped Zach to his feet. "Come on. We've got to go find the rest of our crew. Or what's left of them, if your state is any indication."

CHAPTER
36

Mikivikious

PUSH

I DON'T WANT TO FOOL AROUND, BISHOP.

IT'S *YOU.*

CHAPTER 37

JAYCEE

When the night hit its blurriest stretch, Mik found me. He stepped out of the dark like he'd materialized from it, leaving me to wonder if I'd conjured him.

Deep in the trunk of my drunken brain, I remembered how I'd once longed to be a magician. Not the hokey kind with rabbits and capes, but the chains and leather and near drowning. The year I asked Santa for a tank of electric eels, my mom drew the line, but still it had been a large part of my childhood. Just like Mik.

He hunkered before me on the swing, and I thought about asking if he remembered the day I finally twisted out of my straitjacket, but instead I stole a hand through his hair. He touched my face, and I slumped against his chest that—according to Natalie—was remarkable in some way. I suddenly imagined Mik with scars. Many, many scars. I tugged at his shirt, desperate to see what lay beneath.

"Are we interrupting?" Zach said, stumbling out of the night with Natalie holding him up.

"Nope," I said more loudly than necessary.

Natalie took the swing beside me, and Zach sprawled out on the turf. "Where's Bishop?"

"He's making something." I pointed toward the deserted road that ran around the backside of The Ridges. "He's dragging broken bricks out of the creek."

Natalie stopped swinging. "He's doing *what?*"

"Oh, he's fine. You should be happy that I decided to sit here and feel sorry for myself. My first instinct was to go climb the bridge." I looked up. All the booze had boiled through me until I was nothing more than mad. "You know what's great? After this, there's nothing. Isn't that great? I mean I'm not even being sarcastic. I've been looking for ghosts and spirits for years, and it finally hit me. There aren't any. When we die, this is all over."

Mik took my hands, looking over the bloody scrapes that I couldn't feel.

"Liquor makes you stupid," I told him. "I scrubbed away his footprint in the stain room. It's gone now. I made room for someone else." I laughed maniacally, and Zach laughed too for whatever reason. "I made room," I said again. "What the hell does that even mean?"

Bishop approached. He was sweating, and his teeth were bared like he'd just wrestled a wild creature. "Did you let your brother out, Zach?"

"Natalie did," Zach said. "He totally pissed himself. It was so cool."

"We'll talk about that later," Natalie said matter-of-factly.

Mik kept looking at my hands, and I leaned my forehead into his. "You going to talk to me now that you need to fix me? This is all about fixing me, isn't it? It is for Natalie. Ask her. She needs to go to New York with a clear conscience."

"This isn't about Cornell," Natalie said. "I love you, you jerk."

I looked up at her. "Dad's going to send me to Stanwood Crazy Hospital. I can even room with my mom. Will you come visit, Natalie, when you're on break from your wonder education? You can write a paper on me."

"She's a mean drunk!" Zach kicked his legs out like a dog scratching its back.

"You're not going insane, Jaycee," Natalie said. "I've researched your behavior *many* times. You're depressed and lonely with a serious self-destructive streak. That's what you are."

"Hey, what the hell do you look forward to?" I snapped. "My dad wants me to 'look forward to something.' He seems to think you're good at this."

"I look forward to getting out of this small town hell," she said. "Starting over."

"Should I be offended?" Zach asked.

"No. Be quiet." Natalie turned back to me with her eyes sparking. "I'm planning my life the way I want to live it. That's what I look forward to."

"What if your plans don't work?"

"I'll think of a new plan," her voice wobbled. Maybe none of us knew how to grow up.

I hung my head and felt Mik's hand on my cheek. "I can't get to the other side of this."

"That's the whiskey talking," Zach said. "It always makes me feel like I'm dying in a good way."

"We're on the other side of this," Bishop said. "We're your friends."

"More than friends," Natalie threw in. "Right, Mik?"

I stared at Mik's face only a few inches away. The darkness

of his brown eyes was unbelievably deep. "Do you know what I realized tonight?" I asked. "I hate him."

Mik flinched.

"Oh, you don't hate Mik," Zach said. "You guys got something happ…en…ing."

I got to my feet, but every step was soggy. "I hate *Jake*. I hate him for being in my life. I hate him for leaving it all fucked up. I hate him. You know what? He was kind of an asshole!"

Natalie smiled. "Hate is a good step. It's a—"

"If you say it's a stage of grief, I'm going to run at you like a bull."

Zach laughed riotously. "What? That was sooo funny."

"Excuse me for trying to understand you, Jayce. You freaked out when those kids burned Jake's journal, but now you're voluntarily destroying his stuff. What the hell?"

"Because my brother is not his stuff!" I stepped toward her and almost fell. Mik's arm circled my waist, and I gave him my body. He sat down on the swing and pulled me onto his lap. I was surprised to find that he was better than a couch, and I let myself go loose into him.

"None of it makes him feel real anymore," I said. "Not the clothes. Not the stories. Nothing. The only thing that worked was climbing that chimney." The playground started to spin. My stomach twisted. "No offense, Zach, because I know this is your favorite pastime, but I think I hate liquor."

"Give me the map." Natalie grabbed Jake's map out of my pocket and held it up to the moonlight. "Cleveland. We're going next weekend. No. Tomorrow. We're finishing this so that you can move on. So we all can. This is important."

"Hey, wait." Zach sat up, struggling with his phone. "Say

that again, Natalie. I'm going to play the *Braveheart* soundtrack in the background for effect."

"Zach," Natalie warned, but suddenly we were all laughing. Even me. Even Mik, his face so close to mine. I'd somehow smeared my blood on his chin, and when I tried to wipe it off, he stared into my soul.

"Hey," I said. "That's private."

He kissed the side of my face, and I laughed a bizarre, hyena-drunk laugh.

"We need to take her somewhere to get her cleaned up," Natalie said. "If we bring her home to her dad like this, he'll have heart failure. That is not an exaggeration."

"Basement sleepover!" Zach surged to his feet and nearly toppled. "Let's go!"

Natalie herded the two drunken boys toward the parking lot. "Don't you dare get sick in the Bonemobile. Either of you."

"Are they really my friends?" I asked Mik. He lifted me onto my feet. The fact that he wasn't going to answer seeped through my drunkenness, and I realized that I could say anything to him. This was suddenly a challenge. As much of a challenge as trying to walk without falling down. "I went into the attic and found all of Jake's old stuff, but you know what I also found? *My* stuff. Stuff I'd completely forgotten about.

"Remember my straitjacket?" I asked. "Remember when I dragged you into my room to play audience? It was the first time I got out of it in less than two minutes, and I was so excited that I jumped on you and we fell over on my bed, and Jake came in screaming that if we loved each other so much, we should just get married. He threw the blanket over us, and I kissed you."

Mik cleared his throat like a whole traffic jam of a response was lodged in there.

"I don't think that kiss counts," I said. "We were just kids."

He laced his fingers with mine, and I wanted to kiss him. No, I wanted him to kiss me. For real this time. I pressed my cheek into his shoulder and held on tighter.

"When I look at you, I don't think about Jake anymore. Feels terrible. Feels great."

CHAPTER

38

BISHOP

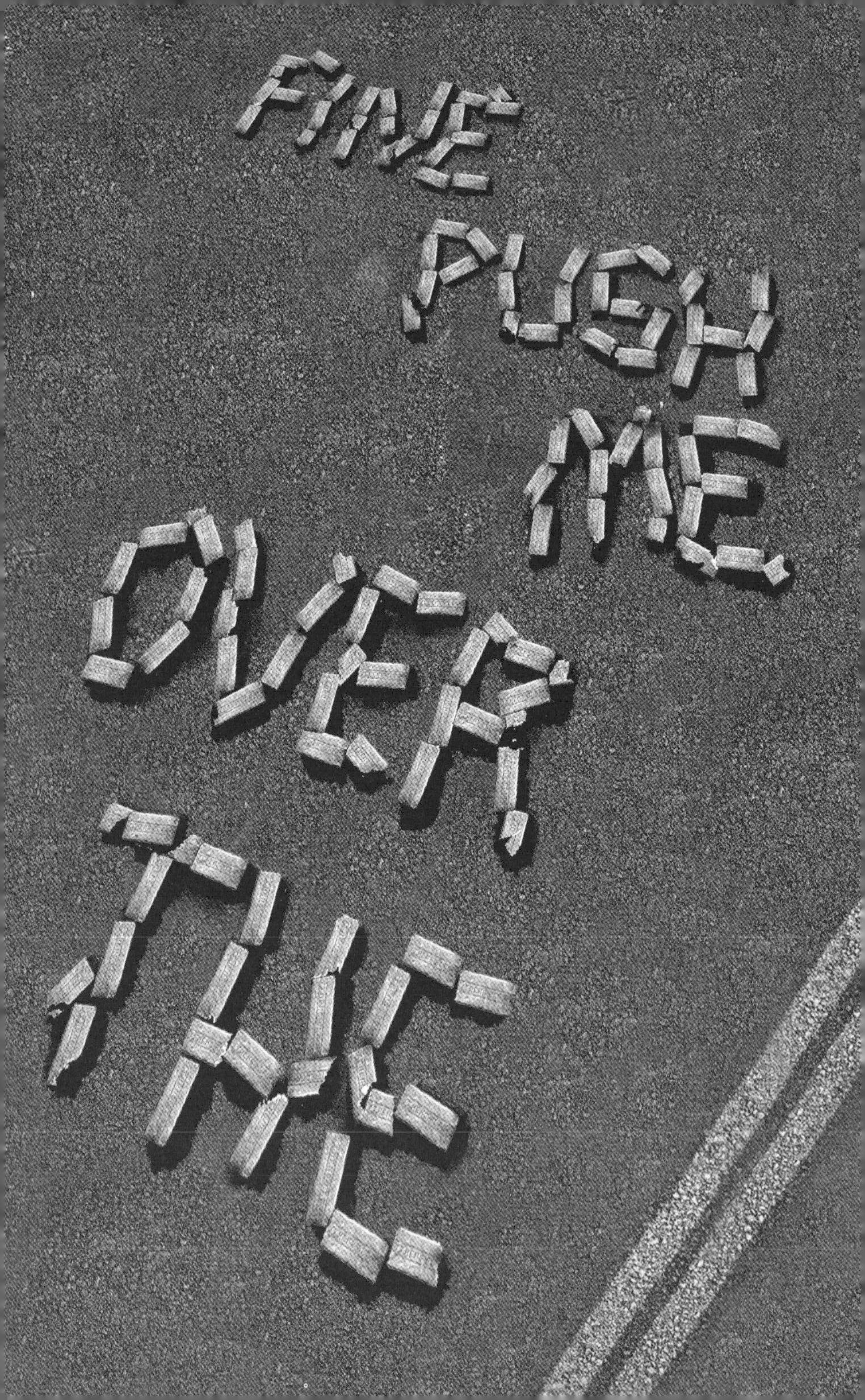
FINE
PUSH
ME
OVER
THE

RANDALL PARK MALL

CHAPTER

39

Natalie

NATALIE NEVER REALLY FELL ASLEEP, SO SHE NEVER REALLY woke up. Instead she lay between a now snore-whistling Zach and a silent-as-death Jaycee on Zach's king-size bed. Dawn threw an orange pall through the rectangular basement window.

Her parents weren't as absent as Zach's or forgiving as Jaycee's. She needed to get home before her mom noticed that she'd been out all night. Zach had moved the desk that she used to climb out the window, so she headed up the stairs, pausing to glance over her night's work.

Bishop was asleep on the couch. He was the only one of the "Drunkateers" (copyright Zach, three a.m.) who hadn't thrown up. Whatever Bishop had been doing in the creek had burned all the booze out of his blood, which begged the question, what *had* he been doing? Natalie thought that he was emerging from his Marrakesh nightmare, but now she wasn't so sure. Something had spooked him.

Zach was another story, and one that Natalie had a read a few too many times. He was passed out on one side of his huge bed—coincidentally his parents' pre-divorce mattress, although that fact was glossed over with the help of the cartoon sheets she'd gotten him for his sixteenth birthday.

On the other side of the bed, Jaycee and Mik were spooning, their hands entwined and resting on Jaycee's hip like it was no big deal. She was wearing his trench coat, and even though her skin looked pale from her hangover, she seemed more human than ever. More like the girl who had insisted she wasn't scared while clutching Natalie in a headlock when Jake made them watch *The Ring*. That girl was still in there somewhere, under all that demigod-quality sarcasm.

Natalie snapped a picture with her phone. "Evidence," she muttered.

Mik heard the faux-shutter *click* and glanced up at where Natalie crouched on the stairs. She waved. He lifted one finger as a response like he was petrified of waking Jaycee, and Natalie didn't blame him. Which Jaycee would open her eyes? The Jaycee who glared at all boys as if they were muskrats wearing pants? Or the Jaycee who'd whimpered on the bathroom countertop while Mik scrubbed The Ridges' filth out of her scraped palms, and who'd then buried her face in his neck and wrapped her legs around his waist like she'd been waiting her whole life to do it?

Mik closed his eyes and turned his face into Jaycee's hair, and Natalie took that as her cue to sneak home. While she swept the Bonemobile for evidence of the night's wildness, she couldn't help remembering Jaycee on that swing set, sitting there looking lost and delirious. Like maybe she'd never left the place where her brother died—the place where Natalie had abandoned her all those years ago. Natalie flooded with familiar guilt. How could she *really* help Jaycee? This was beyond getting Mik to kiss her. Beyond getting Jaycee into college or on a career path. Jaycee needed something much more basic… like hope. But then, so did Natalie, damn it.

When they were kids, everything had been possible. But then they split up, and high school played out like a sitcom full of prom dresses and pop quizzes and movie dates that barely bumped the bar of interesting. When Jaycee had been with Natalie, life had skewed dire. Fights were toothy. Laughter made you fall off the bed. Natalie sighed deeply, unsure if she was longing for Jaycee's friendship or for the simplicity of childhood, or if the two were so tangled that she'd never be able to tell them apart.

"Hey."

Natalie jumped as Jaycee leaned through the open passenger window. She was no longer in Mik's trench coat and squinting from the sunlight. "Give me a ride home?"

"Mik." Natalie straightened her glasses and pushed down her memories. "You should let Mik drive you home. He'll want to do that."

"Too weird." Jaycee got in the car. "We were holding hands when I woke up."

Natalie relented and started to drive. "Did you at least say goodbye?"

"I said I was going to the bathroom." Jaycee seemed nervous—confused and disgustingly pretty for someone who'd thrown up all night. "I think maybe that wasn't such a nice move."

"True." Natalie tried to put herself in Jaycee's shoes. There was something holding Jaycee back that wasn't Jake. It wasn't Mik either. At the stoplight, Natalie thumbed through her phone until she got to the picture of Jaycee and Mik spooning. "A memento for you."

Jaycee stared at it. "That doesn't look like me."

"It looks like you when you have your guard down. I'm not surprised you don't recognize yourself." Jaycee was still staring, and Natalie added, "Your children will be giants."

Jaycee snorted or laughed or gagged. It sounded like all three. "You have to sex to have kids, Natalie."

"And that's not in the cards for you?" She tried not to beam too brightly. Girl talk—she was actually girl talking with Jaycee Strangelove. "Come on, Jayce. If Zach looked at me the way Mik looks at you, it wouldn't have taken me three and a half years to sleep with him."

Jaycee was turning red. "I don't know…wouldn't know… Nat, I'm one hundred and eleven percent out of my comfort zone when I'm with him." She looked at the fine gauze on her palms. "That's not what it's supposed to feel like, is it?"

"You've really never had a crush on anyone before, have you?" Natalie pointed at Jaycee's hands. "That's what a crush looks like. Last night, Mik cleaned out your cuts so you wouldn't get an infection. He studies medicine. Did you know that?"

"Don't." Jaycee tipped her head against the seat and closed her eyes. "It's bad enough that he won't talk to me. Don't go bragging that you two are great pals."

Natalie swelled with justification. If Jaycee was jealous, than her feelings really were genuine. "He's quite talkative once you get him going. He even told me about his longtime girlfriend back at school."

Jaycee opened a wary eye. "What girlfriend?"

"Ex." Natalie turned onto Jaycee's road.

"Then you should have said 'ex.'"

"But then how would I prove that you're one hundred and eleven percent into him?" Natalie tried not to look too smug. "Why don't you just ask me how I got him to talk?" Jaycee didn't say anything, and Natalie took that as an invitation. "All I do is speak to him like he'll answer. Not like I'm waiting for him to answer, but like, at some point, he might chip in. Mik said it took the pressure off. His condition is all about social anxiety, you know."

Jaycee scratched her ear and acted like she wasn't listening. She tried to turn the radio on, and Natalie knocked her hand away.

"I'm going to say thank you now, and you're going to say you're welcome."

"What am I being thanked for?" Jaycee asked.

"For Tyler. For getting to the bottom of everything last night." Natalie squeezed the steering wheel. "Thank you. I...I needed to, well, not knowing was making me malfunction."

"No problem." Jaycee looked down. "It was a bit insane. No clue what came over me."

"Oh, I know. You were being you. Crazy Jaycee who got suspended from school for kicking the shins of that girl who pushed me off the monkey bars." Natalie dug deeper. "Crazy Jaycee who stole Jake's favorite baseball bat after he stomped my American Girl doll's head in."

"That bat is still buried in the backyard," Jaycee said, her voice low.

"Maybe we should dig it up. Bury the hatchet instead." Natalie pulled into the driveway. She took out her notes from last night and set them on Jaycee's lap. "I did some planning while you were hurling. We leave for the greater Cleveland area at dark. I've found us a hotel so we can sleep and then enter the mall around dawn. There will be fewer people outside, and from what I've read on the Internet, we'll need the light from the skylights to explore. Oh, and I even talked to this urbexer about his entry point on the side of the mall, by the old cinema."

Jaycee touched the notes. "Nat, I don't think we should go. I…I was drunk when I agreed. I don't want to go on any more of Jake's adventures. They never turn out the way I need them to. And what about you? Don't you have to pack for college or something?"

Natalie bit her lip, aching to tell Jaycee the truth. And not just about her worries and paralyzing anxiety, but the truth about *everything*. How would she take it? "I have enough plans," she said. "I want something different. Maybe that's what *I* need."

She was just about to open her mouth, about to let the words, *I don't even want to be a psychologist*, spill out.

Jaycee beat her to it, staring at her house. "I'm afraid to go in. My dad's going to bring up sending me to Stanwood again. Do you know what's the worst? He's right. I'm cracking. I belong there with my mom."

Natalie shook her head vigorously. "No. You're going to be okay." Jaycee had to be okay because Natalie had to be okay, and they were now, as much as when they were kids, linked. That's the way it'd always felt. That's what felt best. *Yin and yang.* "I'm going into psychology so you should listen to me. You're coming out of the grieving process. This is all good. Natural."

Jaycee chuckled sadly. "Remember when you said that thing in Moonville…about how you see yourself in the dark?"

"Yes."

"That's me too. I thought Jake was the light, but now…"

"He's the shadow?"

"I'm starting to wish him away." She looked at Natalie, and her eyes were streaming silent tears even though her expression was flat. "I have these flashes when I'm, like, Jake who? My dad's not wrong. It feels *so good* to pretend like he was never here. It's goddamn heroin."

"What do you know about hard drug abuse?" Natalie managed. "You're not even good at getting drunk." Jaycee gave her a sad smile. Natalie wanted to take her hand, but Jaycee had never been one for hugs or holding. "Come to Cleveland. We're…something together. You, me, Bishop, and Mik. Even Zach. There's something important when we share our crap feelings."

Jaycee let the tears fall like she didn't even notice them. "Zach wants you back."

"I want him back too. He's my drug. That's what's so hard." Natalie took her glasses off and cleaned the lenses on the edge of her shirt. *Be brave. Do it.* "Jaycee, can I tell you something?" She struggled for the words. "Bishop thought I was trying to find out what happened with Tyler so that I could tell Zach, but I…I was going to let Bishop tell Zach."

"Okay." Jaycee got out, and Natalie had to yell out the window to get her attention.

"Okay? That's not okay. That's sick. I'm turning into a monster. I mean, am I any better than Tyler? I sabotaged my relationship with Zach, and I don't even have the guts to admit it."

"You just admitted it to me. That's something." Jaycee stood by the driver's door and shoved her hands in her pockets.

"Maybe you should stop overthinking everything, Nat. If you were truly a monster, you wouldn't care about Zach. Or me. Or yourself. But you do."

Natalie wanted to scream. Here she'd wanted to open up to Jaycee, and Jaycee was being so *casual*. "You're all so unpredictable. You scare the crap out of me!"

Jaycee smirked. "Now that? That's a good confession."

"What if something happened to one of you?" *Like Jake.* "I'd never forgive myself."

"What if nothing happened to us? Isn't that worse?" Jaycee asked. "I don't know about you, but I'd take something over nothing any day."

CHAPTER

40

JAYCEE

TRYING TO GET BY MY DAD AND OUT OF THE HOUSE WAS proving impossible.

"You come home at dawn, and now you say you're going to Cleveland for two days, and I'm *not* supposed to be curious?" He eyed my backpack.

"You wanted me to make plans. So I'm going on a trip with my friends." Strange words from me, and my dad's disbelieving expression proved it. I glanced over his shoulder, through the front door's rectangular, prismatic window to where Mik's car had just pulled up. I had about thirty seconds before Mik would come knocking and fan my dad's little hope flame. I didn't want that to happen until I knew what was going on. I tried to sidestep him again.

"Not so fast." He narrowed his eyes, no doubt wanting to tell me to have fun while also restraining me in a death grip.

The doorbell rang. Great. I reached around him and swung open the front door. Mik was standing there looking awfully shy. I changed tactics, grabbing his sleeve and pulling him next to me. "This trip is sort of an extended date, Dad. Surprise."

Again, my dad looked like he was either going to call bull-shit or start tap dancing. "Nice to see you, Ryan," he said. "I take it you're the sober driver?"

Mik nodded. His eyes skimmed my face, my neck. I had a flash of the previous night. Of how close I'd let him get. Of how close I'd let him stay.

My dad looked out the door. "And who is in the car?"

I glanced out. "Eric Bishop."

"OU president Terrance Bishop's son?"

"Yep," I said, thankful that Bishop's family came with a certain level of respectability. "Natalie's coming too, so you know we'll be more responsible than we'd all prefer to be."

My dad looked over Mik and me like we were one person. "I'm going to allow this on one condition. Text every few hours. Don't leave me hanging here."

I hugged my dad around the waist. "We'll be fine. We'll be back on Sunday."

"Okay. Get going," he said when I didn't let go.

"I love you," I told his T-shirt, giving in to those words and their pesky sense of mortality.

"Yep," he said. I squeezed him until he added. "Love you too." His face blotched, and I left sniffing, suddenly grateful that Mik didn't say things just to fill the silence.

We drove to Zach's house and parked on the street, only to find Natalie and Zach standing in front the Bonemobile, their bags at their feet and their arms around one another.

"Nooo," Bishop said, getting out of Mik's car. "I thought we were beyond this."

"Don't judge the love," Zach said, kissing Natalie's wrist.

Mik and I got out as well. We threw our bags in the open

trunk, and when I passed Natalie, I whispered, "Off the wagon already?"

She shrugged. "Look how happy he is."

"I'm looking at you," I whispered back.

Natalie turned away and tossed the keys to Mik. "Mik drives because he knows the area. He goes to school up there." Her eyes darted to mine like she was trying to shove me with her words. "He goes to Kent State."

Bishop had been opening the passenger door, but he pointed at me. "You take shotgun."

"I can sit in the back," I said.

"No way. Favored girl always gets the front."

"Man Commandment Number Eight," Zach added. I glanced at Mik, and his eyebrow jutted high as if to say, *It's true.*

Zach crawled in the back. Natalie took the middle with Bishop on the other side. I knew Natalie was right about me trying to talk to Mik, but it still felt weird. Two hours passed, almost two-thirds of the drive, before I found the courage. The back trio was sound asleep.

"So you go to school up here?" I asked, immediately wondering if that was too much pressure. The dark path of I-77 flicked a strobe light of streetlamps on his profile. What would Natalie say? She'd talk about herself. "I'm not going to college. Maybe you don't know that." I picked at the hem of my shirt. "I'm planning a trip across the country," I added, wondering why I was admitting that aloud. "I mean, I might do it, but probably not. My parents would croak."

My backtrack statement made Mik glance at me, and I was unnerved by how much concern lined his face. Things were different after last night—after I'd drunkenly criticized him for not talking to me and then puked into a wastebasket while he held me upright. Then I'd woken to him lying beside me. His hand in mine. And I'd been happy.

That was the craziest part. How did a hangover and massive embarrassment and waking up on Zach's ridiculous sheets leave any room for happy?

"Thanks for last night," I said quietly.

"No problem," he said.

I tried not to jerk my head at the sound of his voice, but I failed. And I liked his voice. Not too deep, but still flecked with attitude. What would it be like to fight with him? Scream at him? Shut him up with a kiss? I went full-body hot. Too many movies. People don't really kiss in the middle of a fight... do they?

We were silent until we reached the hotel, a Holiday Inn Express. Assigned to room 317, Natalie and Zach took over one full-sized bed, tangle-cuddling like puppies.

Bishop claimed the other one. "I slept on the couch last night," he added. "It's my turn for the bed. I don't care who sleeps next to me."

"Someone can sleep in the tub," Zach said unhelpfully.

"No, it's cool," I said, pretty certain that I wasn't going to fall asleep. I grabbed a pillow and tossed it on the floor. "One time, Mik, Jake, Natalie, and I camped out in the backyard and we only used one pillow. Remember, Nat? We fanned around it like a pinwheel?"

"I remember that." Natalie rubbed her eyes. "Ugh, that was the night with the firefly butts." She fell back on the bed, and Zach pounced. I dragged one of the comforters to the floor so that I didn't have to watch them get all handsy.

"What about lightning bug butts?" Bishop asked through a yawn.

"If you pinch off a firefly's back end while it's glowing, it'll keep glowing and you can write with it on anything. On Natalie's forehead, for example." I risked a smirk at Mik. He smirked back. He remembered. "Although it's sad, because it kills the firefly."

"It's gross," Natalie added. "And it's sociopath behavior."

"Thank you, Dr. Cheng."

Mik was leaning against the wall, standing over the bed I'd made on the floor like he was assessing the whole situation—like he was trying to figure out where he fit in, which was a really good question. On one hand, we'd kind of slept together last night, no big deal. On the other? I had been out of my mind drunk, and right at that moment, I'd never felt more sober.

I lay down on one side of the pillow. "You can sleep on that side. Like when we were kids," I added awkwardly.

Mik pried off his boots and trench coat and joined me on the floor, except not really because his body was facing the other direction. His head, however, was next to mine, and I could smell his shampoo and see all the winding curves in his ear.

Natalie turned the lights off, and the darkness slapped. "We're getting up at four a.m., so"—she yawned—"don't fool around."

"That goes double for you two," Bishop said. "If I hear the slightest groaning, Zach…"

Zach pretended to snore, and Mik chuckled from mere inches away in the dark.

My eyes began to adjust, filling in the gray. I turned my head, and Mik turned his, and we were two inches apart and looking at each other upside down. People look demented upside down. I turned back to the ceiling and traced the concrete slabs that hung over us. *Don't suppose I'll be able to sleep*, I thought in the moments before my heart went slow, my body curling up into a ball of post-hangover exhaustion.

I woke up when I got stepped on. Bishop mumbled an apology and kicked a path toward the bathroom. Desperate to get out of the way and keep sleeping, I crawled to the other side of the pillow and collapsed…until I felt the warm stillness of Mik's body beside mine.

And suddenly I wasn't sleepy.

Zach and Natalie were both breathing hard enough to prove that they were out. And a bathroom fan-turned-asthma-monster sounded on the other side of the cardboard walls, followed by the shower. I cracked an eye open. Mik's breath was even, his chest rising and sinking. His mouth was open a little, and I couldn't help wondering what he did with those lips. Did Natalie make up that ex-girlfriend? Were there many girls? Who did he hang out with at school? Did he talk to them? Probably.

I hated those people all of a sudden. And I hated that he was sleeping, and I wanted him to stare me down with his well-deep eyes. When he did that, I could tell that he was looking at *me*. Not my Jake obsession or tomboy clothes or my status as a "beautiful disaster," as Zach so callously put it. Just me. Whatever Mik saw, he liked, and I wanted to ask him what he was seeing exactly.

I made my move fast and without too much thought. I tossed onto my side and felt my pulse *bang* as I dared to let my arm "accidentally" flop across Mik's stomach. He didn't react, and my heart got way too excited to feel the edge of his black T-shirt—and his skin beneath it. I touched him for a solid minute, feeling downright crazy. When I was about to flip onto my back and give this up as pure dark o'clock madness, Mik's hand moved to my waist.

Guess who was no longer asleep.

What my fingers had done to his stomach, he did to mine. Light touches. Curiosity with moments of heat in his palm. When his hand went still, I realized he'd matched my move. Would he do it again? I reached under his shirt, tracing the edge of his rib cage down to the lip of his pants and back again. Then I waited. And almost gasped when his hand slid under my shirt to the top limit of my stomach, to the spot where my ribs rose sharply to catch my breath. His hand swept down to my waist, and in a move that was both gentle and sure of itself, he turned onto his side and pulled me closer. Nearly touching.

I kept my eyes tightly shut because I knew that if I looked at him, I'd stop. And I didn't want to stop. This was quite possibly the best series of dares I'd ever engaged in, and it was my turn again.

I reached even higher and felt his chest. His heart. It slammed against my fingers, and my mind hummed with, *This is Mik. This is Mik. Holy shit, this is Mik.* But through the head rush, there was more.

This is me.

My hand slid over one side of his chest, which didn't feel scarred or hairy—thanks, Natalie—and back down to the edge of his pants where I found a belt loop and claimed it as a lifeline.

Mik's breath was sharper, and I still couldn't open my eyes.

His hand slid up the center of my chest and rested on the spot where my heart was going insane. It stayed there a hell of a lot longer than mine did on his, and I wondered if he was backing down.

I was breathing so hard that I was scared. No one had ever touched my breast before—no one had ever done anything to me before—and as his hand slid over my bra, I couldn't stop a sigh that somehow felt insanely embarrassing *and* awesome.

Mik's arm pulled tight around my lower back, bringing us together. Matched. Hips to hips. Chest to chest. With his height, my face was pressed into his neck, my lips on his throat.

My pulse hammered like I'd just dashed over a finish line, which made me think of track, of all things. Junior year, my dad won an epic battle to get me on a sports team. My long legs found hurdles, and at my first meet, a blue-haired eccentric-looking boy from the other school asked me if I liked to trip. Thinking he meant acid, I nearly spit on him, but then he pointed to my untied laces. It actually made me laugh. After I'd run my event, I found him waiting for me along the fence, only to overhear two boys from my school hassling him.

"Don't bother," the first one had said. "She's as deranged as she is hot."

"Possibly a lesbian," the second one chipped in.

I snagged the lead ball from the shot put gear and nailed the second boy in the stomach. That was my last day on track, although the coach did bemoan the fact that she hadn't sensed my natural gift for shot put before she had to kick me off the team.

Why was this memory coming now while I was in Mik's arms with my legs somehow wound up with his legs? Was it to prove that I wasn't a lesbian? Because I definitely wasn't. I was as attract-ed to Mik as he, um, definitely was to me. It was more than that. My impulse to touch him had tangled with my doubts too fast. Was I still Jake's little sister to him? Did I even want to be? Crazy thoughts. Of course I wanted to be Jake's little sister. But now… things were so different. And I'd worried so much about what Mik wanted from me that I hadn't figured out what I wanted from him. A kiss? A first kiss? More than that?

What kind of more?

"Mik?" My lips brushed his neck.

"Jaycee, I—"

An alarm went off, and Natalie jumped up and flicked on the light like she'd been foghorned awake. I tried to slide away from Mik, but our bodies were tangled, and it was so obvious that Natalie watched with her arms crossed, her eyebrows sky high.

"*Morning*," she said with ten kinds of emphasis. Zach sat up, following her cocked-head stare to where Mik and I were sit-ting, looking so damn guilty.

"No way. Were they hooking up?" Zach squinted tiredly.

"Better than that," Natalie said. "I think they were cuddling."

CHAPTER

41

MIKIVIKIOUS

THEATRE

CHAPTER

42

ZACH

VAMPIRE-CAVE BLACKNESS. PLUS THIS PLACE REEKED OF MOLD and damp.

Bishop stumbled forward and into a row of seats. "Christ," he said. "This is hands down the creepiest place yet."

"My spine is tingling," Zach said. He bumped into Mik, who lit his Zippo, throwing a dull glow over the old rows of stadium seating. Silver faces looked back at them.

Zach screamed. A falling-to-his-death stormtrooper kind of scream.

"They're mannequins," Jaycee said. "Someone staged mannequins all over this place!"

Zach held Natalie's shoulder in a death grip while his girlfriend swung the beam of her headlamp left and right. Jaycee had already climbed up the seats and was sitting next to one of the blank silver faces. "How cool is this?"

"Magic Johnson Theatres," Zach read off the wall.

"The basketball player?" Bishop asked. "He had movie theatres named after him?"

"They used his name as a way to develop first-rate multiplexes in urban areas. The first one was in Harlem," Natalie said. When Bishop hooked an eyebrow at her, she added, "I googled it. You guys should try that sometime. I don't have to be the only one who knows what's going on."

"My girl researches everything." Zach slipped an arm around her. "Which was a real neat-o surprise when we started doing it."

"Zach," Natalie warned, but she was almost laughing.

"What? I'm proud of my girl. Can't I brag?"

"No," Jaycee, Bishop, and Natalie said at the same time.

Zach looked at Mik. "At least you're on my side, man."

Mik patted Zach's shoulder and shook his head. He moved up the aisle, his Zippo lighting the way. Jaycee scurried to follow him, and Zach thought he saw them link hands. There was a different energy between those two since The Ridges. Natalie said that they had been cuddling this morning, but Zach wondered if it was more than that—like they now knew the high of getting too close. Once you've had that, you want it all the time. For Zach, that moment had been the first time Natalie sat on his lap and put her arms around his neck. It had felt so good that he'd never wanted her to move, even when his leg fell asleep.

They should call it cuddling crack. Or maybe hugging heroin.

Zach kept his hand on Natalie's shoulder as they walked up the aisle. At one point, he heard Bishop swear, staring at the screen behind them. Zach turned around. The white, plastic wall had been slashed apart as though by some wild animal or blade-wielding ninja.

"Freddy Krueger was here," he said. No one laughed.

"It's art," Bishop said. "Someone set this up as a statement. The mannequins are watching everything fall down around them."

"I don't see it," Zach said.

"You don't try," Bishop countered. He started to walk away and then came back. Zach wondered what kind of woe-is-me Marrakesh crap he was about to be subjected to. "Zach, we need to talk about your brother."

Zach laughed hard. "My brother?" At first it was a real laugh, and then he was just faking it, holding his sides and slapping his leg.

"What's wrong with you?" Bishop asked.

"My brother is not my problem."

"He's sick, Zach. There's something I need to tell you about the other night."

Zach pushed past him. What the hell was wrong with Bishop? Didn't he know that Tyler was the *last* thing he wanted to think about? Tyler with his hands all over Natalie? Tyler who'd *kissed* her? Tyler who'd probably put his dick on her? Didn't Bishop know that Zach was doing his damnedest to pretend like Tyler didn't even *exist*?

Zach swore, wanting to have it out with Bishop once and for all. Maybe Zach would run through his grievances: Bishop's endless moping and his horrible girlfriend. Maybe he'd even let Bishop know how shitty it felt to have him floating in and out of his life whenever Bishop didn't feel like scribbling a poem. Zach's sharpest thoughts edged toward his heart with each beat—just like that chest-dagger scene from the second Hellboy movie. Maybe he, too, would need to venture into the underworld for salvation while Natalie traded in her soul's eternal happiness to save Zach from Bishop's treachery.

Okay, maybe Zach was being melodramatic. He kicked at a dark mass on the ground. His foot tangled in something that made a weird whipping-kite's-tail noise when he tried to stomp it loose. Using his phone's screen, he illuminated a nest of filmstrip that someone had left in ribbons on the floor.

"Help," he called out. Everyone had left him. "Anyone have a knife? Hello?"

Natalie came back. "Oh, who would do such a thing?" She stooped and helped him free his sneaker. "Film is one of our most important cultural treasures."

Zach read the label on the canister. "Well, this was *Wild Hogs*. I think even the Smithsonian would pass on treasuring this Tim Allen slash John Travolta travesty."

"Oh, you used the word 'travesty.'" Natalie kissed him. "I love when you talk like me."

Despite the fact that Natalie had had sex with him three times yesterday afternoon, he wanted to dump her on the spot. Her IQ might outstrip his IQ, but it didn't make him an idiot. Zach didn't dump her though. He was never the one who broke up with her. He was the one who swallowed all her backassward insults and treated her like a queen. He was the one who got dumped and then opened up the covers to let her snuggle back in.

He freed himself from the rest of the filmstrip and walked away fast. Yep. This whole summer was turning into a dagger to the heart. And sadly, Zach Ferris was no Hellboy.

The hallway opened up with early morning light. The front entrance of the cinema was all glass, and though it was dirtied from birds and leaves, it streamed daylight over the chaos. The concession stands had been raided. The food displays were smashed and register drawers dangled, spitting out coupons and napkins.

They walked from the theater section into the grand central

heart of the mall. Zach wasn't prepared for what he saw. "This mall was open ten years ago? No way."

"It's like it tore *itself* down," Jaycee said. Mik was touching her lower back, and both of their heads were tilted up in unison, looking at the black empty spots in the ceiling where the panels had fallen two floors to become spongy piles. They walked through the endless crunch of broken glass, past planters filled with shriveled brown plants, and water fountains displaying their plumbing and lighting guts like they'd been victims of an anatomy class.

The floors were flooded in several areas. Blue, carpeted ramps climbed in a crisscrossing pattern from the first floor to the second and from one side of the mall to the other. Wheels marked where skateboarders had broken in and made use of the ramps, while everywhere else, there was unbelievable, mad destruction.

"You think people just come here to break things?" Zach asked. He was the first person to speak in what felt like hours.

"Yes," Jaycee and Natalie said together.

"I'm going to look upstairs," Bishop said, heading for the frozen escalator. "I want to know what this place looks like from up there."

Jaycee and Mik headed toward the black hole of a massive storefront.

"Come on," Natalie said as though she expected that Zach would go along with her. She walked after the misfit couple, not even waiting to see if he was following.

Zach stayed put. He turned his face up to the numerous skylights that poured in warm morning light. He imagined that at any moment, the mall doors might open to music playing and fountains springing. People would wander in for the blowout shoe sale or a Robert De Niro movie or to kill time on a bench with a mouth full of soft pretzel.

An echoing creak sounded through the abandoned mall like the wind was breaking in. Zach blinked away his daydream and felt the weight of the huge empty building all around him like something carved hollow and leaning in to collapse. November's jack-o'-lantern.

"Wait," Zach called out to Bishop. "I'm coming with you. We need to talk."

CHAPTER
43

JAYCEE

"DOES ANYONE ELSE FEEL LIKE THIS PLACE JUST MIGHT…COL-
lapse?" Natalie's voice was tiny. A mouse scurried through the
cavernous floor of what had once been a Dillard's.

Large, boxlike stands for clothing displays littered the store,
and the dark doubled as we stepped farther from the glow of
the central skylights. I took it all in. Unlike all the other places,
looking for Jake's marker wasn't distracting me. I hoped someone would find it, but it wouldn't be me. Whenever I searched
for Jake, his absence only grew larger, and I was done screaming into that hollow blank space.

I stepped on something that made a warbling, plastic crack.
Mik squatted down to look at it, finding a huge, dust-coated
customer service sign that someone had ripped from the ceiling.

"The destruction here is…"

"Palpable," Natalie finished. "From everything I've read,
urban explorers don't ruin things. 'Take nothing but photographs. Leave nothing but footprints.' That's their motto."

"Yeah, but there have clearly been vandals here. Probably
homeless people too," I said. Mik left us to check out a

strategically piled collection of sale signs, and I noticed his ears, specifically the left one, which had a slight point to it that the right didn't manage. How could I have known him forever and never noticed such a perfect imperfection?

"You love him," Natalie said. "Admit it. You're totally standing there thinking about how cute he is and how much you want to kiss him."

I turned away. "If you must pry, I was thinking that he has one hobbit ear."

Natalie groaned. "You're hopeless. I almost give up."

"Almost?"

"Well, you know I don't back down."

"Truth or dare, Nat?" I asked.

She glowered.

"So you do back down."

"I hate you," she said, and I wanted to be friends again. Not urbex partners or trip schemers, but real friends. I dragged a circle in the thick layer of dust on the ground and stood in the center. "Nat, do you remember when we tried to figure out how to disapparate?"

"Of course." Natalie grinned and drew her own circle to stand in. "We spent the whole summer trying to magic ourselves from one hula hoop to another. Every time I wanted to give up, you'd blindfold me and make me concentrate harder. Some days, I really thought we'd make it." Natalie closed her eyes, and I remembered all the muttered incantations, wands whittled from tree branches, and eyeliner lightning bolts drawn on both of our foreheads.

"I should have been Hermione," Natalie said, opening her eyes. "Why did you always insist that we were both Harry Potter?"

"Because Harry is the best." I shrugged. "And you're *not* Hermione."

"Well, I am the token overcautious know-it-all."

"No, you're brave like Harry. You never let Jake get away with anything you thought was wrong, no matter how he tried to punish you for tattling."

"Technically, that would make me Neville."

Natalie edged forward like she needed to say something, but I shook my head. "No, we don't have to get into it. I know you didn't like Jake, but I know you didn't want him to die either. It's okay, Nat. Really." I squinted into the black veil at the back of the store until I found the small flame of Mik's Zippo.

He flipped the lid closed and walked toward me so unwaveringly that I flushed. When he was close enough for me to reach for him, I did. It was so strange. So compulsive. Parts of my body felt like they were taking cues from my hormones or my subconscious, or something that clearly wasn't ordinarily in charge. And the weirdest part? I loved it.

His fingers slid between mine, and I remembered them beneath my shirt in the gray dim of the hotel room, and it made my mouth dry. "Jesus Christ," I muttered. Mik started out of the store, and I followed him, our hands linked.

"It's sweet," Natalie said. "You guys are sweet."

"Don't," I warned her, a smile creeping up my face.

"What?" She motioned to our hand-holding. "Looks like you guys are aboveboard now. I was simply commenting on how much I liked it."

"Don't take credit," I said, even though I was pretty sure she deserved credit.

We left the old Dillard's and walked down row after row of storefronts. The ones that had been glass covered were now smashed, making each step crunch, and the ones that had been barred were mangled, their accordion-styled gates bent outward like some giant had yanked on them.

"Really, this is a commentary on the decline of the American economy," Natalie said. "Did you know that this was once the largest shopping mall in the country?"

"Yes."

"You did?" Natalie asked, surprised.

"No, but I thought I should teach you a lesson about phrasing your know-it-all-isms as a question." I couldn't stop myself from laughing at the pinched look on her face. Mik pulled me close, and he was grinning so hard that I was dying to hear his thoughts.

"Nice. Real nice," Natalie said. "You'd think that no one wants to hear what I have to say, but you guys would still be peering into the mall windows without my research."

My laugh died away while happy tears dotted my eyes. "I'm sorry. I couldn't help it. I really am glad that you're so ana—" She glared. "Prepared," I said.

"Nice catch."

I caught the ghost of a smile on her face. Mik's hand was on my waist, and I glanced up, and he was looking down, and our smiles morphed into wanting. That fast.

"I'm almost afraid to ask," Natalie said, breaking my staring contest with Mik. She peered up at the second-floor balcony. "What did Jake do when he was here?"

"He climbed things," I said.

"Surprise, surprise. I'm going to murder whoever thought up parkour."

"He was mostly excited about climbing the elevator suspension ropes. He called it 'spidering.'" As if fate wanted me to have a window into my brother's weird brain, we turned a corner and faced the guts of a partially stripped elevator. The doors were held open by a broken chair, and inside, someone had piled red, fake Christmas presents that the mall must have decorated with during the holidays.

I stuck my head inside the shaft. Looking up, the dangle of rubber and metal and chains greeted my eyes like a scene from a horror movie. Bloody finger streaks ran down one of the metal panels as though someone—maybe Jake—had cut themselves while attempting the climb.

Natalie stuck her head in, glancing up at the wires and ropes hanging down. "Get out of there. It's psychotically dangerous."

"Of course it is! Everything he did was psychotically dangerous." I kicked a Christmas present before storming out. Mik and Natalie stepped back while I removed the chair holding the doors open and then pushed them shut with my shoulder. When I turned around, Mik was looking down, and Natalie's eyes were too large.

"Give me a second, will you?" I walked to the other end of the mall and sat on an old planter, scuffing my shoes against the dried, curled leaves on the ground. The poor tree at my back had been abandoned along with the mall. Its death pose reached toward the skylight, and I wondered how long it had tried to grow when no one came to water it. A month? A season?

For five years, I'd put Jake in the center of my life. At first, I'd felt better. Close to him. Then I'd started to forget him and grew desperate, and now…was I crazy? My dad's threat to send me to Stanwood didn't scare me as much as my own fear that

I belonged there—that I would never be able to get myself out of this black hole.

And if I did, what would my life look like without Jake? What would it feel like?

Would I be as ashamed of myself as I was with my dad for forgetting him?

Mik and Natalie crept up on me, and I demanded a bottle of water from Natalie's pack. I emptied it into the flaky soil at the base of the tree.

"It's dead," Natalie said. "Long dead."

"The water is for its next life." I stared Mik down. "Let's do something unbelievable. No talking about Jake for the rest of the day. Just us." I glanced at Natalie. "Sound good?"

Natalie grinned.

"Look less happy about it," I warned.

Her grin halved.

"Better."

We turned down a new corridor of the mall, one that had been painted sunshine yellow and held the remains of the food court. Farther on, we came across a Hot Topic. The signature rusted-iron gates were relatively intact, and we pushed through to look around the graffiti of wall skulls and dated *Twilight* references. Mik took a look at the back of the store, and Natalie got close to me like she was afraid.

Wrong. She wasn't afraid. She was prying.

"Did he kiss you yet?" she asked. "Did he ask you out? What's your status?"

"Cease and desist," I said. "We haven't talked."

"Are you doing what I told you to do? Are you making it easy for him to answer?"

"I'm…I'm trying!" I said wildly. "I don't know if it's working."

"Oh, for crying out loud." Natalie twisted my elbow and hauled me into a narrow fitting room. The door banged shut behind me, and before I could even attempt to escape, Mik was shoved inside as well. He rammed into me in the dark, and I hit the wall.

"Sorry," he said so automatically that I knew he hadn't meant to speak.

We pushed at the door, but Natalie was putting all her weight into keeping it shut. "I'll let you out once you know what's going on," she yelled. "I've been patient long enough. It's time for you to talk to each other."

"I'm not talking to him while you spy and give pointers!" I yelled back.

"I'm putting my headphones on," Natalie said. "Full volume!" I pictured her sitting against the door on the other side, earbuds in. I even heard the thunder-rumble of her classical music. Mik's Zippo clicked as he opened the cap.

"Don't," I said. "Leave it off." I wanted the dark. I wanted to keep my eyes open and touch him and not have to worry about him seeing how much I blushed and fumbled. My pulse started to run downhill. Doubts turned me around inside. Was I really going to let Natalie force this? I shook my head. This wasn't just what Natalie wanted. This was what I wanted. "Mik," I started.

"Ryan," he said.

A moment pushed between us.

"I haven't called you Ryan since I was in second grade."

"Jake gave me the nickname," he said. "He thought it was cool. I didn't speak up to correct people, so I've lived with it ever since."

"And that's how you became Mik? And you don't even like it?" I was suddenly angry with my brother, and then I was mad that I was thinking about him. "We weren't going to talk about Jake. Remember? This is about us today."

Us was a big word, and it blew energy into my hands. I grabbed his trench coat by the lapels and pulled him closer. My fingers found his neck, his scruffy jaw. His lips. I was so amazed to be touching him that I didn't realize right away that he wasn't touching me. His arms hung at his sides, and I sensed more than the rush of being close; he was shaking.

"Are you going to kiss me? I've never been kissed for real, and I'm probably terrible at it. Natalie and I practiced on each other like a decade ago, but I'm pretty sure that doesn't count."

Nothing. Not even a chuckle.

"Ryan?" His name felt wrong. This whole thing was starting to feel very wrong. What had I done to screw it up? I stepped back, bumping into the wall.

"I have to tell you something."

"What?" I waited, but he'd frozen up again. "What?"

"It's the truth, Jayce. I respect how much you value the truth." Mik's voice seemed to punch me on a spot that was already bruised. "Jaycee, I have to tell you if…if you want…this."

He touched my cheek, and I clenched my jaw. My heart thundered, and I felt dizzy—like my body knew what he was about to say long before my mind did.

"I dared Jake."

CHAPTER

44

BISHOP

CHAPTER 45

ZACH

ZACH'S ATTEMPTS TO UNLOAD ON BISHOP WEREN'T GOING well. Bishop had retreated into one of his graffiti spray paint whatevers on one of the old mall directories, and Zach had been forced to sit against the second-floor balcony, glaring at Bishop's back.

"I thought you wanted to talk."

"I thought you didn't," Bishop returned.

"Not about Tyler, I don't." Zach growled and rubbed his hands over his face. "Do you have any idea how hard it's been to erase what Tyler did with Natalie from my brain? If I hadn't, I wouldn't even be able to look at her. And you just want me to *talk* about it?! Yeah, Bishop, why don't we talk about how Marrakesh dumped you? Wouldn't that be fun?"

Bishop's hand went astray, a line of spray paint messing up a letter. He turned, and his glare was very dark. "I'm only going to say this once, Zach. Don't belittle my broken heart."

"She was horrible, Bishop! A cheater! I think she slept with half of Tyler's frat. I definitely saw the pictures when Tyler texted them at me, and I *tried* to tell you!"

Bishop surged at him. Zach leaned back against the balcony bars with an echoing *bang* that made the railing shake and show off all the places where the screws had come loose.

"I don't care why I shouldn't have loved her. I care that I did. I don't expect you to understand that. You're narrow, Zach. Shallow. Immature." Bishop pulled a phone out of his pocket and waved it at Zach. "And I know all about Marrakesh's exploits because I found them on your brother's phone when I was trying to delete the half-naked pictures of Natalie he took. I didn't want you to have to see those."

Zach looked away. "Thanks."

"Your brother is sick, Zach. Not sick like a dirty frat boy, but something is *messed up* in his head." Bishop's eyes glinted strangely. Damply?

"Are you crying?"

Bishop's fist tightened around the phone. "I've spent the last five months trying to find something that put my pain over Marrakesh in perspective. I've found it, and now I wish I hadn't. There's something you need to see. Well, no one needs to see it, but I can't get it out of my head. So, here. It's four seconds." Bishop turned the phone on and called up a paused video. He held the screen out to Zach. "He's your brother. You tell me what the hell I should do. Call your dad? The police? Get your brother in trouble for having a snuff film?"

"Jesus," Zach said. A *what* film? What the hell could have Bishop this riled? Was it porn? Because for fuck's sake, Tyler liked gross porn, and Zach did not need to see that. He glanced at the paused image of a few dozen people outside on a sunny day.

He pressed play.

The camera pointed up to where a boy in a cap and gown stood atop a swing set.

Zach stopped existing for the four seconds that it took for Jake to grin madly, flip—and *crack* against the blacktop. As fast as it had started, the clip ended, cutting off with screams and a jerk of the screen.

Zach dropped the phone. He staggered a few feet away and started to gag.

"I know." Bishop gripped his shoulder. "It's… Can you believe your brother has that on his phone? What does he do with it? Show people at parties?"

Of course he does, Zach thought miserably, but he couldn't respond because his brain was frying. Surging. All the black feelings he kept locked up in his mind's basement flew out of control, and he attacked Bishop. His fists flew into Bishop's stomach and face. They rolled on the ground, through plaster and broken glass. Bishop didn't want to fight and kept trying to get away, but Zach went at him harder and faster. He went at Bishop like Tyler always went after Zach when they were kids—with bared teeth and fists that aimed for kidneys.

Finally Bishop swung back. He landed a punch on Zach's side that left a shooting ache every time Zach lifted his arm. But the pain felt great. Fantastic. Distracting.

At some point, Jaycee ran by them, sobbing and holding onto her shirt like she'd been attacked, but not even that made them stop. It wasn't until he heard yelling from across the mall that Bishop managed to pin Zach down. "Did you hear that? Was that Natalie?"

Zach put a quick kick to his stomach. He didn't care who was yelling. He couldn't stop. If he stopped, he'd remember why they were fighting. He'd picture that disgusting, twisting, snapping end, and he'd hear all of those people crying out. Zach's body went insane. His arms spun fiercely until Bishop was knocked hard against the railing. A huge section of it broke away, smashing into the floor with an echoing chaotic crash.

From across the mall, Jaycee started screaming. But Zach's eyes were fastened to Bishop's as he grasped at the air, one leg dangling over the drop and the rest of him tipping back…

CHAPTER

46

Natalie

NATALIE SAT AGAINST THE FITTING ROOM DOOR AND TURNED
on her party mix, which just so happened to be her London
Philharmonic Orchestra jams. The run of brass and timpani set
her heart alight while she really did try to distract herself from
whatever was happening behind her. Was Jaycee getting her
first kiss? Were they confessing their love for one another?

Anything was possible. If she and Zach could come off of the
Tyler disaster with renewed energy for one another, anything
really was possible. She even thought that maybe, just maybe,
she was becoming friends with Jaycee again, and that was such
a relief that she wanted to cry out *Braveheart*-style. God, Zach
had made her watch that movie way too many times.

Natalie turned the volume down on her music and eaves-
dropped. Whispers and slight rustling. She smirked and left
her guard at the door. They would come out when they were
ready. Mission accomplished. She walked to the balcony and
looked over the railing at the chaos of the ruined mall below.
Everything was going to line itself up now. She could feel it.

She walked around the cavernous, cave-in of a mall, ignoring everything in favor of the gleaming skylights. She found the second-floor elevator door. This one was propped upon a few feet like the one below, and she wanted to look inside. *Bad idea. You could fall.*

I am Natalie, and no, I won't.

She stepped to the edge and glanced down, down, down. It wasn't so hard after all.

Rather proud of herself, she leaned in farther, thinking about Jaycee's mom at that behavioral hospital. Jaycee probably thought she was going off her rocker because all she had to compare herself to was her mom, but Natalie could tell her the truth. She could teach Jaycee all the things she'd memorized in her years of therapy—about asking for help and talking to people.

Then maybe all those things might actually work so that Natalie didn't wind up letting someone like Tyler touch her ever again. Natalie looked down even farther at the dangling, greasy suspension ropes and the support bars that, stripped of their elevator, now had nothing to support. Across the way, her eyes caught on a little piece of graffiti next to the counter weights. Jake's signature and a scribble that might call itself a spider.

It felt like Jake Strangelove was screaming, *I'm right here!* And Natalie shouted back, "Not anymore, you jerk!" Her voice echoed fiercely.

Ultimately, she could tell Jaycee the hard-earned truth that had taken Natalie all of these years to figure out. She'd tell Jaycee that uphill was slow and steady and cautiously planned. It was all about college visits and SAT prep classes and counting dates between sexual advances. But downhill? It wasn't a slope or progress. It was as simple as changing directions. Turning around. Like swallowing a whole handful of pills.

Or watching a boy snap his neck.

Natalie pulled herself back to the safety of the walkway, just in time to see Jaycee.

She was running in Natalie's direction and holding herself. Sobbing. "You just have to force everything, don't you?" Jaycee yelled. She flew toward Natalie in a way that pushed Natalie right up against the wobbly, broken elevator doors. "You ruined him and me!"

"What happened?" Natalie had never known Jaycee to be so upset—which could only mean one thing. "Oh no. Mik told you about Jake? Right now? What an idiot!"

Jaycee's face went from destroyed to irate in a flash. "You knew what he did?"

Natalie tried to back up but only slipped closer to the crevice and what could only be described as a suicide fall. "Jaycee, did you let him explain?"

"Explain what? That he *started all of this*?" She was shaking so hard, but Natalie couldn't reach out to her. She had to hold on to the elevator and hope that Jaycee didn't push her farther.

"But this is the truth, Jayce! You know, that thing you prize above people and possessions. That thing you've had a death grip on your whole life! And you know what? There's more to the story, so if you want to know what happened, you have to listen."

"That's hilarious coming from you! You're so good at lying that you don't even know when you're doing it!"

Natalie felt like she was bursting. Her chest was heaving, and she wasn't against the elevator anymore because she was pushing Jaycee with both hands. Back, back, back to the second-floor railing. "Jake was being awful to Mik that day. Egging his stupid drunken friends on so that they were all making fun of Mik for not drinking. For not talking. Think about it, Jayce. Make yourself remember how cruel he could be!"

Jaycee struggled to speak. "So that's it...you and Mik... you've had long chats about this? Is it fun for you two to reminisce about how he died?" Jaycee tried to clasp her hands over her ears, but Natalie pulled them down.

"No! Mik and I have never talked about this."

"Then how do you—"

"Because I was there, Jayce. Hiding under the slide so I could tattle on Jake for drinking." The words flew out, and Natalie was empty. She nearly fell over and took hold of the wobbly railing. "I saw Mik dare Jake. I saw Jake climb the swing set. I watched him break his neck, and then I ran away and lied, and I've been in a permanent anxiety attack every single day of my life since. So there."

CHAPTER

47

JAYCEE

"Did you see me?"

My voice sounded like it was coming from another human, another state away. "Did you see me after he hit the blacktop, and I was standing there calling out his name and staring at that blown-fuse look on his face?"

Natalie opened her mouth, but nothing came out. She nodded.

"And then you ran home and lied?" My eyes were flooding, but the tremble in my chest was the worst part. Mik's confession had hatchet-slammed my heart into half throbs, and then less. Fractions of beats. And now Natalie's words were grinding whatever was left into splinters.

"So you do know how bad that day really was, and yet you still spent the last five years passing me in the hall and looking at me like I'd lost my mind?"

"I've always felt bad about Jake," Natalie said, her voice shrunken to a hundredth of the volume it had been moments ago. "But I'm dead inside over abandoning you. The guilt...it makes me doubt everything I do. Every decision. Every friend. Everything. It makes me feel like I'm not even me."

"You deserve it," I growled, trying to get back to anger and not being able to. Jake was gone, and this? This was the truth that couldn't be rejected. Couldn't be embraced. It could only exist with me tangled inside of it. Maybe this *was* the other side that I ached for when I was drunk. Maybe this was as good as my terrible life could get.

A huge, crashing, echoing sound shot Natalie and me to the balcony. All at once, I was sure that the mall was coming down around us. We looked out across the open center of the building to where Bishop and Zach were fighting on the far side.

"They're trying to kill each other!" Natalie yelled out to them, but they only fell over, wrestling, and Zach landed a kick to Bishop's stomach that sent him slamming against the railing.

Another earthquake of a crack ripped through the second floor, so much stronger than the first, and a huge section of the railing fell, fell, fell.

I looked down with it.

"Mik!" I screamed.

Too late.

CHAPTER 48

Mikivikious

GEAUGA LAKE

CHAPTER
49
ZACH

ZACH AND BISHOP SPRINTED DOWN THE FROZEN ESCALATOR. They beat Natalie and Jaycee to where Mik lay unmoving. They tried and failed to pick up the huge section of railing.

"He's knocked out," Bishop yelled. He reached through the bars and felt Mik's neck. "I think he has a pulse."

Jaycee and Natalie arrived. Natalie was holding Jaycee upright as though she'd dragged her all the way down the stairs. "We have to lift it together. Everyone get to a corner." She shook Jaycee and pointed to where she should stand. The four of them collected around the railing, and Natalie yelled, "On three!"

She counted and then they lifted it together. It started to fall apart before they'd moved it far enough, and Bishop and Zach both swung their side out so that the whole thing spun when it hit the floor, breaking into smaller sections.

Mik was all twisted, and his head was bleeding from an ugly spot by his temple.

"Don't move him. He could have spinal damage." Natalie held her ear toward Mik's mouth. "He's breathing."

Zach couldn't believe how focused she was. He couldn't even think straight.

Natalie thrust her phone toward Bishop. "Call 911."

Bishop dialed the number, swearing. Zach stood there watching Natalie tug on Jaycee, trying to get her to come closer to Mik. To talk to him. Jaycee looked like something had broken inside, and when Natalie pulled too hard on her hand, she slumped to the floor like someone had taken out her knees.

"Zach! Zach!" How long had Natalie been yelling his name? "Zach, go outside, flag the ambulance down, and lead them straight here."

Zach ran for the front entrance. He snagged an old cash register off the floor and threw it with everything he had through the glass door. The burst of shattering shards filled the air with chaos, and he ran outside into the dawn.

When the ambulance and cop cars roared across that cemetery of a parking lot, he waved his hands and jumped up and down, screaming until his voice broke. They came straight for him at a million miles an hour, and though he'd seen just about every blockbuster movie on the planet, nothing prepared him for the stabbing reality of true emergency.

He stayed outside while the paramedics rushed in, slumped on the curb with his head hanging between his knees. They brought Mik out on a stretcher and took him off in a blare of lights. When Zach looked up, Natalie, Jaycee, and Bishop were standing there talking to a cop who was busy filling out a report.

"Are you going to arrest us?" Natalie asked the woman.

"I need all your information, but you can go to the hospital to wait on your friend."

"We were exploring," Natalie said, holding up her head-lamp. "We didn't break anything. We weren't vandalizing. Well, Zach broke the door, but that's because he needed to get your attention."

The cop sighed loud and long. "That's beside the point. You're not the first kids we've had to pull out of here. Not the last, I bet. We need to contact the property manager. He'll decide if he's going to press charges, but you might get lucky."

"How are we lucky?" Jaycee asked, her eyes as red and dark as something rabid.

"They're planning on ripping this place down really soon. I doubt the property manager is going to want to deal with the headache, especially after you...nearly lost your friend in there."

"Give it a little more time," Bishop said. "It'll rip itself down."

Natalie led Jaycee away, and together the four of them crossed the parking lot to Natalie's car. Zach offered to drive, and he immediately felt better when he was in the front seat. His hands twisted on the wheel as Natalie gave directions to the hospital.

Zach drove mindlessly. All turns and speed. When he pulled up in front of the emergency room, Jaycee and Natalie jumped out without even looking back at him.

Bishop got out too, but he leaned back in and looked at Zach strangely. "You all right?" Zach squeezed the steering wheel and managed a small nod. Bishop reached in and placed Tyler's phone on the passenger seat. Zach glared at it. "Go park. I'll see you inside."

"Yeah," Zach said, his voice cracking, but when he peeled out of the emergency room turnaround, he didn't stop. He got on the highway. He headed home, and his mind hardened around one impulse. There was nothing he could do for Mik, but there was definitely something he could do about Tyler.

He'd never felt so lucid. There were no superheroes in his head. No trees turning into Groots or plastic LEGO blocks to make him feel safe. There was only the highway running beneath him and his foot holding down the gas pedal.

Zach pulled into his driveway around nine in the morning. Tyler's car was inside the garage, and Zach's father's car was missing—probably at his girlfriend's house. *Two brilliant strands of luck*, he thought as he made his way inside.

He busted open Tyler's bedroom door. His brother sat up in bed, and Zach went at him.

"What the—" Tyler started, but Zach was too fast.

He dragged Tyler to the floor. He didn't want to fight him; he wanted to hurt him. He yanked Tyler's old football injury arm behind his back until his shoulder popped at a horrible angle and Tyler howled.

"Get off me!"

Zach used his weight to pin him down and pressed Tyler's phone against his face. "How could you be so sick?"

"What? Where'd you get my—I knew you bastards stole my phone!"

"I stole it. Explain yourself!"

"I take pictures of the girls I bang. They know I'm doing it. It's not a crime!"

Alianna appeared in the doorway in her pajamas. She looked terrified.

"It's okay," Zach said. "I'm teaching Tyler a lesson."

"Call Dad," Tyler yelled.

Alianna didn't move.

"Call Dad, you failed save-the-marriage baby—"

Zach pulled his arm back harder. "Say something nice to her! Now!"

"Okay, okay," Tyler yelled. "You're kind of a smart girl."

"Say something I don't already know," Alianna said. Her face was burning red, but her stance wasn't yielding.

Zach tightened his grip until Tyler started to talk. "Fine. You're smarter than me! Is that what you want?"

Alianna had tears in her eyes that made Zach ache to hug her, but he wasn't done with Tyler, not by half.

"Go," he told his little sister. "I need to talk to him. He won't bother us anymore after this. Promise."

Alianna nodded, backed out of the room, and shut the door behind her.

"What went wrong with you?" Zach screamed. "Why are you so evil? I mean, I understand that we got fucked up as kids. Believe me, I'm the only one who gets that as well as you, but why do you have to be vicious all the time?"

"You're a weak, whiny woman, Zach. That doesn't make me evil."

Zach pulled his arm back even farther. It was going to snap out of Tyler's shoulder socket at any moment. And yet the tears were burning in Zach's eyes. It hurt to harm his brother, and that was hands down the worst part. "This is not about your sick pictures of girls. I'm here about the video. Of Jaycee's brother. Of him *dying*."

Tyler stopped struggling. "You watched that?"

"I can't *unwatch* it, you asshole. You've completely scarred Bishop. And Jaycee…what if she knew that you had that? It'd kill her!" Zach threw the phone at the wall and it burst into pieces. "Why did you have it?"

"BECAUSE HE WAS MY FRIEND!"

Tyler whipped his body around and threw Zach off of him. He held his arm to his chest and backed into the bed. "He was fucking nuts, but he was *my* friend. I was his 'photographer.' He was trying to make a demo tape to become a reality TV host for those dumbasses who explore abandoned buildings. I was taping him when he died because I always taped him." Tyler grabbed a box out of his closet and pulled out a small video recorder. "Here. There's probably seventy hours of Jake being Jake on that. Give that to Jaycee if you're so desperate to bone her."

Zach punched his brother in the face.

It was a beautiful sort of punch. The kind that sent Tyler flying backward.

"She's my friend. Don't you ever talk about my friends like that." He paused, his fist still ready for another go. "You know what? Don't talk about *anyone* like that in my presence again. You make me sick, Tyler. Even if you were Jake's *photographer,* why would you have that video on your phone?"

"Because sometimes I watch it. I want to remember that all we have is seconds. Why be careful? Why be cautious or hold back? It doesn't matter in the end, because sometimes your neck just snaps." He clapped his hands, and Zach jumped.

"You need help."

Angry tears glazed his brother's eyes. "Oh, so you saw a video of Jake dying? And that makes you so traumatized and noble? I was there, you fuckface. I was there, and he was my friend. Work that out. Go on, I'd like to see you do the math. I know you can't put numbers together for shit."

Zach stood there watching his brother for a long moment. It was the damnedest thing; Zach *knew* that Tyler wanted him to leave so that he could cry alone. Zach knew that because they'd grown up together, fighting over Halloween candy and NERF weapons. And yet, the fact that Zach knew Tyler so well had become its own sort of roadblock. Tyler didn't want people around who knew his softer side. He wanted Zach to see him like the world saw him: a selfish, foul playboy.

"Stay away from Alianna," Zach said. "Stay away from me."

"Fuck off."

"Okay." Zach moved to the door. "I will. I am."

"You going to go cry and say that I'm not your brother anymore?"

"You'll always be my brother, but I don't have to let your life touch mine. I'm not going to turn into you. Not for anything."

Zach left the room and ran straight into Alianna eavesdropping in the hall. She threw her arms around him and sobbed into his chest.

"I hate him," she said.

"What'd you tell me?" He looked down at her. "He hates himself. That's enough."

CHAPTER 50

Natalie

THE HOSPITAL WAITING ROOM SMELLED LIKE STRONG CLEANER. Bishop was dead asleep in the corner, and Natalie sat on the sofa with Jaycee collapsed across her lap. It had been six hours since they'd arrived, four hours since the nurse came out and said that Mik had a bad concussion but was otherwise all right.

An hour ago, the cop who'd taken their names showed up to give the good news that the property manager wasn't going to press charges, so everything had worked out okay. But then, if everything was okay, how was Natalie going to get Jaycee back into a sitting position? And where the hell had Zach taken off to? She checked her phone, but he still hadn't responded to her fifteen hundred texts.

At one point, she called her mother and told her what had happened. Natalie was shocked that the phone didn't erupt into flames in her hand. Honestly, she was shocked by her mom's rather relaxed interpretation of the whole situation. "The neural insulation of your frontal lobe won't be finished developing until you're in your midtwenties. You're not fully aware of the consequences of your actions," her mother informed her.

Was that it? Was it her frontal lobe's fault that she felt so disconnected all the time?

Jaycee slowly sat up.

"I thought you were asleep," Natalie said.

Jaycee shook her head. "Can't."

Natalie handed Jaycee her phone. "Text your dad. Something vague and positive so he doesn't worry why we're not on our way home yet. We'll explain to him what happened in person."

Jaycee thumbed a text and then leaned back, her eyes closed. "Heard from Zach?"

"Nope. And yep, I am going to kill him when he resurfaces."

"Leave him be. That was a lot to take. Maybe he needed to get away." Jaycee opened her eyes and stared at Natalie. "I couldn't move…couldn't think… I think you saved his life."

"I only did what you would have done." Natalie thought back to Mik beneath the bars, and her mind burned. The truth was that she'd wanted to run again. To hide from what was happening, but Jaycee was there falling down beside her, and she had to be the strong one. "Any perceived bravery is just me doing my impression of you. You and Jake."

"He wasn't brave," Jaycee said with so much resignation that the words felt heavy. "He was courageously stupid. That's what I keep thinking about. All of Jake's ideas and challenges, what was the point? The adrenaline? The fear? The notoriety?"

"I think it was a potent cocktail of all three." Natalie picked at a hole in her jeans. "I thought I was being brave by going out of state for college. I thought I had to get out of town to become a new person. Fresh start. Reinvent myself into someone who is not so controlling. I've even had this countdown going for almost two years." She sat up and sniffed hard. "But you know what? I don't *want* to be different. I want to be myself, and I think you're the only person who's ever made me feel strong enough to do that."

"Zach does too, in his own way."

"He's not enough. Leaving isn't enough. I need to be okay with who I am."

"So do that."

Natalie sat up, excited but not in a good way. "See? Right there. That's the huge difference between us. I can't just accept myself. I doubt, and I question, and I make up stories that seem more interesting than my own experiences. I've been in therapy for years. I've been on half a dozen antidepressants, and the only revelation I've had is that I can't stand that I ran away from you five years ago."

Jaycee scowled. "Don't let that pull you under. I can forgive you. I suppose I have to."

"No, you don't. And I don't want you to. I don't deserve it." Natalie looked down and twisted her hands together. "Jayce, I tried to kill myself." She'd never said the words aloud before. They come out in a gust, leaving her throat chafed.

Jaycee shrugged. "Who hasn't?"

Natalie shook her head. "Listen. Three years ago, I took fifteen Motrin. I researched it online and found out how many I needed to take for my weight. I put the bottle back in the cabinet afterward and went to take a nap like nothing happened."

"Did you panic and call 911?"

"My mom canceled her class unexpectedly and found me passed out in my own vomit."

Jaycee's stubbornly unaffected look transformed. Natalie realized with a start that what she was seeing was Jaycee's fear.

"That…that certainly is trying to kill yourself." Tears glassed Jaycee's eyes, but she set her jaw. "Your mom canceled a class? That's unbelievable."

Natalie choked on a laugh. "You think it's fate?"

"Nah. We don't believe in that crap." Jaycee wound her arm in Natalie's.

"I can't believe how sure you are of everything. You've always been so sure, like you know me inside and out. Like we're both these permanent, mighty beings." Natalie was crying, but she didn't care. "When I wasn't your friend any-more, it was also like I wasn't *me*."

Jaycee laughed sadly. "That's funny, because I was the one having an identity crisis. I think I became Jake for a few years, and then when I started to forget him, it was like there was nothing else inside of me. Who is Jaycee Strangelove anyway? I'm the damaged girl. No hobbies. No passions. No future."

"Oh, I know this one!" Natalie sat up tall and faced Jaycee. If she was going to go full know-it-all, she was going to do it right. "You're the girl who read about King Tut's tomb and spent all her allowance money on a digital video camera so that we could do a reenactment. You're the girl who talked me through a mile of pitch-black sewer pipe with such elab-orate descriptions of Narnia that I was never once afraid. And disapparating! You convinced me that we could *magic* ourselves from place to place when we were way too old to believe that."

Natalie shoved the tears out of her way so that she could keep speaking. "You're the girl who loved her big—albeit brash— brother so damn much that I ached to have a big brother of my own. And when I figured out that that was impossible, I made

Jake my big brother. That's what it felt like that day. I wasn't watching your big brother die. I was watching mine."

The nurse came in, and both Natalie and Jaycee looked down, embarrassed. "I… Sorry to interrupt, girls. I wanted to tell you that Ryan is awake, and we're going to process him to be released. You can go see him now, if you'd like."

Natalie thanked the nurse, and when she finally worked up the courage to look at Jaycee, she found her staring at where the woman had stood. Natalie took a deep breath. "I never wanted to tell you that. I know he's *your* brother. I just…well…"

"I understand," Jaycee said, distracted and rubbing her arms nervously. "Go see Mik."

"I think you should do that."

Jaycee shook her head. "I think I'm furious with him, and that's cold considering he almost died a few hours ago." She scowled hard. "How could he want me to picture him there? Standing with Jake's friends on the playground, laughing and drinking? Saying the words that sent Jake up there…" Her voice sputtered out. "And what about now? Does Mik want everyone to know? My dad? My mom?" Jaycee choked on her own breath. "Picture it, Nat. 'Hey Mom, Mik is my boyfriend now. He's studying medicine at KSU. Oh, and he's also responsible for Jake's death.'"

Natalie was trying to figure out what to say, but Jaycee's voice recharged. "You want to know what's *really* unhinged? Want to hear me sound so girlie you might get nauseous? I'm mostly mad because Mik ruined it all before anything even happened. I just want to talk to him. Hang out with him."

"Kiss him?"

"Well, yeah. Hell yeah."

Natalie was quiet for a moment. "So wait, are you mad that Mik ruined it all by daring Jake, or did he ruin it all because he wanted you to know the truth?"

"Is there a difference? It's ruined either way."

"There is a difference, but it doesn't have anything to do with Mik. You either accept what happened as part of this grand, sad scheme, or you reject it—and you reject him too."

Jaycee crossed her arms. "You know I always accept the truth."

"So what are you waiting for? Go talk to him. I dare you."

Jaycee's expression hardened the way it always did when she had a challenge. She stood up, and only the slow pace of her steps proved that she was terrified.

Natalie watched Jaycee leave, and then she slumped in her chair. She glanced over at Bishop and found him watching.

"You two make sense," he said, rolling over onto his back across three chairs. "It's that whole 'opposites attract' thing."

"Yin and yang," Natalie corrected, closing her eyes and feeling strangely at peace.

CHAPTER

51

JAYCEE

I WALKED DOWN THE NEON-WHITE HOSPITAL HALLWAY, PAUS-
ing outside of Mik's assigned room. I'd come by once while he
was sleeping, peeking in at him while my fear sucked me under
and whipped me around. What would I feel when I looked at
him now that I knew the truth?

I leaned against the wall until a nurse came by, squinting at
me. I ducked inside. "Hey—"

Mik was shirtless. He hunched over the edge of the bed
while he laced his boots. A forehead bandage glared at me
when he looked up, but that's not what caught my eye.

I finally saw what had gotten Natalie so excited weeks ago.

"Tattoos," I said like I had Tourette's. A blush reached up
my neck and cheeks. Mik sat back, and I took a few steps
closer, getting a better look at the black symbols and strings
of words across his chest and upper arms. I cleared my throat.
"You have tattoos."

His eyes were on me, but his mouth stayed closed.

I got closer somehow. "Am I back to the silent treatment?"

"Depends."

"On what?"

"What you want." His dark eyes made something in me kind of scream, and I pressed myself between his knees before I could think twice about it. He took my hips in his hands, and I started to leak those silent, slipping tears that I had no control over.

"The crying…it's not about you. I mean, I was *scared*, but you're all right." I pushed at the tears with my palms, unable to stop. "It's not about you," I said again.

"It's not about Jake," he said like he was correcting me.

"What?"

"How I feel about you. It's not about Jake. Never has been."

"My parents think you've had a crush on me since we were kids." My fingers brushed the tattoo on his right shoulder, a scrolling Latin phrase. *Serva me, servabo te.* "What's this one say?"

"It says, 'I've had a crush on you since we were kids.'" His tone hinted at sarcasm. I couldn't say for sure, because I barely knew the angles of his voice. When I didn't respond he added, "It means, 'Save me and I will save you.'"

I touched the tattoo over his heart. A date written in a circle. My brother's last day on this planet. "And this one? Does this have nothing to do with Jake as well?" I had the strangest feeling like we were on the edge of a fight, and it made me stronger. I wanted to push him over and interrogate him. Or hit him…or kiss him. Or both. "Why didn't I know that you have tattoos?"

"Because you couldn't even look at me while we were playing Zach's stripping game all those weeks ago."

"Did you just call me a coward?"

"Also depends. Are you going to use all this as an excuse not to get to know me?"

I made a note of the way his voice dropped lower when he was riled. And that note read: *Jaycee, you fucking love him.* I touched his face, turned his chin so that I could see the bandage over that evil notch in his skull. "Maybe I'm afraid of you."

"You don't have to—"

"Mik, the last real time we spent together, we were building bonfires in the backyard and feeding Jake's gecko bags of crickets." I kept moving closer even though my words got harsher. "And what am I supposed to do? Tell my parents about your dare? Am I supposed to ignore it? You know I'll never be able to lie about what you…about your part in Jake's death."

He scowled, and if this was Mik getting angry with me, I liked it way too much. "You should major in excuses, Jayce."

I pushed away from him, and he stood, and then my hands were somehow on his chest. He pulled me close, and the world swung like a carousel with me stuck in its center. "You're making me dizzy," I said. "Stop."

He let me go, but I didn't let go of him. I didn't want to.

My pocket vibrated. I turned my back and answered my phone. "Zach. Where are you?"

Mik's fingers slipped through my hair, and for a solid minute, I felt like I was going to pass out. "What? No, I heard you. Meet you outside." I hung up and realized that Mik had done a terrible job of putting my hair back in its ponytail.

He leaned down to my ear, and every nerve in my body shone. "Give me a chance."

Natalie appeared in the doorway, literally skidding when she saw us so close. "Just wanted to say, uh, that Zach texted finally. He's outside, ready to go." She looked from Mik's shirtlessness to me. "Why do you have sex hair? You guys making up?"

I stared at the floor.

"You guys making out?" she asked hopefully.

"Like I'd know how to do that," I growled as I walked by her. Mik had at least one ex-girlfriend. He had *three* college years on me. And tattoos. Maybe I *was* scratching around for excuses, but Mik—Ryan—was an enigma. And kissing? There's no way I wouldn't embarrass myself. And all this came secondary to the life-altering confusion that I'd finally found a person to blame for Jake's death, and I no longer wanted to.

CHAPTER 52

ZACH

BISHOP WAS SITTING OUTSIDE THE HOSPITAL WHEN ZACH pulled up.

"Is Mik all right?" Zach asked, rolling the window down.

Bishop climbed into the passenger seat. "They're releasing him now. How are you?"

"Better."

Bishop stretched. "We need to get out of here. Too many parades of senior citizens in wheelchairs, trailing IV bags. I'm having flashes of my own mortality. Can't believe something worse didn't happen. Can you?"

Zach stared ahead, his knuckles drawn tight on the wheel. A few minutes clicked by.

"So, Zach, where'd you go?" Bishop's question hung in the stiff air of the Oldsmobile. "You don't look so great. Should we put on the *Guardians of the Galaxy* soundtrack or something? I mean everything is cool now."

"Cool?" Zach stared at Bishop. Was it possible that this guy really didn't know how uncool his life was? "What's your first memory?"

"What?"

"Tell me."

Bishop closed his eyes and exhaled. "Something about a funeral. My great-grandpa's funeral. People were telling stories and laughing, and I thought that was weird because my dad said we had to be serious."

"My first memory is my fifth birthday. I ran into the kitchen with my new toy bow and fired one of the suction cup–tipped arrows at my mom. Shot her in the butt. Surprised her. She dropped my cake on the floor. It had Darth Vader on it, and I always picture the way his helmet kind of slid off the icing and onto her shoe. She cried *really* hard, and I was in the middle of thinking, 'Wow, Mom, it's just a cake!'" Zach paused. "How many five-year-olds have that sort of perspective, do you think?"

Bishop's brow was bent down in a *v*. Good, he knew this story was going to get worse.

"My dad came in and caught her scooping up the cake. He started screaming about how stupid she was. He said she had one job for my birthday, and she'd ruined the party." Zach put on his best dad voice. "'You ruined his birthday, Carrie. Look how he's crying!'"

He glanced at Bishop again and was pleased by his horrified expression.

"Of course he felt bad about it later. So much so that mom woke me up that night and said, 'Guess what? You're going to get another present. How about a little baby brother or sister?' She was totally beaming. I think she'd wanted another kid for years, but my dad had said no. So that's how we got Alianna. Because I shot my mom in the butt, and my dad felt guilty about ripping her down to the fibers over floor cake." Zach felt his body grow cold. He pictured himself looking just like Tyler, squinting maliciously at the shards of his life. Searching for the sharpest piece. Something to cut his steak with.

"Damn, Zach. I didn't know there was verbal abuse in your house."

"You think Tyler's cruelty just sprang from the earth? That shit is passed down, baby. Like heart disease and the ability to roll your goddamn tongue." Zach reached into his pocket and pulled out the pieces of Tyler's phone. He dropped them on Bishop's lap. "I've talked to him about what was on there. He doesn't have a real excuse, but he's not what you think he is."

"You talked to him?"

"I had to hold him down, but yeah."

Bishop rubbed his face. "Zach, you drove to Athens and back today?"

"I did."

They were silent for a long time. Zach eyed the entrance, waiting for the girls and Mik to come save them from this conversation. He didn't want to think about that video ever again…or about Tyler's I-have-to-cry-so-fuck-off face. Bishop was staring at him strangely. "What?"

"Nothing. I just…man, I feel like I don't know who you are right now."

"Of course you don't. You think I'm a kid who's wandered into a movie, asking what's going on. You think I'm simple." Zach's hand tightened around the steering wheel. "What did you call me exactly? Narrow? Shallow?"

"Zach, think about it from my perspective. All you've ever showed interest in is getting boozed, playing video games, and making out with Natalie in your basement. I'm sorry if it seems like I don't respect you."

"Don't apologize. It's what I like about you." Zach thought about giving him the real truth, and then...he did. "When I started to date Natalie, she was doing a project for a class. Something about the end of childhood. Coming-of-age bull-shit. I think it was a request from her therapist to help deal with Jake's death. But anyway, she started telling me about how kids who see horrible things stop being kids. And I immediately thought about my parents. About how they'd stolen all the best times of my life from me. So I went backward. On purpose. It's like you said. All I want is to escape to my basement to make out with my girl and play Tetris with my best friend and pre-tend that everything can fit together like those falling bricks."

"Christ, Zach."

"Don't worry about it. You can head off to Michigan next week and never look back." Zach smiled sadly. "To think that at the beginning of this summer, all I cared about was finding a way to make you stay around. Thinking about life without you and Natalie? Now that's terrifying. Well, when you come home on the holidays, you can check in on me. I'll be in the basement."

"You've got to move out, Zach. Live in the dorms while you go to OU."

"And leave Alianna? Are you *stupid*?" He couldn't breathe all of a sudden. He hit himself in the chest until his mouth opened and let in air. Those words were his father's favorite insult, and they were always right on the edge. Ready to pop out. He had to be more careful. No, he had to be carefree Zach. That was the only true defense. "I'm sorry, Bishop. But think about it: How long before my dad marries his girlfriend? How long before everything is not heaven, and he starts tearing her down? Or what if it isn't his new wife who pisses him off but Alianna?"

Bishop looked as shocked as Zach wanted him to look. "Can she live with your mom?"

"Maybe. Mom only has a one-bedroom apartment. My dad took the house in the divorce. I actually think that's the cruelest thing he ever did to her. Ali and Mom don't have the best relationship either. I've been trying to get them to talk more."

"And Tyler?"

Zach shrugged. "Lost cause." They were quiet for a long moment. "We should go inside and get them. We need to head back to Athens before our families send out a search party."

Bishop touched the pieces of Tyler's phone in his hands. "I've been thinking, Zach. About Jake. About Jaycee's map and how she's been trying to find her brother."

"You think we need to go to that last place." Zach had been thinking it too. "That abandoned amusement park?"

Bishop nodded. "For all of us. Not just for her. This feels like something we have to see through, you know?"

Zach felt the same way, but there was an immediate problem. "Natalie is going to freak. That cop made us promise we wouldn't trespass again."

"This is more important." Bishop opened the car door and let the pieces of Tyler's phone spill out onto the parking lot. Zach agreed, but he still felt old and cold inside. "Maybe you can talk Natalie into it," Bishop added. "Use your charm."

Zach smiled genuinely. "Holy shit. I actually forgot she was my girlfriend again."

Bishop lifted an eyebrow. "She'll kill you if you tell her that."

Mik came out with one girl on either side of him. He looked pretty good, considering the last time Zach had seen him. Bishop and Zach jumped out of the car to greet him.

Zach was stiff, exhausted from driving all morning. And yet, there was a new lightness in his mind. Whatever he'd unloaded on Bishop had needed to be let out of his mind's basement. He only hoped that the feeling lasted.

"You all right?" Bishop asked Mik.

Mik nodded. Natalie kept trying to walk him like an invalid, and he gave her a *bug off* look. Jaycee stood apart, seeming lost.

"You okay?" Zach asked her.

"She's okay," Natalie said. "We should get going. That is, if Mik's up for the drive."

"Well, *we*"—Bishop looked to Zach for confirmation— "want to go to the amusement park." He looked to Jaycee, and her face lit up. "What's it called?"

"Geauga Lake," Jaycee said. "At least that's what it was called once upon a time."

Natalie started listing all of her reasons why they shouldn't, but Zach was distracted. He leaned against the passenger door, staring at the rectangular light of his phone's screen. He had two missed texts from Tyler.

Told you. Was his photographer.

The second one was a video attachment. Zach's finger hovered over the play arrow. This could be a trap. Tyler could have sent him something horrible to watch as a repayment for the beating.

He pressed play but then paused it two seconds later, his heart storming.

"Guys." He pushed in to the center of the group, holding out his phone. "You have to see this."

CHAPTER
53

MIKIVIKIOUS

CHAPTER 54

Natalie

No one said anything while the video went to black, but Natalie knew that she no longer had a case against going to the abandoned amusement park. They had to go.

They had to go now.

Natalie's brain clicked into action. "We need supplies. I left my bag somewhere in the mall." She shook Zach gently by the shoulder. He looked like he was seeing ghosts.

"I forgot that he used to go by Ty," he murmured. "Did you hear him laughing in the background? Like *really* laughing?"

Natalie didn't know what to do with that, so she turned to Mik and Jaycee. Jaycee was holding Mik's hand and grinning excitedly, while Mik seemed determined.

Natalie ushered them into her car. She jumped in the driver's seat and looked up directions. Anything to keep Jake's smiling, happily crazed face out of her thoughts. In the end, all she could say was this: he would have made a fantastic TV show host.

Geauga Lake—or what was left of it—was surprisingly close. She actually had to drive farther to find a Walmart. Natalie left all the quiet, disconnected humans in her car and bought a hundred small things. When she got back in the driver's seat, they were all still silent. "I've got food, water, an emergency kit, and this is for Bishop." She handed him a plastic bag.

He opened it and looked at the spray paint cans and a book of letter stencils. He grinned at her. "Aw, you remembered."

"I remember everything. And all of you should be aware of that and take it into consideration."

Mik chuckled from the passenger seat, along with Jaycee in the back.

"Now everybody say, 'Thank you, Natalie. You make all of this possible and fun.'"

They laughed some more, but she waited, and finally the three of them said it in unison. Mik kept a quirky little smile like he knew something she didn't. He probably did; no doubt all that quiet was hiding a warehouse of life experience.

Their first view of the amusement park was of a green courtesy fence that blocked all eyes from what lay behind it—all except the mounding peak of an old, wooden roller coaster.

The Bonemobile had to pull a wide turn and half go into a ditch to get around the cement blocks that cut off the driveway from the parking lot, but after that, it was easy to find a spot in the jungle of weeds growing up through the pavement to hide the car.

The front entrance had been partially dismantled. The pictures Natalie had found online bragged a looming redbrick gate with a large clock tower. But that was when the park was active. All that was left was a series of brick pillars connected by a platform roof. Anchored to the pillars, a metal mesh gate securely blocked their entrance.

Natalie looked through it. The first thing that made her

pause was the saplings. No—small trees. *Trees* were growing inside the park, up through the broken concrete and straight through some of the remaining structures.

"How long has this place been abandoned?" Bishop asked.

"Almost ten years," Natalie said. "It's a sad story, actually. This park was built in 1887. It survived more than a hundred years. Then Six Flags kinda ran it into the ground. And then another company bought it and closed it so that it wouldn't compete with their park in Toledo."

"Where are all the roller coasters?" Jaycee asked.

"They sold them," Natalie said. "Piece by piece. They're as far and wide as Germany and France. I read a listing of the sales on Wikipedia."

"But not that one." Jaycee pointed to the high crisscross of wooden tracks and rusted rails. The last remaining roller coaster. Natalie knew that Jaycee was thinking of the marker on Jake's map—or maybe the final image on Jake's demo tape of him standing with his arms out, the wind throwing up his messy hair while his grin showed off that infectiously unabashed nature that seemed to run in the genes of the Strangeloves.

Natalie shook the secure metal fence. "What do you think? How do we get in?"

"Up and over," Zach said. Bishop offered his linked hands, and one by one, they boosted each other to the top of the redbrick pillars and then jumped down on the other side. Mik was the last one, and he scaled the pillars without needing a boost. Natalie marveled at his skills, flashing back to all the times she'd watched Mik and Jake repel from trees or climb the two-story-high fences around the baseball diamond with fake rubber daggers in their teeth, Rambo style. Jaycee always wanted to try it; Natalie never let her.

Once inside the park, Natalie didn't feel the ghostly pinch like she had at The Ridges, Moonville, and in the rotting collapse of the mall. And the park was, thankfully, nothing like the cement incline of the Gates of Hell that swept toward that iron wedge…

Geauga Lake had been stripped.

The buildings, bathrooms, and shops were mostly missing. Leveled. The pathways showed where someone might have walked without revealing where they might have gone. They followed one route toward the shore of the mud-green lake that the park had been named for. Bishop and Jaycee climbed onto a huge cement block, one of many that rose out of the water all the way down the shore, dotting a mysterious path.

"What was this?" Zach asked.

"A roller coaster," Jaycee and Natalie said together.

"The platforms for it at least." Natalie closed her eyes, briefly imagining the *whoosh* of what standing here might have been like when the passengers screamed by. A roar of metal and sound and air. Of excitement and heat and the full-body sticky sensation of ice cream, candy, and sweat. She opened her eyes, and birds flew overhead, landing in the water with a slight splash. The sun was beginning a pink-blue sunset, sending its last warmth across her back.

Bishop pointed across the lake at the multicolor swirl of water slides. "What's over there?"

"A water park," Natalie said. "It used to be a SeaWorld."

"SeaWorld in Ohio?" Zach gave a short laugh but then

immediately shivered. "You guys ever see *Blackfish*? I still get nightmares about being eaten by a killer whale."

Natalie held her hand up to her eyes to take in the small outline of the rides across the water. "The SeaWorld was sold to this park. Conjoined, Six Flags turned them into the largest amusement park in the world in 2002."

"SeaWorld…" Bishop shook his head like he couldn't believe something. "Guys. I've been here. Right here. Back when we first moved to Cleveland, my dad brought me here. I was eight, so 2007."

"That was the last summer it was open," Natalie said.

"And this is all that's left of the world's largest amusement park?" Jaycee asked.

They looked around, letting the quiet sink deep.

"Do you guys know what a Gordian knot is?" Bishop asked. "Some people think that it represents time. A tangle of sorts, but basically, it implies that anything that happened is still happening. That the past is never gone. The future already exists. Spirals upon spirals." He cleared his throat. "So really, everyone who was ever here is still here. In a sense."

The wind picked up, pushing into them. Natalie thought she smelled the fall.

Zach broke the silence first. "Well. I officially have the willies."

Mik laughed, Bishop shook his head, and all three boys started back to the center of the park. Jaycee and Natalie left the lakeshore together, turning their backs on the cement headstones that now remembered the path of some monumental roller coaster. Everywhere they stepped, nature was trying to come back, to crumble the walkways, to make trees.

Natalie watched Zach walk next to Bishop. The two of

them were different. Zach hadn't been trying to get Bishop's attention, to drill him for his opinion. They were just walking a few feet apart. Two boys, one broad shouldered and one tall and thin, and yet they both had the same silhouette when the setting sun threw their shadows askance. Zach had also been distant with Natalie since the mall. She remembered with a start that they were supposedly dating again.

Oops.

Jaycee ducked away from the group when they passed one of the only remaining buildings, a faded-yellow, old west–styled structure with a porch that looked like it was a sneeze from collapsing. Natalie followed her, watching the three boys head off toward the front gate. Jaycee was drawn to a deep winding chute that must have been some sort of log ride. She looked over the edge. The water had pooled and drained inside with each heavy rain, leaving muddy stains in the bottom and the evidence of animal prints and tail swishes.

Natalie looked around for Mik, but he wasn't shadowing Jaycee for once. "So what happened with Mik in the hospital? You guys looked like you might've been kissing."

Jaycee's face fell. "Nothing. Happened."

Natalie cocked her head. "Is that what you meant by 'Like I'd know how to do that'? Are you…scared to kiss Mik?"

"*Hey.*"

"Intimidated?" Natalie asked. Jaycee climbed up on the edge instead of answering. Natalie took it as a confirmation. "Get down. The concrete is crumbling."

Jaycee turned and jumped inside the chute. "Ow, my knees…"

"Serves you right." Natalie sighed. "Now how are you going to get out of there?"

"I'll find my way."

"Are you always going to take off when we're in the middle of a serious conversation?"

"Yes." Jaycee started to walk down the chute. Natalie walked the path above, tagging along in Jaycee's adventures just like when she was a kid. It had been her first bold mission to keep Jaycee Strangelove from succumbing to bad planning, but one that had always felt important. And exciting. Like she'd found her life's calling.

"Freeze!" Natalie suddenly yelled when she saw snakelike wires across a puddle, blocking the path of the chute. "There are downed wires. Look."

Jaycee stepped close to the water. "They don't look live."

"Jayce…"

Jaycee sat down, pulling her knees into her chest, and sighing loud.

"I'm going to get Mik to help pull you out."

"No, wait. Don't." Jaycee's expression was desperate. "I'm not good at being around him anymore. There's too much… stuff between us."

"It's called 'chemistry.' And you two have enough of it to start your own meth lab."

Jaycee blushed. "There's other stuff too. You know I can't date him. I'd be a walking made-for-TV movie. Girl falls for boy who killed her brother. Ugh."

"Jake killed Jake." Natalie muttered the words, but that wasn't enough. "Jake killed Jake!" she yelled.

"Yeah, but—"

"Listen. I've been in therapy for five years because of the day your brother flipped off that swing set. Did I know that he was drinking? Yes. Should I have said something sooner? Of course. Did I have any idea that he was about to kill himself? No!" Natalie leaned over the edge, feeling fired up and more sure of herself than she'd been in a long time. "In the end, he climbed up there. He jumped."

"I guess."

"No, *really*. Jake was a suicide bomber, Jaycee. We are all his collateral damage."

Jaycee stood up, and for a minute, Natalie thought the girl might start screaming or scurry up the side of the chute to wrestle her to the ground. Instead, Jaycee's scowl melted a little. It twisted and turned into a rough, heavy smile. "Jake killed Jake?"

"Yes. And that, my friend, is the butt end of it." Natalie had so much trouble not grinning back at Jaycee. "Wow, I feel better. Now I'm going to get Mik, and he's had a head injury, so be nice." Natalie turned to leave, but Jaycee called out.

"Just so you know, I think you did figure out how to disapparate. After the railing fell, I couldn't move. And then suddenly we were downstairs, saving him. You magicked us there. That's why you're Harry."

Natalie sighed. "You forget that Hermione can do magic too."

"Yeah, but Harry saves the day. You saved us all this morning."

Natalie found herself blushing. "This time, maybe, but I was still terrified. And last time—"

"Nat, everyone's afraid. Everyone's afraid all the time."

"You're not."

"Are you kidding me? I'm actually thinking about turning my back on Mik because the idea of kissing him petrifies me. What if I suck at it?" Jaycee's mouth stayed open, but her voice seemed to zoom off without her. "That, ugh, sounds really bad when I say it aloud."

Natalie nodded solemnly. "They tell me confession is good for the soul. What if I tell you the things I can't tell myself and vice versa?"

Jaycee smiled impishly. "That might work."

Natalie was about to leave, but then she leaned over the edge. "No tongue."

"Huh?"

"Too much tongue is the fastest way to make a kiss feel sloppy. Work up to the tongue slowly."

Jaycee put her hands over her face and yelled, but Natalie could tell that she was also laughing in there somewhere. She left with such a sense of pride in her chest that she wanted a goddamn picture of it.

Mik wasn't really that far. He was never far when it came to Jaycee. Natalie pointed him in the direction of Jaycee's most recent danger, but this time, she didn't go along to chaperone.

Instead Natalie stood by the oval brick of what was once a fountain. If she closed her eyes, she felt as stripped as Geauga Lake. She could take down all the buildings and rides—all her beautiful plans—and still be right here, foundations intact.

She thought about her three matching suitcases full of Jaycee-styled clothes and shuddered. She had some shopping to do over the next eleven days. No grunge clothes this time. No uptight clothes. Maybe she could mix and match. What would a cardigan look like with holey jeans? Could she pull off a pixie haircut? She'd wanted one for years, and her mom had expertly talked her out of it each time. Now she had to do it.

But first? She had to go break up with Zach.

Natalie looked toward the top of the front entrance where Bishop and Zach's silhouettes stood out against the setting sun. Bishop was spray painting. Zach was sitting beside him, swinging his legs. The words came to her sort of magically as she felt the sun's rays light up her cheeks.

I'm Natalie, she'd say to the people she met in New York. *And it's been a rough few years.*

CHAPTER 55

JAYCEE

BEFORE TODAY, THE UNIVERSE HAD KILLED JAKE.

It was my parents' leniency or whoever bought him the beer. Or it was Natalie's fault for not telling someone that he was drinking. Maybe it was God's fault or whoever endowed him with that revving, broken-braked personality. Or maybe all of that was crap, and Mik was to blame because he had been the one to dare him.

I buried my head in the fold of my arms.

No.

Natalie was right; Jake killed Jake, and now I had to live with that crystal clarity. That's what Natalie brought to my madness: method. After all, I might have been the one who came up with the idea to make a video of us discovering King Tut's tomb, and I was definitely the one who spent all my money on a camera, but Natalie did the research. She painted all the vases and turned a cardboard boot box into the most elaborate, bejeweled sarcophagus imaginable.

And she was the one who watched the YouTube video over and over so that she could teach me how to get out of my straitjacket.

I moved the toe of my Chucks toward the puddle. Then I hunkered and stared at the water. Reaching one finger then two, I was about to touch the surface but pulled back. I didn't actually want to die. I never did. I just didn't want to feel so separated from my brother. So left behind. "Sorry, Jake," I muttered at the dark water. "Guess you're on your own."

Mik jumped into the chute, exploding the narrow space with the sound of his boots.

I held up my hands in surrender. "I'm not going to touch the puddle. Promise."

He didn't say anything. Looking up from where I was crouched, he seemed even more like the boy I used to know. The boy who came to our house dressed as the headless horseman one Halloween, wearing an actual hollowed-out pumpkin on his head and his father's long, black trench coat. I might have told him that I loved his costume, and he might have worn that trench coat ever since.

I stood up, and he moved closer. My whole body leaned in, and I knew I couldn't trust myself around him. Was that a good thing? A bad thing? "Mik…" I paused. "Ryan?"

"Better," he said quietly. "Are you going to let me explain about that day?"

"Natalie already told me. Jake was being a jerk to you." I turned and started walking down the chute, but his voice stopped me.

"Melanie Howard."

"What?" I snapped, swinging around, and then, "Who?"

"When I started high school, Jake wanted to hang out again like we'd never stopped. Only he wanted me to fit in with his new friends. Drink with them. Date the same girls. Go on the urbex weekends. You've met Tyler, so you can imagine how appealing that idea was. Jake was always pissed at me, and that day, graduation day, he kept shoving beers in my hand and sending Melanie Howard over to talk to me. I tried to tell Jake to leave me alone, but he just kept *pushing*. I didn't know how much he'd had to drink. And I said that dare to get him off my back for five minutes. He'd done that flip a hundred times before. We both had."

Mik took a jagged breath, and emotion ripped through his voice. "It was *his* fault."

"I know." I leaned against the chute and put my hands over my eyes. "But that doesn't make me feel better." *Would anything ever make me feel better?* I felt Mik's hands on my arms, and my sneakers slipped on the curved bottom of the chute as I looked at him closely, newly. "You should have told me a long time ago."

"Couldn't," he said. "I…my feelings made it impossible to…say anything."

"I still don't know much about you, Mi—Ryan."

"So ask me. Ask me anything."

I dug into my mountain of questions. "Start with where you live. Where do you go when you're not with us?"

"Home. I live with my parents in the summer. During the school year, I live near here. I go to Kent. I'm premed, starting my junior year. I talk much more when I'm up here. It's easier when people don't assume that I won't. What else?" he asked.

I liked his voice. A lot. I liked the way he looked while leaning in. I liked *him*.

"I'm turning twenty-one in three weeks," he added.

"Why are you studying medicine? You want to be a doctor?"

"Something like that," he said, blushing. "I like the healing process. It's fascinating."

"But you don't like talking to people."

"Strangers I don't mind. The more I care about someone, the harder it is to…" His voice disappeared, and he kissed me. And I didn't do a thing. Mik's lips met the wall of mine, and I froze. He stopped short. "You know, Jayce, when I imagined this, you kissed me back."

I opened my mouth, but nothing came out.

Mik stepped back. His boot hit the water, and he yelled and stamped. "Those wires are definitely live." He deadlifted my hips toward the top of the chute. I grabbed the wall and climbed over the top.

On the other side, I scrambled away while Mik used his height and reach to get himself out. I half expected Natalie to appear and tell me that she'd seen everything, and that I'd both completely botched my first kiss and was swiftly ruining everything with Mik.

My heart hammered painfully as I watched him trip on his trench coat, only to rip it free and leave it as a black puddle by the edge of the chute. He started to walk away, and then he turned back around, his face unlit. We were standing in the long twilight shadow of the fake, old west building.

"You're giving me mixed messages. Last night in the hotel, you were the one who started touching me and—"

"That was a game. A series of dares," I said in a rush, attempting to joke.

"A game." His tone was either furious or wounded. Maybe both.

I looked down, feeling a burn across my cheeks. "I don't

know what I'm doing, Ryan. I've never done anything with anyone. Never been on a date. You've probably had sex."

I couldn't look at him. Sometimes I felt like a girl with a silly crush around him…but not always. No. Sometimes, when I got too close, I wanted to take him down and claim him like a flag.

He sighed. "Well, *this* is going to be awkward, but I did say you could ask me anything. Yes, I've had sex. My ex-girlfriend's name is Sam. We met at school and dated for a year."

Dammit. She even had a cool name. I broke my hair free from its ponytail. A year? I might as well jump back in the chute. "So why aren't you still together?"

"Because last June, I spent the whole night walking around with a girl who proved that my feelings for Sam were nothing."

I glanced at him. "That night meant something to you?"

"Meant something? I had a crush on you when we were kids, Jaycee. It's not a crush anymore."

The words looked like they hurt him, and I reached out. My fingers wrapped around his wrist, touching the burn scar that ran up the inside of his right forearm.

"The bottle rocket," he said as if to explain.

"I remember."

Jake and Mik were setting off fireworks in the backyard, and one didn't pop. It skipped into the grass. Jake went to pick it up, but then Mik—or he was Ryan then—slapped it out of Jake's hand, and it went off, setting his sleeve on fire. I had held his arm under the kitchen faucet while Jake went to get Dad so that we could take Ryan to the hospital. He was shaking so hard, and I told him to *just cry already*, because in trying not to, he'd bitten his lip bloody.

A flood of knowing Mik came with the memory, and not just knowing him as a kid but the person he was now. He was still the boy who'd rather bite himself than reveal too much.

"I wasn't trying to give you mixed messages." My fingers went to his stomach, to the edge of his shirt, daring him like I had on the hotel room floor. *A game*, I thought. Was that the answer to beating my fear? Natalie would kill me if she knew I was boosting my courage this way. But whatever, because Mik caught on. He reached for my stomach, touching me in a way that was stolen from the previous night.

I slipped my hands around his back, and he did the same. We were chest to chest, and I kissed his neck, damp with sweat. He kissed my neck in return, and my heart blazed as I reached for something more than a dare. A truth. Maybe Natalie *would* be proud.

"When you put your hands in my hair," I whispered, "I feel like I'm falling open."

He made a deep sound in his throat, and his fingers slid up to the back of my head. I wondered if that was his next move, but it wasn't. He had a truth for me.

"Stop hurting yourself. It's killing me."

I leaned away so that I could see his face, planning on telling him what I told Natalie, my dad, myself: that I was never actually trying to hurt myself. But that's not what came out.

"I was trying to feel closer to him." The tears appeared, the silent ones that never asked permission, and I realized for the first time that they had nothing to do with Jake. They were my tears. For me, about me. They sprung from all my swallowed-back and buried feelings. Tears for everything I pushed aside so that I could spend every waking hour chasing a ghost.

I kissed Mik, and the suddenness of wanting his lips made me smile and then laugh. "I'm sorry," I said. "I'll get better at this, I swear."

And then I did.

I kissed him hard and with everything that ached. I wound my fists into the front of his shirt and pressed him back and pulled him into me, and I was aware of his hands through my hair and our bodies getting hotter, and then his back slammed into something because I'd pushed him all the way against the porch brace of the old west house.

It creaked. Moaned. And I ripped the neck of Mik's shirt as I hauled us away from the collapsing porch.

We stared, still wound up.

"Was that more like you imagined?" I asked.

"Yeah." His voice cracked.

CHAPTER 56

ZACH

ZACH AND BISHOP WATCHED THE OLD WEST COLLAPSE. THEY had climbed the redbrick towers at the entrance and were standing on the roof. It was soggy in spots but otherwise surprisingly sound.

Bishop had been busy painting over a nasty bit of graffiti on the teal dome top of one of the side buildings when they heard the breaking wood of the old west's porch snapping off. A few moments later, the rest of the building went down with a few cracks and snarls and a huge exhausting puff of dust. The gnarliest part was that Mik and Jaycee barely stopped kissing long enough to get out of the way.

Natalie rushed over. "What was that crashing?" she called up.

Zach pointed toward the spot where the old west had been. "It's just Mik and Jaycee's love taking down the world."

"What's happening?" she yelled. "I can't see anything from down here. Are they okay?"

"Oh yeah," Bishop said, squinting. "They're kissing again."

Natalie cheered, dancing in a circle and waving her hands in the air.

"Do you ever feel like whatever's happening between them is way bigger than the rest of us?" Zach asked.

"Yes," Bishop and Natalie said together like they were both surprised Zach had noticed.

"Do they remind you of Marrakesh?" Zach asked.

Bishop stopped spray painting one of the stencils. He glanced at Zach from the side.

"Stupid question. Everything makes you think about Marrakesh," Zach answered for him.

"Mostly not in a good way," Bishop said. "It was always intense between us. Everything dire. I never just went to visit her and gave her a hug and watched a movie. I'd always find her singing at the top of her lungs or cutting herself." He started painting again but kept talking. "One time, I grabbed the knife and started cutting my arm and said that I wouldn't stop until she promised me she'd never cut herself again."

Bishop rolled up one sleeve and showed off a whole series of slash mark scars on the inside of his upper bicep.

"Hell," Zach said. "That's insane."

Bishop put his arm down. "Yes. It was."

"You know, cutting is a rather common psychological disorder," Natalie called up. "Asking her to stop won't work in the long run. She'll have to make that choice on her own."

"Thank you, Dr. Freud," Bishop yelled down.

"Natalie, you should pretend like you know half as much as you do. Especially when it comes to other people's lives." Zach's words were quite possibly the harshest he'd ever given her, and they stirred up a storm in his chest.

"I'm not going to pretend to be stupid," Natalie yelled.

"Not stupid, Nat. *Sensitive.* You think Jaycee's honesty is the scariest thing around? I've got news for you. Your honesty is pretty damn sobering."

"You're supposed to be honest with the people you're in relationships with." She had that look on her face. That *I'm about to dump you* look.

"Do you mind taking a walk?" Zach asked. "I'm talking to Bishop about something important."

Natalie scowled and headed down the path.

"What's so important?" Bishop asked, in the middle of spray painting.

"I don't know." Zach sat on the edge of the platform roof, his legs dangling and swinging. Ever since Bishop had talked about time being a knot, he'd imagined Geauga Lake alive. People streaming through the gates. The wave of screams coming from the upside-down twist of a massive, hurtling roller coaster…

"For the record," Bishop said, "I miss your goofy side. You've been too quiet since…"

"Since you showed me a video of Jaycee's brother dying?" Zach asked.

Bishop faced him, revealing the spiral upon spiral image he'd drawn in the center of his words.

"Is that Gordon's knot?"

"Gordian knot. Yeah. Look, Zach—"

"It's cool. I'm just…well, maybe I'm like that knot. I'm goofy Zach, but at the same time, I'm also all the shit things in my life. All at once. All tangled. One side of me daydreams nonstop," he admitted, thinking of all the times he'd turned the world into pixels or LEGO bricks or both. "The other side thinks this whole struggle isn't worth it."

Bishop sat next to him. "Sounds like a good balance."

"Neither one of those Zachs can sleep by themselves though." He rubbed his face. "And lately, well, when I hang out with you guys, the fanciful Zach is starting to feel more and more ridiculous. Maybe I'm supposed to get boring and annoyed with global politics or some shit."

Bishop laughed hard. "No, please don't. We give you a hard time, but we do love you. You keep things light."

"That sounds like a secret insult."

"Take it how you will. Just don't fight your nature." Bishop stood and returned to his stenciled poem. "And for fuck's sake, don't stop daydreaming. Particularly if you can't sleep. That'd be like having no dreams at all."

Zach's gaze trailed to the spot where Mik and Jaycee were still locked together. "I want to know what that feels like. Soul-igniting love, or whatever's going on there."

"I highly suggest it," Bishop said. "Marrakesh and I were doomed from the start. I see that now. But I've gotten a lifetime of words out of my feelings for her."

"Wow," Zach wondered aloud. "What am I doing with Natalie?"

Bishop laughed so hard that he dropped his can. "Do me a favor. Go ask her that."

Zach climbed down the brick pillar and jogged over to where Natalie was inspecting what might have been a wave pool. Zach found himself imagining laughing people. He had to. He didn't want to see the world for its bad spots alone. After all, without perspective, Tyler was Hitler and Natalie was an ice queen. Oh, this was fun. He kept going. That would make Jaycee the Mad Hatter and Mik had to be the Headless Horseman. Bishop could be the Artist Formally Known as a Good Time.

And Zach? Who was he? He wasn't the sad teen with a growing drinking problem who lived in his dad's basement. Well, he was, and maybe he should do something about that, but he was also the kid who'd won the eighth grade science fair—not because of his project. No, he'd made a volcano out of papier-mâché like the other low-level achievers. He'd won because he'd beat out the other boys by making Natalie laugh *and* kissed her on the cheek.

Natalie smiled at him sadly now. "Zach, I think you and I should—"

"Hang on a second. Picture this with me." He stood behind her and pointed at the crumbling park entrance. "You come with your family, but you ditch them at the gate. Your dad tries to give you a high five, which makes you flee in embarrassment. You have to meet your parents by the main fountain at three o'clock, but you have four hours to do anything you like."

Zach pointed to the old wooden coaster and zoomed his fist over the profile of the rails. "There! Right there! You stand so close to the lines for the huge roller coaster that the screams roll over you when the cars hurtle by. You're too terrified to ride. Next year, you promise yourself, watching every twist and turn and taking notes so that when your dad asks you if you went on it, you'll say of course you did."

He moved Natalie by the hips to look left, sneaking a peak over her shoulder at her smile. Then he swept his hand over the imagined slopes of slides. "You walk by the water slides where people are screaming down at a million miles per hour, only to stand up and pick their bathing suit wedgies out of their small intestines."

"Gross, Zach!"

"Shh! Listen. You hear that?" He held her around the waist. "It's the Wave. It comes about once every fourteen years, but it's coming now, and the crowd of unsuspecting people bobbing in the pool is about to figure out what it feels like to take a swim in a blender."

"I would look away," Natalie said.

"No, you don't. You watch because this is as close as it gets to seeing a live train wreck." He used his hands to conduct the full effect of smashing bodies and limbs. "In the wake, children cry for their moms and floaties scatter all the way up to the line of sunbathers."

He pretended to unfold a map before Natalie. "You turn to the billion-fold park directory, and you keep walking around the whole park, maybe looking for someone to practice your brand-new flirting skills with. But instead, you see a fistfight, the kind that always gets stopped at school before it goes this far. Blood flies from each punch landed, and you hurry away, scared that the fight might spread like a fifties Hollywood movie about greasers versus jocks. You go over there"—he pointed—"and buy a frozen lemonade that's already mostly melted but still tastes bitter and yet at the same time so sweet. In front of you, two teenagers are kissing. Like *really* kissing. Exactly the way you want to kiss somebody someday. One of the park cops walks up and taps them on the shoulder, telling them to move along."

"There was a log ride here," Natalie whispered. "Jaycee and I found the chute."

"You'll get there," he whispered back. "First you go past the games. People call out to guess your age or weight.

'Climb the ladder and you can take home a stuffed lion as big as your bed!' one yells. 'Throw a Ping-Pong ball in a bowl and win a goldfish!'"

Natalie jerked around. "Which is incredibly impractical and borderline inhumane. How many of those fish survive the day, let alone getting shoved in a sweatshirt pocket while their new owner rides something called the Texas Twister?"

"So true," he said. He'd accidentally killed a few goldfish at carnivals in his day.

She leaned against him, giving him all her weight. "Log ride," she reminded.

"You walk past the log ride where limey water is sloshing around scared-silly people in a plastic tree trunk. You wonder if you're going to work up the courage to ride all by yourself when your dad sneaks up behind you, surprising the crap out of you. The two of you head up to the farthest roller coaster, the one that people tend to avoid because it's off the beaten path. Your dad convinces you to sit in the front seat, and you both hold your arms up the whole time, which is *loco* because the clacking and thrashing throws you from one side of the seat to the other.

"When the ride finally comes to a jarring, neck-jerking stop, you're laughing so hard that you can't breathe. You head down to check out the picture of you on the roller coaster coming down the steepest drop, and it's so ridiculous that you have to buy a key chain of it to show your mom. Your dad holds up a high five, and you smack hands with him and laugh like you're no longer twelve trying to be twenty, but just twelve being twelve. It feels perfect."

For a long moment, Zach and Natalie were quiet, wound up

together in the way that had always felt like home. His throat was a little dry, but he'd seen every single word. He'd felt the rumbles of coasters in his chest and tasted the oil in the air from a hundred sizzling deep fryers.

"I love you," she said.

"I love you too." He sighed. "We've had a good run. Years and memories and whatnot."

"Will you remember me like all of that? With color and sounds and flares of happiness?" Her voice dropped. "Will you remember me beyond what happened with Tyler?"

"Natalie, the best thing about me is that I remember everything. I can't stop remembering."

"That's me too. See, maybe we are the same species," she said. He laughed, and she hurried to add, "But we can still be friends. I mean, I want to be friends."

"Friends that sometimes have sex? Like when we're both single and bored?"

She sighed. "I won't say yes to that. Or no. Just promise me that we'll never ever get back together."

"Oh man, we're a Taylor Swift song." He grinned.

Natalie laughed, and she looked beautiful. "Yes. Finally."

He gave her a crushing hug and kissed her hair.

Bishop had finished his art and climbed down from what was left of the front gate. Natalie and Zach joined him, and they read his stenciled words.

"It's a little depressing," Zach pointed out.

"All my stuff is a little depressing. It's a stylistic choice," Bishop argued.

"*Shhh*," Natalie said at both of them. "I want to take a mental picture."

CHAPTER
57

BISHOP

WE ARE HERE
FOR MEMORY

FOREVER

CHAPTER 58

JAYCEE

AFTER KISSING MIK FOR A SOLID HALF HOUR, I NO LONGER felt like I wasn't in his league. Instead I felt like I'd joined the league, tackled the entire team, and become the captain.

I never wanted to stop kissing him, but the sun was only a few inches of red at our backs, and the image of Jake standing atop the roller coaster during a sunset five years ago made me pull from Mik's mouth. My lips were raw, and my hands clenched in frustration from where they'd almost succeeded in tearing his shirt from his body.

His hands were doing something similar to mine.

"Coaster," I said. "Must climb."

"Yes. Demo tape," he added.

Apparently we already had a shorthand dialect. We started walking hand-in-hand toward the roller coaster. The sunset's rays threw a sideways heat on my cheeks, and when I closed my eyes, everything felt orange. We met Bishop, Zach, and Natalie by the ramp in front of the roller coaster. Zach whistled like they all knew exactly what we had been up to.

"So," I said, having to clear my throat before I could

continue. I stared up at the roller coaster. "What's this old guy's sad story?"

Natalie looked up too. "It really is sad."

"Has to be," Bishop added. "He's the only one left."

"He's called the Big Dipper, the oldest standing roller coaster in Ohio," Natalie said. "Seventh oldest in the country. Twelfth in the world."

I glanced around. "And everyone just forgot about him?"

"There have been attempts to sell him. Even on eBay, but they've fallen through. Now there's not much to save."

I walked up the ramp that led to the little pavilion where riders would have been strapped into cars and sailed around the track for a solid minute or so of clacking screams and wind and rush. Mik touched the rails. Bishop ran his hands over the yellow gates that would have divided and funneled the passengers into each car.

Zach stepped inside the tiny little control booth. "Hey look! The controls are still in here. Jaycee! You've got to come see this!"

I jumped the tracks to see what he'd found.

Jake's marker was on the control booth's glass. It stood out amid the other graffiti, and I rubbed my finger over my brother's scratchy left-handed signature. An arrow reached from the E and pointed toward the high bend of the track beyond.

"Easy to find this time," I managed.

"I meant this, Jayce." Zach pointed down at the floor of the control booth.

I gasped. An honest to God, bad-acting gasp.

A bare footprint had been left in the dirt and dust. It had a high arch, and the second biggest toe didn't leave an impression. Tears spotted my eyes as I imagined my brother here.

Right here.

"Jake," Natalie said like a swear. "Only he would be stupid enough not to wear shoes in this place."

I almost laughed and pushed the tears away with the back of my hand. Mik's arm went around my waist, and I leaned into him. If I closed my eyes, I could imagine my brother climbing the Big Dipper. Barefoot and jumping, so much wiry energy that he always seemed destined to blow a fuse before the rest of us. I took a picture of his footprint with my phone. Then I started up the path of the roller coaster. Mik was behind me, followed by Bishop and Zach.

"That's not sound," Natalie called out.

"You said you'd climb the roof next time. Remember?" I threw back. "This is it."

We were getting farther from her, and I stopped at the top of the first peak to look back. She seemed smaller and more scared than I'd ever seen her, and yet I had the feeling that it had nothing to do with the roller coaster.

"Ask me, Jayce," she said. "Ask me. I'm ready."

"Truth or dare?"

"Dare."

I smiled and glanced at Mik. Zach and Bishop had stopped their hike up the rails to watch our exchange. "Major in history," I said.

"Hey, that's not what I—"

"That's the dare, Nat. Take it or be a wimp."

Her scowl was fierce and set on me. I loved it. She took forever on her first steps, carefully picking each foothold on the ladderlike platform that ran beside the tracks.

When she finally reached me, I linked arms with her. "If we go down, we go down together," I said.

"Let's not go down at all."

We made our way around the rails, feeling how loose the metal joints had become and even seeing spots where the wood had rotted away. When I looked down, I realized that all that separated me from the ground were crossing supports, too many to count but enough to see through. We kept climbing, and around the downhill, I lost my footing, sliding away from everyone toward a spot where the tracks disappeared.

Snapped apart by a fallen tree.

Mik's hands caught the back of my shirt. I stood and tried to lean forward, but he held more tightly.

"I want to look over the edge," I said. He shook his head, his mouth set in a line. I took his arm. "I won't let go."

Natalie had caught up, and she took my other arm. "I want to look too."

"Liar," I said, but I inched toward the drop with her, understanding for the first time what my dad had meant about telling a lie that you want to be a truth. Natalie wanted to be brave. I wanted to feel connected to people. Two lies we'd have to tell ourselves until they became true.

Natalie and I leaned over the edge, and it wasn't until I glanced down at the massacre of the track, the long, long drop, and the broken tree branches like spears at the bottom that I realized that Zach and Bishop were holding on to Natalie and me as well. I stepped back from the edge, climbing the tracks to the highest spot on the U-shaped bend of the roller coaster. My friends followed.

The sunset was getting over itself with a spray of brilliant reds and pinks. In the near distance, the lake glittered with the last of the light, and though poor Geauga Lake resembled an archeological ruin more than a relic of the world's largest amusement park, I felt its beauty.

Bishop started doodling on the wood with a fat black marker while Zach did some rail balancing that was near comical. Natalie ordered him to sit. She had a death grip on the supports, and her whole body was as rigid as a statue.

"Breathe, Nat," I said.

She did, reluctantly.

"Say, what happened to Mik's shirt?" Zach asked with a smirk, motioning to the rip.

"Jaycee happened," Mik said.

Zach stared at Mik, astonished. Bishop laughed.

"He prefers to be called Ryan." I moved closer to him, fitting myself between his knees.

"Hey, Jayce. Truth or dare?" Natalie asked.

"Dare."

"I really hate you, Jaycee Niagara Strangelove."

"Niagara?" Bishop and Zach asked at the same time.

Natalie sat forward, looking entirely too pleased to provide this information. "The Strangeloves have middle names reflecting where they were conceived. For example, Jake Albany and Jaycee Niagara."

"My parents have a thing for New York."

"Ew," Zach said.

I pointed at him in agreement. "Jake and I had a running joke about our fictional little brother, Joey Manhattan." I laughed. It felt strangely good to remember that, like breathing fresh air after too many months in a submarine. But then, oh hell, what do I know about submarines or even air? What do I know about anything—other than how fast the world can break and how very long it takes to put all the pieces back together.

Mik's arms wrapped around me.

"By the way, Zach," I said, "if I hear a Niagara Falls joke, I'll twist your ear off your head with my teeth. Got it?"

Zach held his hands up in surrender.

Natalie laughed. "She really will, Zach."

"I believe you," he said, grinning. "So what do you guys want to do now?"

I took Jake's map out of my pocket and looked over the worn creases and scribbled words. "I think we should get lost."

"What does that mean exactly?" Natalie asked.

"We drive across the country without a map. Just winding up places," I said. "There are some pretty amazing forgotten buildings on the old Route 66."

"Hell yes." Zach stood up like we might take off right here and now. Natalie grabbed the edge of his shirt and made him sit back down.

Bishop nodded. "I'm free next summer."

I looked over my shoulder at Mik. Ryan. He leaned into my ear to speak, and his words made me kiss him. And not stop.

"Why do I have a feeling that they'll still be doing *that* next summer?" Zach asked.

I pulled from Mik's lips and looked to Natalie. "What say you, Nat? A trip like that will need some serious organization."

"Organization but no maps? That's a headache. That would require a hundred contingency plans. Think about the scale of packing alone, Jayce."

"True," I agreed. "You up for it?"

"I'm up for anything you've got." She crossed her arms in triumph.

I closed my eyes and tried to feel Jake's presence like I had on the TB ward roof all those weeks ago. It didn't happen. If he was still here like Bishop said, tangled up in time's twist of past, present, and future, he wasn't waiting around for me. And I knew it was finally time not to wait around for him.

I started to reshape Jake's map into a paper airplane, being careful with the balance of the folds just like he'd taught me a lifetime ago. Then I tossed it onto the wind. It sailed high above our heads for a spell before dipping. I leaned my cheek on Mik's knee and watched the spot of white notebook paper disappear, caught on a current we couldn't see.

Acknowledgments

Off the bat, I thank my bruders, Evan and Conor, for every adventure and misadventure. Also, a supermassive thank-you to my best friends, Missy and Amy, because every time I missed the boat, you ladies gave me a ride. Additionally, the Jaycee in me wants to thank the Weenies for a dramatic education in group dynamics and for all those lessons in falling for my big brothers' friends.

So much appreciation to the Sourcebooks team and my editor, Aubrey Poole, who trusted me to bring such an ambitious story together while encouraging all shenanigans. A huge thank-you to my wonder agent, Sarah Davies, and Sonia Liao, who magicked my characters to life and turned Bishop into a true artist. Also, I thank Modest Mouse for "Missed the Boat" and Wake Owl for "Gold," two songs that were my constant soundtrack while writing this book.

A special thank-you to Gwynnie and Mario Speedwagon for The Ridges and Moonville adventures. I'd also like to thank all the people who made my years in Athens eccentrically memorable. People like Maggie Tapia, Tina Elliget, Justin

Braxton-Brown, Kerri Shaw, Misty Cole, Kim Corriher, and
Minnesota Steve, as well as everyone at Trimble and Chauncey
elementary schools. Another special thank-you to Jeff Riffo,
Dr. Dyer, Missy Carignan, Andy Paul, Tom Bruscino Jr., and
Erica Eckert for mining their memories for Zach's Geauga
Lake daydream.

As always, I'm thankful for my family and friends who
encourage this uphill career choice, particularly for Christian
and Maverick's support. And I'm eternally indebted to the brilliance and guidance of Amy Rose Capetta, officially the first
person to fall for Mik.

While I dedicate this book to Matt, this story is also for the
Harmon Middle School Eighth Grade Class of 1997 and all of
our teachers—because after almost twenty years, it still feels like
we turned around, and he was gone.

Like Natalie, I love the cracks in history. *You Were Here*
came from my love of forgotten places. All of the urbex set-
tings in this book are real, and I encourage you to look them
up. Sadly, The Ridges' TB ward was razed in 2013 and now
only exists in Internet pictures and YouTube videos. Randall
Park Mall has suffered a similar fate and was reduced to rubble
a few days after Christmas in 2014. There is not much left
of my childhood playground, Geauga Lake, although the Big
Dipper may yet stand. The Moonville Tunnel and the Gates
of Hell (Blood Bowl) are accessible to all ambitious urbexers.
Remember that if you do go exploring, leave nothing but footprints, take nothing but photographs. Oh, and Natalie insists
that you bring a first aid kit and wear a headlamp.

About the Author

Cori McCarthy's first job was as a zombie at Geauga Lake Amusement Park. Only slightly less strange, she now writes books for a living. Cori studied creative writing at Ohio University but mostly spent her time daydreaming about The Ridges. She also holds a postgraduate certificate in screenwriting from UCLA and an MFA from Vermont College of Fine Arts. Find out more about her other books, *Breaking Sky* and *The Color of Rain*, at CoriMcCarthy.com.

ABOUT THE ILLUSTRATOR

Sonia Liao is an illustrator and comic artist with a BFA in illustration and a minor in creative writing from the Maryland Institute College of Art. She's illustrated several comics, including "At All Cost" in Issue 5 of *The End* by Shawn Padraic Murphy and *Helena Rose: An Intergalactic Fairytale* by E. O. Levendorf. Sonia spends her free time watching crime procedurals and collecting Alpaca plushies at her home in Massachusetts. For more, visit sonialiao.com.